To fight the Dark One had been one thing. To battle this new intrusion with an alien science sufficiently strong to destroy the greatest of galactic creations, the *Deneb,* was another; a thing that no one had ever foreseen or prepared for. We'd always thought that whatever the problem, whatever the obstacle, in the end a starship could destroy an entire system, with its sun, or suns. But now a starship had itself been destroyed. And now, too, in the place of that starship, in this limited quadrant of the galaxy, there would be just me and the humanoids of Camelot-Fregis—and *Hooli!*

D·S.

The Magick of Camelot

ARTHUR H. LANDIS

DAW BOOKS, INC.
DONALD A. WOLLHEIM, PUBLISHER

1633 Broadway, New York, NY 10019

PUBLISHED BY
THE NEW AMERICAN LIBRARY
OF CANADA LIMITED

Cover art by Richard Hescox.

FIRST PRINTING, JUNE 1981

2 3 4 5 6 7 8 9

DAW TRADEMARK REGISTERED
U.S. PAT. OFF. MARCA
REGISTRADA. HECHO EN U.S.A.

PRINTED IN CANADA
COVER PRINTED IN U.S.A.

"A starship is invincible in war and indestructible to all known phenomena. A starship is also the Federation's potentional bridge to infinity. . . ." So stated the introductory lines, tape EC-16-LK, as reproduced in the handbook *Starships of the Galactic Fleet.*

Great! Except how, by bloody Hestoor, would it ever explain the *Deneb-3* to my Fregisians? It wouldn't, actually. But no matter. For a Fregisian is first an Alphian, a humanoid from the systems of the binary stars, Fomalhaut's I and II. And, to use an archaic metaphor, is therefore from a race "with an unfortunate propensity for advancing from barbarism to barbarism without ever achieving the mellowing influence of civilization."

Moreover, to a Fregisian's thinking, they needed no explanation; indeed, they could hardly care less. For they have sorcery and witchcraft. And it works! And so to them the realities of the *Deneb* were but parallel manifestations of the vagaries of their own potentials. Moreover, too, they didn't have to understand a starship. It was enough that I, their born-again "Collin-mythos," as well as their recent hero and savior in two wars, did.

They were even smugly pleased that it was one of their own, *me*, who'd apparently conjured up this marvelous package from which they now viewed the night side of Fregis against the surrounding blazing aureole of Fomalhaut I. Fomalhaut I's twin sun, Fomalhaut II, was also visible—at about two billion miles, as was the entire starry void; this, from the parabola of platform within the inner arc of the *Deneb's* transluscent nose.

Unshaken, even somewhat amused, my "ambassadors" relaxed in the platform's swivels, sipped Terran and Velas wines and ate their fill of strange fruits and ice cream. A few—and we were a round dozen altogether—leaned against a gravity rail, nibbled confections and preened their body fur. This last was pure ostentation, done only when one of the ship's personnel in shorts and see-through tank tops, and quite obviously devoid of body hair, passed by. On occasion, too, one or the other would wink at me and offer a jolly quip or mot. All in all, they seemed to be enjoying whatever it was they thought was happening.

They wore a mixed bag of satins, velvets, jacquards, tooled leather and the like, sufficient to dazzle a Terran peacock. Slashed sleeves and surcoats revealed the silver and gold washed steel of their mail shirts, which they'd refused to leave at Glagmaron Castle. They were armed too—great-swords and faldirks—as was I. Indeed, I looked as they did except that my blue-purple eyes (all Fregisian fauna have blue-purple eyes) were derived of contact lenses, effectively hiding their natural brown. My fur was black, short, and of a satiny, mink-like texture. It was also of a gene-cultured origin. Coming from a planet with twice Fregis's mass, I had twice the strength of any of these downright *deadly* swords-men. Moreover, as an added, protective gimmick, I'd been subjected to an imposed neural conditioning prior to original planetfall which had made me an absolute master of all Freg-isian weaponry. . . .

Even the gleaming jewels of my swordbelt were not just jewels, but rather links to certain death-dealing laser beams as well as other things, including a communications potential with the *Deneb*, wherever it chanced to be.

We'd come aboard just fifteen minutes before. I'd taken them up myself in the scoutship which had served me so well in the recent bloody months of unending battle and wild sor-cery which had introduced me to some of the most coura-geous and lovable of friends, as well as the most evil of enemies.

They'd called him the Kaleen, or the Dark One. Actually, he was a true alien from beyond the universe itself. And, though we'd finally won, by finishing him off as it were, the ongoing peril for Fregis, indeed the Fomalhaut systems, re-mained very much alive. . . .

The view-deck with its low swivels and servo-tables hung

directly over the control banks of the main foredeck where a half-dozen crew members kept a sharp eye on whatever the ship had been programmed to do.

Nothing seemed to be happening; a paradox, really, since in the Fomalhaut systems "nothing" was anything but the norm. As if to prove my point the viewscreens attached to an arm of each swivel, came suddenly to life. Scanner connected, they were zooming in on what I knew to be Fomalhaut II's first planet, the destroyed Alpha, where it had all supposedly begun—the demise of the Alphians, the birth of the Fregisians—some five thousand years before.

"*Senior Adjuster* Kyrie Fern!" The voice of Drelas, the starship's commander, cut in above the muted though obviously excited voices of other officers in control-central. "Hear this," he said with his usual flat delivery. "We have an interesting monitor check. Lieutenant Dacey's found five more aliens enjoining with the five we've been watching for the last six months. We have something boiling up through the *gateway*, too. Have a look and tell us what you think."

Adjusters Ragan and Kriloy, playing P.R. to my Marackians, were seated to my left as a part of the group at my personal table. They stared appropriately, as did I. Nothing. The scanner zoomed closer. Nothing. Then, at the very edge of Alpha's atmosphere—and it still had one despite the previous nuclear holocaust—two sets of trim-looking craft, each set in the basic pyramid attack-defense formation, became suddenly visible.

Kriloy's moon face showed boredom. His shrug labeled the discovery routine, just more of the same; which it obviously wasn't. He had a right to think that, however. For the aliens to date, though refusing contact, still caused no trouble. They'd confined their explorations to Alpha and the next three of Fomalhaut II's five planets, all equally useless, and let our monitor alone.

Ragan, however—he was the more serious of the two—had apparently spotted something. He frowned, pursed his lips and said, "Hey, Kyrie—" And was immediately interrupted by one of my stalwarts at the rail.

"My Lord Collin." It was the young lord, Lors Sernas. His tone, imperious as usual, seemed to emphasize the acquisitive gleam in his slightly bulbous eyes. . . . "Would it be possible, sir, to possess a bauble or two from among those I see out there? I'm bound to think they'd make a pendant for which there'd be no equal."

He was quite serious. Despite my briefing, he'd obviously failed to grasp what he was seeing.

"For your lovely Buusti, no doubt," I countered, deliberately reminding him of the recent bride whom he'd left in the dread city of Hish in Om. That country—and it had been but recently freed from the slain Dark One's grasp—had appointed him its ambassador to the kingdom of Marack. Thus his presence in the north. He'd also fought bravely at my side; thus his presence aboard the *Deneb-3*.

The delightfully wicked Sernas—he was an uncontrollable, amoral fellow—grinned, patted his privates and smacked his red lips lewdly. "Or whomever, my lord. For I'm still a Hoom-Tet man. And I'd remind you, that Hoom-Tet's a most gracious god who seeks only the best in physical pleasures for all who worship him."

A flurry of Marackian hands moved instantly to trace the sign of the god, Ormon, upon their chests; this, with accompanying frowns and hisses. I sighed. "They are not baubles, sir, but suns, like unto your Fresti, now hiding behind your world there."

He grinned, winked, belched and said disputatiously, "Indeed, my lord. Well, if you say so. . . ." He then downed a full brandy glass of what appeared to be the best of our Terran moselle.

The frowns of the Marackians softened somewhat at that, for they could all understand a drinking man; not a drunk, but a drinking man. . . .

But not *quite* all. For the lovely Marackian sitting to my right, my betrothed, the Princess Murie Nigaard Caronne of the northern kingdom of Marack, was literally grinding her teeth in rage at the young Lors Sernas, whom she dearly hated.

I barely contained my laughter. In any setting she remained what I'd fancied her at our first meeting—a fairy-tale princess to stir the hearts of those ancient brothers Grimm, who'd sketched her so often in their stories. Golden-haired, golden-*furred*, she had a quite elvish face with dainty, slightly pointed ears and a forever demanding tilt to her chin. Petite, she was beautifully formed. At the moment she was dressed in a quasi jumpsuit of white and powder blue; boots that reached halfway up her calves, and a filmy scarf around her neck, also of blue. The epitome of femininity, she also wore a sheathed shortsword across her back and a jeweled faldirk at her waist. She was a master of both. Indeed, pound for pound—and she'd proved it where it counts most, on the field of battle—she was the match of any master swordsman. . . .

Sensing my unheard laughter, she dug her nails into the flesh of my wrist while murmuring, "My lord! I am not at all amused, sir, that you've brought that disgusting creature with us. I've word that he accosted two butter-maids in Dame Goolis's scullery and would have had both of them then and there had he not been driven off by the kitchen help."

The love-hate syndrome, as apparently inspired in the hearts of all females by Sernas, our happy paragon of total lechery, had touched my princess, hard.

I sighed, grinned and asked owlishly, "The *two* of them?"

Her brow paled in righteous rage. "Well, by the gods, he *did* get one."

"I'll speak to him, my love."

"You do that. Hot oil on the ballocks might cool his ardor."

I couldn't help it. I muttered, "You're indeed quite lovely when you're mad."

"Don't cozen me, Collin."

"I know better than to try."

She smiled at that and made a particularly fetching moue.

I whispered darkly, "There's a thing by which I'm not amused."

"Oh?" The frown returned.

"It's that."

I pointed in disgust to the small dumpy figure asleep in her lap. It was Hooli, one of Marack's two sacred Pug-Boos. Flat-footed, he stood about two feet tall, had a rounded basketball head with fur-tufted ears, stubby arms and legs, shoe-button eyes, and a forever runny nose. She'd dressed him for the occasion in a spanking new orange tam (made by her own two hands, as were all his clothes), green booties and a waist-length jacket buttoned down the front. The jacket was a bright vermillion.

The Boo, or Hooli, as of that particular moment, held a half-eaten, wilted, squishy bung-jot leaf in one hand, blew bubbles as he slept, and had already soiled Murie's spotless jump-pants with the goo from his runny nose.

Actually, there were two Hoolis, though Murie, of course,

was unaware of this fact. The first, the one she held, was a low-I.Q. blob, a mindless *rodentius-drusis* described by Great Ap, the Vuun, one of the intelligent saurians that inhabit Fregis's southern mountains of Ilt, as a stupid leaf-eater. "And if the trees do not leaf at their proper time," Ap had told me, "why then the Boos simply wait and stare and stare and wait, until they fall from the trees quite dead. They are that stupid."

The *other* Hooli—he who truly deserved the formality of the name—was an entity-controller, something like myself, Kriloy and Ragan, excepting, as he put it, we were simply galactic whereas *he* was universal!

I'd never seen him in his actual body. For reasons we'll get to, I hadn't dared. Suffice it to say, I had a deep affection for the real Hooli; this, for various reasons, among them that without him there would never have been a victory over the Dark One; indeed, the lot of us could as easily be damn well *dead*!

The blob that Murie held, that all northerners worshiped, was exactly what it was: a snot-nosed, vacuous, bag-assed nothing! It was demeaning. And yet she forever clutched it to her heart. Without a doubt, my feelings were partly jealousy. But to be forced to be jealous of *that* was a contradiction I found difficult to deal with.

Next to Murie sat her companion, Lady Caroween Hoggle-Fitz, a vibrant red-headed valkyrie with a temper to match. Then came Caroween's betrothed, Sir Rawl Fergis, Murie's cousin and my own sword companion across many months of bloody war. Rawl, at the moment, was diligently spooning his third bowl of ice cream; oblivious to either the "music of the spheres," or his own personal viewscreen, in which the scanner had now boxed the alien ships. . . . They were at a hundred thousand miles from surface, in two sets of five each and, as stated, in the basic pyramid attack or defense formation.

The others of our twelve were: Per-Looris, king's sorcerer and wizard to Murie's father. The great lord Fel-Holdt, commander of all Marack's armies. The newly found Sir Dosh, the slain Breen Hoggle-Fitz's son and brother to Caroween; he'd been thought lost at the battle of Dunguring. The aforementioned Lors Sernas of Hish and four of the greatest lords of the remaining northern kingdoms.

Admittedly, they were by no means representative. Still,

there had to be a first contact and they'd been the only ones available at Castle Glagmaron. The wars were over. The single remaining danger to Fregis lay in *that*, out there, the alien ships and the alien-created "gateway." That they were here at all was because I'd insisted upon it and Ragan and Kriloy had agreed. What with all that had happened—indeed, was continuing to happen now—their presence aboard the *Deneb* was most certainly overdue.

Ragan Orr then burst out in a voice which this time would not be silenced. "Kyrie," he demanded, "have a look, quick! Here comes the big one!"

I looked. The scanner had driven in still further toward atmosphere. . . . Beyond the double pyramids and coming up fast in an arc from surface, was a large blue sphere. Of the size of the *Deneb*, it seemed as a great ball of blue-white lightning, and looked somewhat like a nova looks at a distance of ten parsecs—or better yet, like one of Sernas's "baubles."

We watched closely, our curiosity now tinged with alarm.

The scanner, moving ever closer, allowed us to see our shuttlecraft monitor too, in position. Actually we were able to observe it for just about six seconds; then it vanished in a burst of intense light, obviously nuclear.

And that was the end of our shuttlecraft monitor, plus a young Federation Lieutenant named Jal Dacey and four of his crewmen. . . .

In Galactic Foundation listings the planet Fregis of the Fomalhaut I system is known as Camelot-Fregis because of the aforementioned magic. The indisputable fact is that the spells, enchantments and dark wizardry practiced by Fregis's sorcerers really work. Moreover, the place is an occultists', alchemists', metaphysicists' paradise.

Foundation Center had long been aware of this anomaly. Indeed, over a period of two galactic centuries assigned Watchers—opposite-sexed pairs with a high compatibility potential—had forever apprised them of these facts.

To read a Camelot report had been a joy indeed, except for the one received the previous year predicting the onset of a dark and terrible sorcery to encompass the entire planet. Unless we intervened, the report had said, the forces for progress, the five kingdoms of the north, would be ruined, destroyed. The results? Chaos! A new Dark Age, and worse, for all the forseeable future of the beauteous water-world of Camelot-Fregis.

Not liking the prognostication one damned bit, the Foundation moved instantly to insert a bit of magic of its own—scientific magic! In essence, *me*, Kyrie Fern, Terran, an Adjuster-manipulator of the socio-evolutionary processes, the sly introducer at dark campfires of the sharpened stick and the gut-stringed bow. . . . A graduate of the Foundation's Collegium, I'd become at age thirty somewhat of a genius at the art of "adjusting." The very man for the job, said the Prime Council, and I'd agreed, though I'd soon found that Camelot-Fregis wasn't quite what I'd expected. In essence, it was one giant game of misdirection.

At the court of Marack in the greatest of the five northern kingdoms, I'd passed myself off as one of their own, Sir Harl Lenti. And, too, following certain prodigious deeds, I was also accepted as their "Collin-mythos," reborn. He who had returned to save the northlands from darkest peril!

Said peril, I quickly found, came wholly from an extra-universal, alien intruder called the Kaleen, or the Dark One; with his opponents, other than Marackians, being the host-occupiers of the cuddly court Pug-Boos, one or more attached to each of the northern kingdoms. . . . A solid nine months later, during which I'd led them all in two bloody wars, and won, I was still short of the answers to the original questions as posited by the Foundation. . . .

I hadn't the slightest idea, for example, as to who and what the host-occupiers of the Pug-Boos really were. Moreover, though the P.B.'s had explained Camelot-Fregis's magic, I'd so far grasped only its concepts, not its principles. And lastly, the original Alphian gateway to another universe, continued, *open*!

To top that, ships had been coming through the gateway for the last six months; at least that's where we thought they were coming from. More aliens without a doubt. But what kind of aliens? We now knew something of the first alien, the Dark One, and for that very reason could not accept that others of his kind would use such simple craft as we were seeing. Not that they weren't sufficiently capable. They were. Our sensors told us that their drive, matter to anti-matter, held an obvious potential for warp.

But that, precisely, was the contradiction. They were too

damn normal, internally and externally. They were so much like our own as to be unacceptable as true aliens. The original Dark One had operated with a totally different math, a different body of physics.

Whatever the problem's facets, however, it was *the* reason for my ambassadors being brought aboard the *Deneb*. We'd concluded, myself as Senior Adjuster, together with Adjusters Ragan Orr and Kriloy Rog, that to keep the Fregisians in ignorance of the new danger would be both wrong and counterproductive.

I'd told them something of the situation myself. But to believe in tales told by their Collin, a warlock-warrior-mythos in his own right, was one thing. To actually see and to personally experience travel beyond their world, was another. We'd planned a week of briefings. Later, we'd shuttle others up, students, teachers from the collegia. In part, and depending upon what would then ensue, we of the Foundation would also learn how best to continue our manipulation, our "meddling," if you will, so as to advance them ever faster in the face of the continuing danger.

I'd not told them a thing about the host-occupiers of the Pug-Boos. The total effect would have been too shattering. Indeed, there was hardly a point now anyway, since at my last contact with the real Hooli, I'd gotten the impression that I'd not be seeing him again—ever.

Could that, I wondered, be a part of my anger toward Murie's poor little *rodentius drusus*?

The star-blackened face of our sixty-year-old Admiral Drelas Niall now filled the screen. He began to say bluntly and by rote exactly what I'd expected him to say. Indeed, under the circumstances, I wondered why he bothered. His words were that I, as Senior Adjuster Commander, to whose control the *Deneb* had been assigned, was now relieved of all authority; that he, as of this instant, was assuming full battle-command according to code A2 of the Galactic Fleet.

I nodded, felt Murie's small hand grip my own strongly, as if she actually knew what was happening.

"You are on notice, sir," the admiral continued flatly, and I could even appreciate the gleam in his eyes. "We'll be warping to Fomalhaut II's Alpha in one minute. Keep your people exactly where they are. I intend challenging immediately. Any hostility, any attempt at resistance, will be met with total reprisal. . . . For the record, Kyrie, our monitor and its five man crew *were* destroyed by the second pyramid."

The viewscreen snapped again to be instantly filled with a close of the two sets of alien ships. The blue sphere held its distance at the edge of Alpha's atmosphere. But now, as many as five new ships formed a third pyramid directly above it.

There was an obvious connection between the sphere and the pyramids.

The Marackians, with their innate battle sense, were sharply aware that something was wrong. Their eyes were all on me, lidded, waiting. I shrugged for their benefit, said nothing. There was nothing to say. Again. How does one explain a starship and its potential to "Good King Wenceslaus"? The warp would be painless, a few visible pyrotechnics, no more; this, as an accompaniment to the act of a specifically organized mass falling out of its *parent* space-time continuum and then snapping back in again. . . . Taking their cue from me, my stalwarts shrugged too and contentedly returned to their munchies.

—Excepting Rawl Fergis, who was ever attuned to my personal wavelength. He'd winked at me and put his spoon and bowl carefully to one side. Scratching his nose, he then wiped his lips with the napkin provided and leaned across the shapely legs of our two lovelies to whisper *sotto voce*, "I've a mind to know what's happening, Collin—if you'll tell me."

I shook my head. "Whatever it is, there's nothing we can do except wait and watch. Attend to that," I gestured to the viewscreen, "moreso than that," I nodded toward the great window of the *Deneb*'s bow, "and you'll see what I see."

The tensions building within myself, Ragan and Kriloy touched the others strongly. I mentally ticked off the seconds, watched them closely when the pyrotechnics came. There was no fear; no alarm. Indeed, they greeted the shower of flashing, elongated, sleetlike snowflakes as would a group of children—with delight and pleasure. And why not? Colorwise the bursts of bright flakes ran the gamut of the rainbow and back again. Time, even as expressed in nanoseconds, stood quite still.

And then, and *then*, well there we were, hanging at best but a half-million miles of Alpha's south pole. *We'd jumped two billion miles to the system of Fomalhaut II!* Seen directly through the *Deneb*'s bow, Alpha was as Sol's Mars—desolate, wasted, waterless, ruined! After the hypnotic beauty of Camelot-Fregis, it was no pleasant sight.

My twelve, startled, looked instantly to each other for confirmation of this visual horror, the switch from a Fregisian Eden to a burning Sheol. . . . Their responses were of fear and confusion. When it was understood that they all saw the same thing, and a quick glance at me calmed them somewhat, they shrugged away their fear and settled to what would come next. . . . Conditioned from birth to bloody war, murder and the natural (to them) art of stoicism, they were indeed true Alphians or at least true Fregisians.

My eyes were glued to the viewer. While we were in transit, the two battle pyramids—and I was as yet unwilling to call them the enemy (which defines the difference, perhaps, between an Adjuster's thinking and that of a starship's battle commander)—had tightened considerably. The third grouping continued to hover above the sphere, at a considerable distance from their belligerent companions. It was as if they expected something.

Then Hooli came back, and in a way to almost paralyze my brain. He did it physically and verbally; a thing he had never done before.

I'd taken a second to glance toward Murie, concerned for the thoughts that must be plaguing her as to what was happening. My gaze, of necessity, passed over the sleeping Boo. Its eyes opened simultaneously and, being in a direct line with the viewscreen, it saw exactly what I had seen. A normal *rodentius drusus* would have had no reaction at all. But our little bastard sat up to stare in wild alarm at the ships and the sphere. Then its gaze shifted to sweep the parabola of the *Deneb*'s nose; saw the void and our direct proximity to the surface of Alpha. They held for seconds, as if desperately reluctant to believe what they saw, then switched to focus on *me*. The two small shoebuttons were no longer the eyes of a dull-brained rodent!

I whispered hoarsely, "Hooli? What?—Are you back?"

The little black eyes grew big, staring, like twin black holes as seen from a monitor scope. His reply was direct. Gone was any attempt to ape my voice as he usually did, nor did he use the archaic Terran that he so dearly loved. It was as if he too had been caught off base; as if he'd no time at all for nonsense, no time for anything but to shriek fearfully inside my head with a voice that was wholly his. The words were white hot steel: COLLIN! GET THEM OUT OF HERE! FOR THEIR LIVES' SAKE, *GET THEM OUT!* THERE'S NO—"

His voice broke. And so did his little host. Hooli's very fear had apparently created an unacceptable trauma. The poor little beast—and Hooli had somehow gotten him to his feet—sighed audibly, sadly and, like the fabled Camille, put a small paw to its forehead, groaned horribly and collapsed unconscious into Murie's delectable lap. Arms akimbo, its eyes rolled so that only the whites showed. Its small toes visibly curled as if in insulin shock.

Murie, alarmed, tried instantly to revive it, to no avail.

But Hooli, if he'd really sought to aid us, had returned much too late. The Pug-Boo would survive, that I knew; indeed, that little bastard, if let alone, would survive anything but the absence of forage. I'd just remembered *that it had no belly-button. . . .*

The *Deneb* had, in the meantime and simultaneously, zeroed in on the double pyramid. Battle screens were up, all sensors working, all weaponry coordinated to respond to the slightest hostile act. . . . Which bothered the twin pyramids not one bit. Ignoring all "stand and receive" orders, they simply locked in on the *Deneb* and let loose with a number of pencil beams of contra-terrene particles, anti-matter, directed toward us.

That it was CT was instantly manifest in the myriad of small to large points of released energy dotting the space between ourselves and the aliens. Where even the smallest mote—and it had instantly become an enveloping cloud—touched on a mote of space debris, the release was a flash of purest light.

But Hooli's warning had also triggered me, so that even before the CT release, I'd hit the emergency studs of my viewscreen, calling: "Abort! Abort! Drelas! This is Kyrie Fern. Abort the mission. Abort! Abort . . . !"

At a hundred miles the cloud of CT hit the *Deneb*'s first screen. The result, a gigantic play of pyrotechnics across a huge quadrant of blackness. The interlaced web of raging, silent chaos was easily held by the screen, to waste itself: be reduced to intermittent flashes and finally to die.

But that was afterwards. For the *Deneb* had not been inactive. Before the anti-matter had reached the screens a double grouping of tight beams had shot out to touch each separate ship of the pyramids. Like our defenseless shuttlecraft, they too were gone in instant, patterned stars of released energy.

All of it, from start to finish, had happened in a space of seconds!

Only then did the *Deneb*'s commander deign to reply to my attempts to intercede. I doubt much that he'd have responded at all had the blue-white sphere and the five remaining alien craft made the slightest move to counter. But they didn't and he did. . . .

His face filled my personal screen, eyes the color of dead snow, slitted, his lips compressed. He said harshly: "Senior Adjuster Kyrie Fern. You've just thirty seconds to explain yourself to my satisfaction. And I warn you, sir, that you've chosen to interfere with a battle commander in the very midst of an act of war! Now speak up!"

I answered bluntly, calmly. "But that's my point, Admiral. You are *not* in command! *I submit that Code A-2 does not apply*!"

—Hooli, you little son of a bitch, I prayed. If you're not right . . . by the gods, if . . . you're . . . not . . . right. . . .

Ragan had long been on his feet; Kriloy too, his face white, his features twisted in fear. Kriloy was ever for protocol and the "book," to hide, I think, both his own incompetence and his lack of initiative.

He blurted, "Damn you, Kyrie."

"Shut up," I said curtly. "And don't interfere. And keep your viewers locked on that sphere so we'll know what's happening. Do you understand me? That's an order to both of you."

Admiral Drelas Niall watched silently.

"It's like this," I said, returning to him. "Code 17, para L-2 states that the Senior Adjuster retains command at all times, as long as any of his charges continues within the proximity of *any* potential battle encounter by a starship."

"But not *during* a battle encounter, Kyrie. That's crap and you know it."

"You said that, not me."

"What the hell game are you playing?"

"No game. I want my people off this ship. And in my continuing capacity as commander, I *order* you now to punch back to Fomalhaut I, and to allow us time for planetfall. The sphere, Admiral, and the pyramid, will still be here when you return."

"You dare to lecture me?" Drelas's face was suddenly white with rage, and I didn't blame him. "I'd have you in irons right now, were it not—"

A voice interceded. "Attention, sir. The sphere's moving."

And it was, slowly. I could see it in Murie's screen. "I repeat, Admiral," I said harshly, "get us off this ship, *now*!"

At which point, Ragan—both he and Kriloy were still standing—was foolish enough to put a remonstrating hand upon my arm. He'd unknowingly risked the whirlwind. Rawl, coming instantly out of his swivel and to his feet, slid his greatsword with one lightning *sniiick* from the sheath across his back to hold it flat out, the point touching Ragan's throat. Lors Sernas, at the rail, had also drawn, as had my hulking young Sir Dosh. I remember thinking how much he looked like his martyred father; the bulging eyes, the muscles twitching at the corners of his jaw. . . .

Rawl winked at me, saying, "I've a mind, Collin, to show this impetuous lord the color of his blood. What say you? A small prick, perhaps, to keep him honest?"

I shook my head, careful not to show displeasure. But what I denied, our Caroween did not. "Desist, great oaf," she shouted. "You but show your boorishness to these gentle people. Indeed, I'm bound to think, my love, that my soon-to-be Kingdom of Great Ortmund might suffer seriously with your presence. Leave off!"

Rawl ignored her. And all along the slender platform the lords of Marack and the North drew closer to my person. Some, like the level-headed Fel-Holdt, to spread their arms and to place themselves between the threatening Rawl Fergis and the scared-silly Ragan. . . .

Admiral Drelas, ignoring the whole of it, continued, shouting, "But *why*, man? Dammit!" He literally spat the words out.

I sighed my relief. That he'd asked at all was an indication of surrender.

"I cannot tell you," I said contritely. "I'm deeply sorry. Believe me."

"That clause can be interpreted in a dozen different ways."

"Return us, Commander. Please. At once!"

He fell silent, frowning at the slow-moving sphere in the viewscreen. Then, his gaze returning to me, he cleared his throat to say, "Adjusters Ragan and Kriloy, you are witnesses to this: Senior Adjuster Kyrie Fern. You will board your scoutship now and prepare to return these natives to their planet. The warp will begin in five minutes, provided we are not interfered with. A last point, Adjuster Kyrie, is that upon the termination of this action, I intend personally to prefer charges of mutiny against you before the Foundation Council and the Federation Navy. Is that understood, sir?"

"It is."

His face disappeared from the screen.

Five minutes!

I arose. "My lords," I said to the "ambassadors," "there's no time now for converse. But we, all of us, must return to our world at once. 'Tis in the interest of Fregis and Marack that we do this. Accordingly, I ask now that you follow me, please."

They did. And I led them, half-running, down the main corridors of the great starship; through living quarters, dining compartments, and the combo-playroom, auditorium and library. We then descended to the level of warheads, laser banks, and the great, almost silently humming generators and CT converters. A final dash brought us out onto the shuttle and scoutcraft platform. Once there—I'd perversely ordered the reluctant Kriloy to accompany us—we boarded the little ship as rapidly as was humanly possible, fitting ourselves like the proverbial Terran sardine into a space built to accommodate but a crew of five.

Even as we moved toward the wide exit slot the first flashes of the kaleidoscope of color denoting warp appeared through the transparent double-lift doors. The inner doors raised silently. We slid forward; waited. Then the rainbow flakes disappeared and we were back again, just like that. . . . Again, and without wasting a nanosecond, I caused the outer doors to lift and the inner ones to drop behind us.

We were then instantly free of the *Deneb* and heading back toward that beauteous water world of Camelot-Fregis.

Shifting immediately from a modified CF drive to the power of Fregis's magnetic lines, I swung the little craft in an arc to the area of the great southern continent of Om. At which point I came about, for I intended hitting atmosphere at an angle up from the Selig Isles and the River-Sea, and then north by northeast to Glagmaron City.

To starboard, literally, since we were now cutting back, the *Deneb* was clearly visible. Moreover the transluscence of the scoutship's bow was such that when the ice-blue *sphere* and its accompanying battle pyramid *also* broke through warp to be suddenly *there*, just a few hundred miles from the *Deneb*, we, all of us, were then first-row witnesses to what happened.

I am positive to this day that the sphere was unaware of our presence. I'm positive, too, that whatever sensors it may have had were useless in the face of the fact that we'd already switched to the power of Fregis's magnetic field and in an area of surface-matter turbulence. This last was a natural probe deflector. Indeed, I doubt that the sphere's sensors could have tracked us even if it had been aware of us and had chosen to try.

On the other hand a logical assumption would be that as the two battle pyramids were peanuts to the power of the *Deneb*, so were we "peanuts" to the *sphere*.

They ignored us—if they were aware of us at all—and within a second a dazzling shaft of rainbow light slashed directly out from the sphere to play over the entire surface of the *Deneb*—and the great hulk of the beauteous starship vanished! *It was just gone as if it had never been!* Not even the accompanying residue glitter of fused debris associated with such events remained. It was simply *gone*!

For a few brief moments, I think I blanked out at the horror of it. But then I was hearing the cry of absolute anguish from Kriloy. "My God!" he was saying, over and over. "Oh, my God!"

I echoed him, but silently. My Marackians, sensing, but not knowing, really, that an awful tragedy had taken place, fell to muttering and to crossing themselves with the triple circle of Ormon, Wimbely and Harris. Sweat sprang in cold beads to dampen my forehead.

Rawl and Murie were the only ones, I think, to turn to me, to watch me as if for a clue to this phenomenon with its quite obvious indication of ghastly death.

Murie whispered in a small voice, "Have they been killed, Collin? All of them?"

"Yes," I said. "All of them."

But there was no way for them to know the *meaning* of what had happened. A great ship, a galactic starship with a crew of a hundred had died out there; had been brought to instant destruction. And the bloody-damned sphere was still there, as were its five alien consorts. We saw them all just as we entered heavy atmosphere. After that they too were gone.

Being in mag-turbulence, as stated, their scanners would play hell in tracking me; nor could we now scan them. Just as well. I had no desire to see any part of them, ever again. For I now knew what would happen if I did. What was that opening line: "A starship is invincible in war and indestructible to all known phenomena?"

At the least we would now have to write a new intro to the code book. . . .

Physically numb, I took us down to within five thousand feet of zero. We were in "null" plus "five," which involved a distortion factor, producing something akin to invisibility. Good enough. I hit the coast of the northern continent just short of Kelb's capital of Corchoon and zoomed on above a thick cloud layer for the last few hundred miles to Marack's capital of Glagmaron.

We came to earth precisely where I'd landed the first time, and from whence we'd left *but one short hour before* with our package of the twelve "ambassadors." Actually, I'd returned to the same spot for disparate reasons: one, because we'd left our dottle mounts there; two, because the chances were that whatever it was that had destroyed the *Deneb* would also, and soon, be coming to Glagmaron, Corchoon, Klimpinge, Rheen, Saks, and Janblink, and all the cities to the southern continent. For whatever one might conclude of the *Deneb*'s destruction, the heart of the matter was that the lovely world of Camelot-Fregis now stood alone and helpless and was thus subject to whatever the sphere and its accompanying warships had in mind.

To fight the Dark One had been one thing. To battle this new intrusion with an alien science sufficiently strong to destroy the greatest of galactic creations, the *Deneb*, was another: a thing that no one had ever foreseen or prepared for. We'd always thought that whatever the problem, whatever the obstacle, in the end a starship would always be there to protect us. For a starship could destroy an entire system, with its sun, or suns. But now a starship had itself been destroyed. And now, too, in the place of that starship, in this limited quadrant of the galaxy, there would be just me and the humanoids of Camelot-Fregis—and *Hooli*!

And Hooli?

Well that, too, was a toss-up. For this time even he had seen fit to run; had even psyched out his poor little host in the process. That fact was at least as ominous as the death of the *Deneb*, if not more so.

I brought us down in the midst of a veritable cloudburst; one of Fregis's summer downpours that could last for as many as ten hours and bring a solid twenty inches of rain to forest and field. Timewise, we'd left this spot but one hour before. On any other occasion, excepting that of the last event, I'd be amused.

I'd introduced a quasi dark-ages people to a starship; to their own planet as seen at fifty thousand miles; to that same starship traveling through an advanced "hole-punch warp" for a distance of some two billion miles; to their original home planet, Alpha, which their forebears had destroyed long ago; to an alien life form which had first been blasted out of the void, and had then blasted *us* out; and to the great escape of the millennium—ourselves, fleeing the starship before it was pulverized. Now here we were again on home turf where it was raining gogs and flimpls—and all in the space of a single hour. . . .

I deliberately held our dozen to the cramped confines of the scoutship for the time it took to rebrief them. I spelled out bluntly what I expected would happen now. One or more of the five alien ships would land at Glagmaron Castle today, tomorrow, or the day after. I did not know who or what would be aboard. There would be little point in attempting to oppose their weaponry. To try it, I told them, would be suicidal; not just for us but for the populace too. I, their Collin, their *hero*, told them this and so they were bound to listen. . . . A last provision was that if the alien had not landed by nightfall, well then we'd at least have time to discuss our position further with the king's council; the more reason then to be on our way now!

A severe reactive depression had seized upon me as I talked, so that at the end I'd no desire even to ask what they had learned from my discourse. In a sense, I was too fearful of the answers.

Outside again, we whistled up our dottles. They came trooping and whoooing out of the trees, greeting us as if we'd been gone a month instead of an hour. Their three pairs of painted paws plopped up and down in the mud like webbed duck feet. Fat fannies waved happily. Bushy tails wagged. Big blue-purple eyes rolled, and each of them seemed frantically ready to give each of us a big wet kiss if we showed the slightest inclination for such an exchange. At a ton and a half, it was difficult to be puppylike. But they managed. It just might be, I mused wryly, that when all else was lost our dottles would be the one thing left to cling to.

Fel-Holdt oversaw their saddling. Our gear, including serviceable cloaks against the rain, was quite dry, as it had been put beneath saddle tarps against the weather.

Kriloy would not accompany us. I had other plans for him. Inside the scoutship, I told him bluntly, "You're here for one purpose. A scoutship's communicator is worthless beyond a single system. But you've got to break through anyhow into the galactic matrix. And mind you, I don't give a bloody damn how you do it, or how long it takes. Do you understand me?"

He groaned. "There's no way, Kyrie. There's just no power for a thing like that."

"Then find it. Suck it up from the mag-lines; use the juice from the Loog drives. But *do* it! The Center's got to know about the sphere and the *Deneb*—and that damned 'gateway'; and about *us*. Moreover, your *doing* it will be the only chance we'll ever have. Think about that."

He still floundered, his fear as apparent as his anger at me for having dared to do what I had done: countered the authority of a Space Admiral and brought him, Kriloy Rog, an Adjuster Third Class, to Fregis against his wishes; no matter that he was alive! I'd always liked Kriloy, though I knew that he'd never make Second Class let alone First. The computers, in respect to Kriloy, had made a very serious mistake.

"If we use the drive fuel," he said, "we're dead and you know it. We'll never get off, Kyrie."

"You wanna take my place?"

He didn't answer.

"Maybe you don't understand," I told him. "*I'm* going to have to face whatever comes out of those goddamned ships when they land; me and those other poor sons of bitches out there. *Do* you want to take my place? I'll be only too happy to stay here and try for the matrix."

He whispered, "Kyrie. I'm not psyched. I'd be no good."

"Then do what I ask. The node's still at the base of my skull, so you can keep contact. And I can buzz you through the belt. If I'm alive you'll hear from me. Okay?"

"I'll try, Kyrie." He sounded suddenly contrite, even ashamed of his weakness. "What about me leaving the ship?"

"Don't."

"Why not?"

"Because we need you alive. There are *things* in that forest. When I leave, I'll phase you out. You keep it that way. . . ."

We shook hands then and I went outside to stand before the scoutship and orally key the grid numbers: three-seven, two-nine, four-one. It quickly began to shimmer and to fade. Then it was no longer there.

My Marackians had sat their mounts stoically, watching. I swung myself up into the saddle of my mount, Fat Henery, amused as always at their flat-faced approach to "visual" magick; in this case the scoutship's disappearance. Then Fel-Holdt, tall and grim in the saddle, halooed, and we were off—to a long roll of accompanying thunder in the west.

Marack's commander and the four ambassadors from the various northern kingdoms rode to the fore; a concession from me. Somehow, my awareness that I, the greatest of warriors and warlocks, their hero-Collin, would soon, in their eyes, be reduced to second fiddle if not third bassoon by what would ensue from those damned ships, had really reached me. Ego trip. Loss of innocence. Call it what you will. I wasn't ready for it.

That I was plain damned afraid was also a part of it. Hooli'd put his finger on it as far back as the battle of Dunguring, when I'd been forced to fight the great Gol-Bades. "So what's holding you back, buddy?" he'd asked inside my head. "You got a little old crappola in your blood 'cause you'll be evenly matched for a change? Hey, isn't that what you're here for?"

And that other time when I'd been forced to fight and kill the skaiding, a beast something like old Tyrannosaurus Rex, before the dread city of Hish. Young Hargis, a student warrior of mine, had died to hide my cowardice. Murie had bravely attacked the damned thing to give me courage and also to shield me and my fear from the cheering ranks of the finest warriors of all Camelot-Fregis. Prodigious feats? Sure. I'd accomplished them all a hundred times over. I'd destroyed Gol-Bades too, and gone on to kill the skaiding. But there was still that all too civilized part of me that I couldn't control, that small albatross of spine-tingling fear that would forever despoil the image I flaunted before the world.

Murie'd sensed it too; though there was no way she could guess its reason. Usually she talked a mile a minute. Not now. Instead, from time to time and despite the driving rain, she'd simply ride close and allow a rounded thigh to brush my own while she watched me through slitted eyes.

"My Lord," she finally burst out when she could no longer contain herself, "You are my love and I am yours. Indeed, we're but a week from wedlock, at long last—for you do possess some skill in dodging the marriage bed. Still, 'tis precisely now that you withdraw from me, who should be privy to your thoughts. What's with it, love? I've a right to know."

And she did. But I could only say solemnly, " 'Tis that this time there'll be no way I can match their weapons."

She brightened, laughed, gave me an elbow to the ribs. She said, "You joke, Collin. And you harm yourself in the doing. 'Twas you, sir, who fought the hundred of Keilwher; who killed the skaiding, destroyed the armies of Om, and who with nought but twenty-two swords brought down that hellish center of all evil, the black temple of the Dark One. . . . I cannot believe you."

I smiled sadly. "The fact that you cannot but accentuates the problem."

"I fail me, Collin, to see your point."

" 'Tis that no Marackian will believe me either; though they'll still depend upon me while I, in turn, can give them nothing but a useless sword."

"Hey, now, sirrah! 'Tis one that's always been victorious."

I reached across to catch her hand, bring it to my lips and kiss the fingers. Giving it back, I said, "Murie, hear me. . . . Those who come now can destroy this entire world with the snap of a finger. And I doubt not that they'll do just that. If we only had *time*. But there is none."

My voice trailed weakly off and despite her nearness, I settled again to my depression.

No way. She wouldn't have it. She was my love; would be my love. The fighting Alphian in her forced her to take charge in a different way; the way she knew best: to distract me, to channel my thoughts elsewhere in the age-old therapy that has no equal. She first reached out to pinch my ear, hard, to get my attention. She then leaned across—to press her rain-sweet lips to my cheek and throat. She clung tight this way as we rode; so that Henery, my court mount, looked back to see us and actually chortle. Henery had long forgiven me, I knew, for the ear Gol-Bades had taken at Dunguring; though, in the battle's aftermath, he'd turn away whenever I came near him, to moan and twitch his stump.

Murie whispered softly, but with the tiniest touch of steel to her voice, "Let's cross the Cyr when we come to it, Collin."

I shuddered. She held me tighter. The cliché, though I'm sure she thought she'd invented it, was like a man's teeth on a shield front. "We are of Marack," she persisted with the proper hauteur, "as you are too, though I'm minded, if my ears told me true, to think that you also had some command of that great ship we rode in, which is gone now. Still, you are handsomely furred like me, whilst they were naked of such—so pale and ugly. So you must truly be of Marack, my love. Therefore, be this enemy ever so powerful, you'll find a way. *We'll* find a way!"

She kissed me hard again, clung to me like a succubus. I loved every minute of it. . . . And thus, I thought, had the love-smitten, but wholly amateur in war, Cleopatra, counselled her Anthony on the eve of the disaster at Actium.

Instinctively, I knew that she'd thought of Camelot's magick as the answer. To her it was a boundless sorcery which could make all things right; which is the way they would all think. Conditioning guaranteed it—that we would find a way *where none existed*!

For what they didn't know or otherwise refused to believe was that the magick of Camelot-Fregis had serious limitations. If one was good at it, he could rain, hail, sleet or snow on someone else's crops, chickens or festive outing. One could even do better than that: put a boil, perhaps, upon the nose of an adversary to keep him from a dance or rendezvous with his lady-love; upon which the spell-caster could move in on the lady. . . . But there was nothing at all with which to confront an alien battlecraft from another universe.

The lovable but absolutely murderous in battle, Rawl Fergis, for example, had learned just three spells of magick in his two full years at the collegium. The first had made him a veritable devil with the lute, though for the life of me, I couldn't see how he'd achieved this prowess with magick. He could also turn gog-milk into *sviss*, a most excellent Marackian-Fregisian brandy—a handy stunt! And finally, he'd been given a solid spell for love to be used three times only. He'd hastily used all three of them on the lovely Caroween Hoggle-Fitz, unaware that that sweetest of lusty redheads had used the three she had on him.

The true sorcerers and witches were something else, of course. As were the "king's sorcerers" and the "teachers." These were indeed adept, and could do some damned interesting and even powerful things. But that, I repeat, was the extent of it.

I shook my head against her pageboy bob and sighed. We were, I thought, as Terran Druids against a coming night of laser bursts, death-dealing weaponry and even obliteration. I'd no reason whatsoever to be optimistic.

Our fat dottles, loping happily against the fast-setting sun, paced themselves at their usual twenty miles per hour, a rhythm, so I'd been told by certain chirurgeons, to correspond to their heartbeat. The distance to Glagmaron Castle being just twenty-two miles, we arrived upon the military field before the drawbridge in just a few minutes more than an hour. The town of Glagmaron, lying below the field, the bridge and great crenellated ramparts, was also in the shadow of the hill. Lanterns already bobbed in its streets.

The rain had not let up. And though twilight, too, was fast descending, we'd still been spotted from the battlements. Trumpets cried shrilly in greeting. A hundred kettledrums began to cadence our arrival.

I halted our troop at the drawbridge. There was no moat, just a great ravine to split the hilltop with its field from the castle. Once more I cautioned silence about all that had happened: "As if your lives depended on it," I warned them flatly. "For that is precisely the case here."

The courtyard was storm-lashed; the great slate slabs all dappled with a hail of bouncing drops. We parted hurriedly, handing our mounts to as many ostlers. Rawl and I headed for the entry to the west turret. Murie and Caroween ran for the entrance to the great hall and the corridors to their own apartments. I had one last glimpse of Murie, with that damned macrocephalic *rodentius* riding on her shoulders. A sopping-wet tam drooped around his head so that only his lack luster eyes were showing. I swore. I couldn't help it. She really *did* treat that little bastard as if he were the long-lost Terran Bonnie Prince Charlie.

Fel-Holdt and Per-Looris, the king's sorcerer, headed directly for the royal chambers to report our unexpected and swift return, as was their duty.

I cursed again and felt the better for it.

Rawl and I were once more sharing an apartment. It being high summer, the place was always crowded, for fetes, tourneys, dinners and the like, with swarms of heggles (knights), kolbs (lords), and their ladies, plus magistrates and tax councillors, all coming to stay a day or so and to take up space at Glagmaron. The reason beyond the usual? Well there was peace in all of Marack and in all of Fregis. And, too, the previous year had been a bountiful harvest everywhere so that wassail was forever on the order of the day.

Rawl and I had scarce stripped to the buff and taken a quick sponge bath to wash the dust off our fur from the forty-mile dottle ride, coming and going, when a knock introduced a student courier with the urgent demand for our presence in the royal chambers, *at once*!

I'd figured as much. For the grim Fel-Holdt was not only responsible, but also persuasive. And, though he lacked the ability to grasp fully what he'd seen, his simple tested logic was sufficient to understand the quite obvious peril at its heart—for Marack!

We dressed quickly again. Outside the rain lessened, stopped. In the direction of the great snow-lands however, thunder roared and lightning played in a frenzied fire-storm all around the horizon.

We were met in the royal council hall by a somber group. Seeing their faces, I was certain that our good Fel-Holdt, *and* Per-Looris, had deliberately and wisely scared the hell out of them. King Olith Caronne stood tall, thoughtful and worried, to greet us. Queen Merin Tyndil, at his side, was overtly nervous, irritable. A simple light and airy woman, she'd seen too much of war and very little of anything else. The king's council, all fifty of them, waited wide-eyed, angry—and fearful. This last was an ominous portent, indeed, for I'd yet to see so many Marackians *fearful* at one time.

The walls of this small but beauteous room were covered with battle flags and tapestries, all woven with great love and care. They told of a myriad battles, the history of a thousand years of Marack's kingdom. Here and there, where they hid a stone-laced window, they had been pulled aside to allow in the rain-laden night breeze so that the perfumes of various night-blooming flowers now filled the room. Moreover, as if to compete with the braces of candles in wall sconces and along the length of the double tables, there was an occasional brilliant on and-off glow from a number of Camelot-Fregis's large and friendly fireflies—wafted into the hall by the same breeze.

They weren't fireflies in the ordinary sense, but rather a form of large butterfly or moth. A quite singular aspect of these beautiful insects was that they would of their own choice alight on one's hand or shoulder; would allow themselves to be stroked, and would even take honey or nectar from a tendered finger. As pets they were truly a thing of witchcraft; easily tamed if captured directly from the cocoon. Their life-span, unfortunately, was what it was, short and ecologically meaningless—unless beauty itself is a reason for being.

We'd seated ourselves at the "high table" next to Caroween, Murie and the royal family. Hooli was there on a small dais to the rear. Jindil was with him, the second of the Marackian Pug-Boos; Jindil being distinguished by a black circle around one eye. Both were asleep, as usual, on silken pillows under the care of the court pages. Among the great lords of the council was Gen-Rondin, a stern and positive warrior-juror, Per-Kals of Longven, Kol-Rebis of Gleglyn, Gen-Toolis of Fiirs, Al Tils of Klimpinge and our own Fel-Holdt of Svoss. Per-Looris, our sorcerer, had apparently been hard at work. Indeed, he'd just completed his standard protective aura so that the last of his heavily intoned words still hung in the air as we entered.

The result of the incantation was visible in the faint mist that clung like a small cloud to all those at the high table. Physically, it was a form of "null" induced by word-sounds

(Camelot-Fregis's magick), and impenetrable to most phenomena. The area encompassed by the mist or cloud became as the faintest of bubbles, disrupting at that precise spot the matrix of planetary magnetic lines, *i.e.*, no counter-force utilizing the energies of the same lines (the Dark One, for example) could harm or control anyone or *anything* within the bubble without first weakening or destroying it with counter incantations (word sounds) designed to do the job. The complexities that can arise from this form of *magick* are easily understood.

Watching our aged Per-Looris, I was struck by the similarity between himself and the martyred Fairwyn before him. Per-Looris, without a doubt, would do anything—give his own life if need be—to protect the bodies and the welfare of the royal family of Marack. He watched the rest of us like an aging hawk, suspicious, alert to any danger.

I had time to wonder just what he had thought of that which he'd seen through the bow of the great *Deneb*.

The king greeted both myself and Rawl Fergis courteously. He then suggested that I waste not a second of precious time, but that I tell them now my version of this most deadly peril to Marack and the world. "Peril and danger," he smiled sadly, "are certainly no strangers to Marack. But coming now, when we'd thought to have some measure of peace at long last, 'tis a most unwelcome thing to contemplate."

I arose first to solemnly pledge them in sviss for their attention, and to establish the proper mood. I intended wasting no time in trying to get them to understand what they were absolutely incapable of understanding. I would drive straight to the heart of the matter; paint a simple picture that all could see. . . . Outside, as if to help me make my points, a great thunder rolled: Fregis's thunder, like the sound of some monstrous Terran battleground of centuries past. Continuous lightning seemed to blast the very courtyard.

"Sire and my Lords!" I cried above the roar of nature's chaos. "Tomorrow, or the day after—or *soon*, one or more great ships will sail down through our skies to land at our fair Glagmaron Castle and city. The creatures that will come from within these ships will be as unknown to me in shape or form as they will be to you. But though I know them not, I do know their power. And that, sirs, will be more terrible than anything you've ever faced or imagined before. They will instantly set out to control this bounteous land. Their weapons will be such that to offer resistance in any way will be foolhardy, suicidal; conducive only to the inevitable destruction of Marack and possibly your world as you know it. . . .

"And we'll not be the only victims. All cities in the north and south of Fregis will be likewise visited, and in like manner come under the control of these conquerors. So it will be. And my lords, there is nought we can do for the moment but to let it happen." I paused for breath, and a first reaction.

It came, and instantly. A speech such as that and before such a gathering could elicit but one response. Shouts of anger and outrage boomed from every corner. Some came to their feet, hands on sword hafts to damn me, their Collin, as being either bewitched or deprived of my senses . . . "No one in all of time," brave Rondin shouted to the king, "has cried surrender before ever the enemy was tested. How know ye of these dread weapons? Indeed, how knows our Collin?"

"But they do exist!" stout Fel-Holdt roared above the outcry. He arose to challenge the room. "Our Collin does not lie. We, the ambassadors, were witness to just such weapons in a great battle in the heavens. I believe too, with the Collin, that these same sky ships will indeed come here, and soon."

Gen-Rondin, no stranger to fairy tales as an adjunct to Camelot-Fregis's magick, would still have none of it. He turned to face me, his blue-purple eyes snapping, his shadow great and looming in the candle's glow. "Hear me, Collin, and you are my friend as you are friend to Marack. Some months ago 'twas I who was a victim to the mind control of the Dark One. 'Tis now that I see in you what I knew myself to be. Admit it, sir, and let us cleanse you of it—else by the gods, we'll then take other means."

"That you will not!" Murie leapt to her feet. "Would you put yourself against the royal house, Sir Rondin? I am your princess, and the Collin and I will soon be wed. I too have seen the sky ships *and* their weapons, as has your commander, the good lord Fel-Holdt and our court champion, my own good cousin Sir Rawl Fergis—and Per-Looris too. The sky ships exist. They are coming here. The question is, what shall we do?"

"Good Rondin," Rawl called in his easy, friendly way that so often was misunderstood by those who'd settle all quarrels with the sword, "if the Collin's possessed, why then so am I, and Fel-Holdt and the others. . . ."

Rondin, stung, shouted in quick anger, "Well mayhap we'll quarantine the lot of you. Know that I love you, Collin." He turned to me. "But I and mine will not stand aside and let anyone or any magicked *thing* take from us that which is ours by right and history without a fight. Your counsel's bad, sir, and I reject it."

More voices rose to counter. The idea of surrender without a fight was simply unthinkable. And, I might add, it was also unthinkable to Rawl, Murie, Fel-Holdt and the others. In this matter, I knew that they'd stand with me only to a point. In the past I'd always come up with something. They simply couldn't believe that what they'd heard from me was all of it; that I hadn't some tricks up my sleeve whereby we could all enjoin to smash the enemy whatever his weaponry and skill. The king himself finally arose again to demand that I respond. "For surely," he suggested dourly, "you must have thought on some recourse. I cannot believe you'd come before this body to plead surrender only. What say you now to these lords and me?"

That they waited, teeth bared and eyes smoldering, was the first evidence of the deadly frustration that would seriously compound our danger.

For whatever reason, I looked to Hooli before replying. At that precise moment a golden butterfly-firefly with red striations across the abdomen came fluttering to settle softly upon my sleeve. Marack's warrior-lords all oohed and ahed at this, considering it some sort of omen. The Pug-Boo, Hooli, was awake, staring in my direction. I probed him, mentally. "You back, bag-ass? Anything you can tell me that will help?" And then, "*Do* something. Wink. Wave a paw."

No way. Damn him! I could never depend upon him. He'd play it his way or not at all. All eyes were on the great firefly. I stroked its back. Its huge wings moved slowly up and down. More. A full half-inch of the red-gold abdomen glowed purple-white, went on and off, on and off. I couldn't help myself. I looked again at Hooli—and saw an amused glitter in his little beady eyes.

The insect lifted, beat the air to hover directly over my head. It then flew slowly three times around my shoulder-length black hair, dipped, hovered, went on and off before my face (Hooli's contribution) and flew suddenly through the nearest window.

There wasn't a man of the council who hadn't raptly traced the circle of Ormon upon his breast. There was even a small ripple of applause at this obvious manifestation of Ormon's grace. I sighed. If nothing else, Hooli's game's-ploy had soothed that half-centurea of thirsty swords.

And he *was* back. Still, my relief was overshadowed by the knowledge that the little bastard was, as usual, not helping, but instead attempting to use me. The goal was the same for both of us; we'd no problem there. The question, however, was apparently and again: who would be using whom (and he was forever making it this way) to win the victory?

The battles that Hooli and I had fought and won together had each time been a risk of world-death; more, an entire system had been at stake, as it might be now. Each time, too, our victories had involved a bloodbath. I did not want that now.

They were waiting stoically for my answer to the king. Since I had none, really, I'd no choice but to repeat myself. "Sire and my Lords," I said, "to know nothing of one's enemy excepting his strength, and that a thousand times more than your own, and still to prepare to offer battle is to add idiocy to idiocy. To respect his strength and then to begin the search for his weakness is the path of wisdom. And I would remind you now that I have not called for surrender. I've simply asked that we not resist; that we seek out this weakness that *must* be there before we join in battle. . . .

"To know the 'why' of it all," I dared explain solemnly, "is perhaps to know yourselves, the Dark One and this new enemy too; for your fate has been linked with theirs for a full five thousand years."

I then told them, generally, what the Pug-Boos had told me, making it as simple as I could so they'd understand at least a part of it: that the Dark One, a single entity of an alien life form, had been the first of his kind to pass through from his parallel universe to the Fomalhaut binary system. A warp, or "gateway" had been created on the planet Alpha of Fomalhaut II for this purpose. As the first of a potential horde, the D.O.'s purpose had been to seek proper *hosts* among Alpha's humanoids. But, strange quirk of fate, the D.O. had passed through the gateway and directly into the midst of a nuclear holocaust, unleashed by Alpha's warring nations.

Enter the Pug-Boos, the Universal Adjusters—as opposed to our simple *galactic* status. The Boos had been keeping a close eye on Alpha. At the last moment they'd moved to transfer all humanoid remnants to Fregis, Fomalhaut I's second planet. They sought to save these few thousands—while destroying their memories so they would be forced to evolve again. To guarantee that there would be no life of any kind for future aliens to occupy, *they sterilized Alpha*!

Unbeknownst to the Pug-Boos, however, the alien, the Dark One, had escaped prior to destruction and had successfully occupied a single Alphian life form. The Boos had provided twelve great ships wherein the Alphians had crossed the void to Fregis. The Dark One had seized one of the ships. It landed in the far south—and Hish was founded. The great Reptillian Vuuns seized one—and thus their caretakers. One crashed, with a subsequent release of radioactive materials—and thus the mutant Yorns. Six of the remaining nine landed in the north, on the continent of Marack—thus the men of Marack, Ferlack, Kelb, Gheese and Great Ortmund. The remaining three came to ground on the isles and southern shores of the River-Sea—thus Kerch and Seligal.

All ships were then destroyed by the Boos, as were all memories of Alpha . . . All this I told them, *except I made no mention of the Boos' influence*! The ships, I told them, were *theirs*, for such was their greatness then.

The new enemy, I said, was either more creatures such as the Dark One—or something else, the like of which I knew not.

"And 'tis for this reason," I continued, "that I now counsel you to greet without arms that which will ensue from the ships when they land. We must, whether we like it or not, be the first to extend the hand of friendship. I repeat. His strength is such that he has already, and in the sight of your ambassadors and your princess, struck down a great sky ship whose master and crew were *men* such as yourselves; men possessed of great weapons too. Still they are lost and the enemy lives. Greet him therefore in peace. . . .

"*Help us to buy time to study him, to see what he is and who he is—and where his weakness lies*! Since time began there has always been a flaw in any people. *We* have such a flaw; so, too, does he. I repeat. Allow us time to find *his* before *he* destroys *us*. That, sirs, should be our only priority!"

How much of their history had reached them I didn't know. I was met with a vast and stony silence; few brows seemed perplexed or wrinkled in thought at the mystery of it all. No doubt, I'd gotten through to some of them. But for a Fregisian—read Alphian—to be helpless in the face of danger means, essentially, that he's already dead. To be forced to put one's self wholly within the armed grasp of the enemy is unthinkable.

Still, there was nothing now for them to say. After all, I *was* Marack's savior. Indeed, I'd just been given the sign of Ormon's favor. Who could argue with that? The king was silent; lips pursed, eyes flat. Murie was silent too, as was the commander of Marack's host, Fel-Holdt.

They had never been that way before.

The meeting broke up amidst a shaking of heads. The council members straggled out to the great hall for sup. With Murie on my arm and with Rawl, Caroween, Sir Dosh and Fel-Holdt to our rear, we joined the king's entourage and went to eat. Our entry to the tables must have seemed as a funeral march to the row upon row of happy trenchermen and roisterers. From that point on there was little gaiety.

Even later, when I'd traversed the labyrinth of corridors within the castle's hulk so's to knock on my lovely's door, I was hastily told by a simpering maid that she'd gone to tend her lady mother who'd become ill with a "blues" that only a daughter could cure.

"To ghast with the bastards!" Rawl shouted, long-faced and angry. Caroween had slammed the door in his face too. He'd then inveigled me to go with him to the common room for some serious drinking. On the way we'd collected the willing Sir Dosh from an apartment he shared with five knights of Great Ortmund, a part of his sister's entourage. A pervasive gloom touched the three of us. For me it was exacerbated by a picture I'd seen from the corner of an eye as I'd left the council chamber. It was of Jindil, Hooli's twin. That miserable little bastard had awakened just in time to snatch an absolutely beautiful, rainbow-winged firefly from the air. Its antennae still probed the scented breeze as the rest of it went down the greedy Boo's throat.

I was tempted to drink myself drunk.

The common room was in its usual state of bedlam, but more so. Knights, warriors, and boisterous men-at-arms fought for a place at the two dozen or so tables. Competing minstrels tried hard to be heard above the roar of yells and curses. Incessant peals of great thunder drowned it all.

Still, it was the one place in all the castle where one could be truly alone with one's friends. Tossing a foursome of maudlin drunks to the rushes, we took their places; this to the hails of "Collin!" "Fergis!" "Hoggle-Fitz!" from various well-wishers. We ordered, drank—and ordered again.

"*Blast them*!" Rawl roared a second time, alluding to the councilmen. "You'll see, old comrade. They'll come crawling back, the bastards, when the true plan's disclosed. And then, by the gods, we'll make them eat their words!" His eyes glittered and he smacked his lips at a personal imagery of dripping swords and well-thumped pates.

Remonstrating with him for the umpteenth time, I yelled, "Rawl. There is *no* plan. 'Tis a thing that's still to be decided."

"Ha! But that's the one I'm talking about."

I sighed, said softly, "But we must play the game first, the one wherein we do not fight, where no resistance is offered."

"But 'tis after *that* I'm talking about." His eyes had filmed. He refused even to think of an interim. " 'Tis after, when we're ready for them. All Marack will then see who's had the right of it."

Sir Dosh sat unmoved. Like his father, he lived happily from moment to moment, attributing all things, good and bad, to the whimsy of the gods, Ormon, Wimbely and the lost child, Harris. Still, he now said pompously, "Well then, my lord, your plan's to trap them, right? An ambuscade, perhaps of a hundred or so lances; a flight of steel-point shafts from behind some well positioned boulders? I, myself, would prefer the first, sir. That way there's a chance to get in close; with the sword, mayhap. A small splitting of pates. . . ."

"We'll see," I told him, and pledged them both. We emptied our cups—a reflex toast to nothing.

The rosy-cheeked Sir Dosh, his bulging, owlish eyes blinking, then exclaimed as a point of information: "Well now. My good father who, as the world knows, would sheathe his sword in the liver of any liar did the man dare cozen him.

My good father, who stood before the entire Kelbian army and hacked them all to—"

"We know of him, my lord," Rawl growled impatiently.

"My most illustrious father," Dosh glared blackly at Rawl, "who also stood in Ormon's grace, as does our Collin. My father—" His voice then suddenly trailed off; he frowned darkly, shook his head and seemed to stare to nowhere.

We waited. Nothing.

Time passed until the impatient Rawl could stand it no longer. "In all courtesy good brother-in-law-to-be," he shouted in Dosh's ear, "what *of* your illustrious father?"

Young Dosh batted his bulbous eyes, scratched his head as if to bring himself back from wherever he'd been, grinned and said simply, "Well, sir. I forget. But 'twas you who distracted me. . . ."

Rawl's face went gog's-blood red so that I feared for the young Sir Dosh. What with the night and Caroween's refusal, his temper was frayed to the bursting. "*I* distract *you*?" he roared. "If your thoughts are so addled as to accuse me of the addling, then I'm bound to think, sir, that my sword's flat across your thick skull might cure you once and for all." He grinned evilly and thrust his face close to Dosh's. "Look on me," he said, "as your doctor!"

Dosh blinked, sniffed, wiped his nose on a velvet sleeve and looked hard to me. "Is this then," he asked rhetorically, "the man who'll wed my sister, be queen's consort to my father's throne? I think not, Collin. Indeed," and he too now roared, "a single word more from this bladder-head and, despite my sister, I'll have his guts on our table's top for a close divining of tomorrow's happening."

At which point, my Rawl, raging, reached out to seize young Sir Dosh by the throat. . . .

I'd no choice but to roar louder than the two of them, yelling, "Cease now, both of you! No one is served by such intemperance. There is indeed a plan, though 'twill not be carried out by corpses. Save your damned insults for those who'll come tomorrow."

Rawl, hurling the stout Sir Dosh back to his seat, turned happily to me. "What is it, brother? I've a right to know for we've fought all too long together for there to be secrets now between us."

And there it was, the true reason for his heated anger. The coming battle's complexities he could deal with. But to feel that there was a plan—and he really couldn't imagine my not having one—to which he, my closest friend, was not privy was unacceptable.

"Hear me," I said to both of them, "and repeat it to no one." I then told them word for word exactly what I'd *twice* told the council in their presence; except that this time I conveyed a certain deliberate *intimacy*. From now on, too, they'd be a central part of the collective effort of information gathering; of seeking out the weak points of the enemy, if any, and of helping me to forge some weapon to overcome the aliens.

I stressed that there would indeed be red-war; that it would be long and hard. But that in the end we would win, and that those who fought in this, the last great fight, would live in the hearts of Marack for all eternity. . . .

"By the Gods!" Rawl exclaimed in absolute delight when I'd finished. "I've said it before, Collin. Remember? That though you oft' do swear against violence, still, to you, all violence comes! I'll now say again what I said then: I'd not trade your company, comrade, for the kingdoms of the world!"

"You've a point there, cousin," Sir Dosh said calmly, forgetting completely the brawl of the last few minutes. "And I do thank our most gracious Collin for allowing me a place in his small company. And as for you, sir, well I'm minded of my sister's wicked temper and I doubt me not that 'twill be well served by you."

The red gleam came again to Rawl's eyes. If he'd actually understood what Dosh was saying he just may have seized him again. But he didn't, and so the matter lay. When I think on it, I hadn't the slightest idea either as to what Sir Dosh had said. But neither, I mused grimly, had Sir Dosh. . . .

We drank more sviss then. And Rawl seized a lute from someone and sang as we continued to drink until all things became foggy. Indeed, in the wee hours I again found myself in Murie's corridor knocking on her door.

This time 'twas she who answered; stood in her arched entry in a diaphanous shift, legs apart, hands on hips to laugh merrily and say, "Well now here's a pretty sight. The savior of Marack, my own true love. He who has slain his hundreds many times for my favor and my hand. How now, in truth, can I turn such constancy away?" Her smile disappeared. She pressed quite close to me to say huskily, "How now, indeed, could I do that, when drunk, sober or even playing the fool, he's still all that I've ever wished for bed and kingdom. Come in, lout. I'll make a place for you upon my body."

I awoke in the gray dawn, or rather, I was awakened, ruthlessly, by Murie. My mouth was like the inside of an armorer's glove. My head rang to the screams of a myriad of tic-tic birds outside the stone lacework of the windows. Like my own and Rawl's, Murie's apartment was situated some three hundred feet above the winding Cyr River.

I tiptoed out. Protocol permitted one to sleep with one's betrothed before marriage, even when she was a princess of Marack. But one must never be caught in bed with her. The consequences were not pleasant to contemplate. Before leaving, I kissed her berry-red lips and the lid of one stone-bright eye that regarded me with the contradictory light of true love and deep suspicion. She sleepily sought to pull me to her, while mumbling, "Be pleased to wait on me, my lord, after we've breakfasted."

I nuzzled my acquiescence.

We breakfasted, my now happy Rawl, Sir Dosh and myself—Rawl too had somehow managed to insinuate himself through Caroween's chamber door—in the common-room on gog-milk, bread and delicious flatfish from the Cyr. We even allowed a handful of student pages from the city's collegium, on castle duty during the summer months, to join us.

In Marack, I was the students' hero. Indeed, if and when I was killed and supposedly went to that strictest of heavens as ruled by the gods, Ormon, Wimbely and the lost child, Harris, I'm quite sure they would vote me their patron saint. . . . Once, in a needed act of bravado, when I and Rawl and the martyred Breen Hoggle-Fitz had challenged *fifty* of Kelb's best swordsmen who'd arrived at Marack's court, under the spell of the Dark One, and ostensibly to seek Murie's hand in marriage for their Prince Keilwher, we'd chosen forty-seven students to fight at our side to make up the difference. We'd won, naturally, which made our students the heroes of the day. They'd never forgotten it. Indeed, I now, at all times, had a company of students as my personal bodyguards—when I needed them. They attended classes in the town below while being taught the bearing of all arms by Marack's master swordsmen.

Rawl, Murie, Caroween, Sir Dosh and our Omnian companion, the lecherous Lors Sernas, along with myself, spent all the morning hawking in the bright sunlight, though not going too far at any time from the castle. While hawking, of course, we kept worried eyes on the cloud-fleeced skies for whatever might appear.

Murie, as a reward for my nocturnal visit, or so she thought, had left Hooli in her quarters. Actually, I'd looked forward to her bringing the little bastard along. If the real Hooli was back, I wanted to be there when he *came* back. Not that he didn't have other means of contact. Indeed, it was all ninety-nine percent mental anyway; except it made me feel good when the real Hooli would do something, like thumb his nose at me when no one was looking, stick out his tongue, stand on his head and the like. He dearly loved to make me laugh. Indeed, he delighted in what he referred to as "Terran humor," *humanoid humor*, the like of which he'd not found anywhere. In any event, she'd left him home.

The others of our party, in true Fregisian style, had put the thought of the enemy ships from their minds as soon as the subject was dropped. So, while our dottles trotted gaily over the meadows and through lush stands of great trees to the south of the castle, and our fierce birds of prey knocked pitty-docks, tic-tics and fat bartins out of the skies by the pound, the danger was ignored.

We had lunch in a sparkling meadow at high noon, entertained the while by our Sernas who told a wicked tale of incest in a branch of the Hishian ducal families (there were no kings in the south; the Dark One hadn't allowed it), which brought blushes and statements of "Fie!" and the like from Murie and Caroween, though they'd listened avidly and on occasion licked their lips. Then, we descended a ravine to swim in the Cyr River, after which we rested on the river's bank. 'Twas very pleasant, flies and insects buzzing and my head in Murie's lap.

When she too dozed, I used the moment to press one of the brightly colored stones that adorned my belt. It glowed warmly pink. . . .

"Come in," I called mentally. "Come in. Come in, Kriloy."

He did, his voice worried but sleepy. "Kyrie? What's happening?"

"Nothing yet. What's with you? What's with the ships?"

"They're not moving; haven't moved an inch since the *Deneb*'s destruction. They're just there."

"And the galactic grid, the matrix?"

"I'm working on something. If you hear a loud bang and see a big cloud to the south, you'll know I failed."

"You're going to play with the CT pack?"

"Yup."

"Okay. It's probably your best chance. Still, don't give up on the mag-lines. You tap 'em right and you got all the power you could ever need."

"I tap 'em wrong and who know's what'll happen."

"Couldn't be worse than CT fission."

"So. How's everyone taking it?" He changed the subject.

"As well as can be expected."

"Sheeee!"

"Okay, look," I said. "You'll hear from me if anything breaks at all. And I expect to hear from you, right?"

"Right."

But somehow it wasn't right. You can "work on something" in two ways: play at it, or be serious. I'd give him another twenty-four hours. . . .

At three p.m. we returned to the field for a bit of archery. By five we'd thumbed our noses at the idea of the enemy showing up at all, this day. We returned to the castle.

At six, in our respective apartments, Rawl and I had just completed our ablutions and I was patting cologne into all the right places, preparatory to going to the common room for the hour before sup. He called hastily and excitedly from where he stood at one of the south windows. "It's here!" he yelled. "And there's just one of them. . . ."

I ran to look. Sure enough, a single ship of those constituting the remaining pyramid of the alien warcraft was floating lazily some miles to the south. It seemed to be coming in our direction, but at a slower speed than a dottle's trot.

Before it reached the field, we'd raced for the corridors and the courtyard exit, throwing on our clothes as we went. I whistled up a couple of student pages who quickly brought our mounts from the stables. The great courtyard was bedlam as dozens of dottles in all their finery were brought to be mounted and pranced as a part of the entourage of the royal family, and others, all preparing to move out to greet the "guest."

Our plan, such as it was, provided for myself, Rawl, Fel-Holdt and a dozen or so of Marack's proven leaders to take a low profile. We would follow in the wake of the king, but at a short distance. I'd pleaded vehemently that the royal family not go at all; that the task of welcome be left to a handful of older lords as heralds, and with certain of the merchant class as representatives and the like.

The king would not hear of it.

"Nay! Collin," he'd said strongly. "In the main we accept your counsel, sir. But I could not wear this crown did I not truly lead my people in bad times as well as good. And to lead them is to take all risks pertinent to kings. Say no more."

And off he went. I'd begged that Murie, at least, stay behind. She would not. She but looked to me proudly, leaned from her high saddle to kiss me, hard, and trotted off in the wake of her father to be at his right hand.

Both sets of ponderous gates in the huge double walls had been flung open. Even as the king stared out the enemy craft had arrived to hover and then to settle precisely where I'd thought it would, on Glagmaron's military field. The king rode with Murie to his right and the queen to his left. After them, Per-Looris, Gen-Rondin, Gen-Hargis, the great lord Ap Tils and his companion, Gen-Vrees of the sea city of Klimpinge, the Lord Dols-Kieren and many more. The king made sure that he'd not be lacking in retinue. With him, too, went the five hundred men of the castle guard, the commanders of which, down to the lowliest sergeants, had been warned by Fel-Holdt himself to stay the swords of any man who sought to draw—on pain of instant death!

Knights, ladies and castle visitors swarmed after them. And all this with only those of the council aware that this ship that had flown down from heaven might take their lives.

"And I warrant!" Rawl exclaimed as we rode out, "that if trouble comes, 'twill be from them. For they'll react to any threat of danger as they've been taught to do. They are Marackians."

I grunted noncommittally for he'd said it almost as if he wished it to be that way.

At two hundred yards to the inner wall's left we came to the second main gate to the bridge and trotted through and over. The king's party, bright banners waving, advanced leisurely. All those who'd been at joust, swordplay, or just picnicking on the field, also moved curiously but cautiously toward the ship. Their numbers, plus the knights, ladies, mendicants from the castle and the garrison, made up a sizable crowd of a few thousands. When my twenty or so caught up, we were hard put to force a way through; this, since we wore no armor and had even covered our blazonry a bit so as not to attract too much attention. We managed, finally, to get within fifty feet of the royal family, and then to the fore of the mob who'd made a semi-circle at about seventy feet from the "visitor."

I had time to observe it. It was indeed a warcraft; certainly no merchant or passenger hulk for colonizing. We could easily have designed the thing ourselves, its lines were that simple. Sleek, rounded in the right places, elongated in others; generator-converter pods; sensor bulges, command-control and weapons sections, it was but a quarter of the size of the *Deneb*. Its nose and bridge, potentially transluscent, were opaque now, for whatever reasons.

It just sat there sort of brooding, and nothing happened.

For this reason the waiting crowd became apprehensive, quiet. Time passed and still nothing. The great red-gold orb of Fomalhaut I was already low on the horizon. I didn't like it at all.

Then Sir Dosh spoke *sotto voce* to my rear. "By the gods, my lord. Here comes the other one, the *big* one."

I looked back quickly. Sure enough, the blue sphere, appearing from straight above seemed to be falling rapidly toward us, an optical effect. People screamed, thinking it was actually falling on them. Little coveys of the more timid ran this way and that. Instead of landing, however, it hovered for but a few minutes then slowly wafted back toward the west like a great blue balloon, going finally to ground on a barren hilltop some three miles beyond the winding Cyr. From where we watched it now looked like a small blue marble.

Only then did a port in the warship's side open to extend a telescopic ramp which first formed a platform, then a series of steps to the ground. This last was the first small indication of the nature of the life form aboard. The first of the aliens then appeared, to be followed by five companions. They *walked* casually, arrogantly, if you will, to the very edge of the platform. There they halted, placed hands on hips and gazed down at us with that certain look that I'd seen so often before and on so many worlds. It was the easy, familiar, *scan* of the conqueror, the overlord, the master!

The creatures were humanoid! They also had blue-purple eyes, and showed here and there a patch of brown, black, or golden *fur* through cunning slits in their resplendent raiment.

The creatures were, without a doubt, men. Moreover, they were *Alphians!*

To my Marackians they must have seemed at first glance as nothing less than gods—and had not all men been created in the image of Ormon? Their clothing was of metallic silvers, golds, bronzes and shimmering iridescent weaves. They wore a sort of fitted jupon-suit over a white on white collared shirt beneath a spun-steel hauberk. Each jupon showed a blazonry of lords who had no doubt lived on destroyed Alpha so many years before. They wore short yellow boots and a broad belt with a tooled leather pouch attached. At the side of each belt was a holstered weapon. To the left a blaster, I was sure, and to the right, perhaps a heat-ray or laser gage. . . . And then, and here was the anachronism of all anachronisms—across each individual back was a sheathed greatsword; each haft and pommel glistening, as did the sheath itself, with a wealth of jewels to dim the light of even those "baubles" which Lors Sernas had so desired.

They were *indeed* as gods!

And if they'd had but a single ounce of brains to match their beauty and their *manliness*, they would have instantly been accepted as such. The *ooohs* and *aaahs* sweeping the field were solidly indicative of our Marackians' pleasure. But they had neither brains nor that pinch of humanity that somehow exists in each true humanoid, else they could not have done what they did. More! That they were not gods could be excused; that they were to immediately prove themselves the opposite could not!

Two fresh-faced squires raced forward on the orders of the king to halt in a swirl of dust and to cause their dottles to rear upon four of their six legs and to wave their painted forepaws in the intricate "court salute" to visitors.

The act completed, they then called out in unison, their

eyes gleaming with pleasure at what they saw: "Oh great lords from beyond our skies, hear now this greeting from our noble king. He salutes you all right kindly and begs that—"

Which was as far as they got.

The leader of the six—he'd been the first to step to the platform's edge—held up a hand. His eyes were cold, contemptuous. In the face of the silence *he* had ordered, he then smiled fatuously, drew his blaster and deliberately sent two glowing shafts of crimson energy into the chests and stomachs of each of the youths. Their shrill death screams were instantly echoed by their dottles; indeed by *all* our dottles. For dottles, though they are used in war, do not themselves fight, since they cannot abide the sight of blood and slaughter. . . . The heralds' cringing dottles too were then shot down.

The effect was an instant total fear and loathing. A Fregisian warrior is quickly inured to blood himself. Still the sight of the wanton killings plus the brutal slaughter of the gentle dottles produced pure trauma.

To a ground-swell roar of absolute rage a movement began toward the ship from the block of men-at-arms and warriors—to be held back only by the most frenzied efforts of the sergeants appointed by Fel-Holdt. But no such hindrance blocked the castled knights and gallants. At least a dozen of these dashed forward, swords drawn, to range themselves below the platform and to scream a demand that the visitors, "account for their cowardly act, and now!"

But weapons had now also leapt to the hands of all the insanely laughing half-dozen from the ship. The twelve *and* their animals were instantly cut down by blazing blood-red bolts and penciled shafts of blues and greens.

The crowd, falling back of its own accord, moaned its terror. But still more white-faced but courageous Marackian swordsmen surged to the fore, and more. And the six slaughtered them; butchered the cringing, piteously crying dottles too, so that within seconds the field within the half-circle around the sky ship was a charnel house of blasted bits and pieces of the bodies of Marackians and dottles alike. Some even burned with an unearthly, hellish glow.

It stopped only when the king, inclusive of myself and those with me in his entourage, deliberately put ourselves between those who'd still fight and the enemy who'd be only too happy to destroy them all if they tried.

With the king's first movement, I'd said quickly to Rawl and Dosh: "Now here's the real danger. Prepare yourselves! For if they even begin to level their weapons at the House of Marack, I'll kill them all as is my prowess. Which means, of course, that we'll have to attack the ship at once, to seize the entry. We'll have little chance of victory, but we've not much choice either."

The satisfied, almost *relieved* hiss of their indrawn breaths was comforting. But the five and their leader made no move to destroy Caronne, so the moment passed.

At that point they'd killed many hundreds, deliberately.

There was then an awful silence, until the aliens holstered their weapons, folded their arms upon their shining, emblazoned chests and stared contemptuously down at us.

Their leader again stepped out. "Who among you barbarian scum," he roared in great bell-like tones, "dares call himself the leader of this stinking, unwashed pack." His insults, like the unwarranted killings, were intentional; designed to put down, intimidate—and destroy. "I am Tarkiis Rolls," he continued, "of the great race of Kentii (the name of the original Alphians). I command a fleet of ships such as the one you see before you. We have come to give this world and all upon it to *Diis,* our god. Let him stand forth who is your leader!"

"Now!" I again warned my stalwarts.

But again their was no need.

The language of Tarkiis was stilted and slurred of tonal inflections. Still it was understandable for it retained the words of protocol—and this across a full five thousand years. I thought it strange, to say the least, that this should be.

The king came forward, pale, proud and unafraid. I noted his almost surreptitious gesture that none accompany him. He announced simply, "I am he."

"And *what* are you?"

"I am the king, the ruler of this land. I am the head of the royal family of Marack, and of the Council of the kingdom of Marack."

"Show me at once the others of this family and this council. And I warn all of you—" His voice lifted, became almost stentorian as he looked out over the gathered throng, "that an order from me, or from any of mine to any of *yours,* must be instantly obeyed—on pain of death! Pass the word on, for I will say it no more."

Murie, Caroween, and the trembling Queen Tyndil rode their mounts a few paces forward—as did we fifty of the privy council.

Tarkiis's grin revealed perfect teeth, capped or otherwise. "Come closer," he demanded. "Two things do I know of you already: One, that you call yourselves warriors. Two, that you're actually scum. I'd advise you, therefore, not to let the first confuse you as to your worth, for you have none. Moreover, do not attempt to test us again, else all that you've known will be as if it had never been. Halt now!" he ordered with an accompanying snap of his fingers.

We halted.

I could see Murie clearly; still, I flicked my contacts to four powers so that we were staring eye to eye. Hers were filled with icy anger. Tears of rage lay on her apple cheeks. Flecks of blood shone on her lips where she'd bitten them in helpless rage during the killing. Queen Tyndil, at best of a light and airy substance, was now out of it, her large eyes blank and staring. Just as well, I thought. . . . With few exceptions the looks on the faces of the rest of the council bespoke a simple suicidal hatred. Had not the king and others who'd clung to sanity held them back, they'd still have attacked—and we'd all be dead.

The ascetic Per-Looris had, through it all, been able to maintain his limited "null" around the king. Though uncertain of its potential against the Alphian's weaponry, I knew it would have *some* effect. Indeed, I was tempted to press a belt stud for my "null," but thought better of it. The reason? Well, since *I* was aware of Per-Looris's limited "null," perhaps Tarkiis would be too; which meant that their sensors would also hit in on me. Why take the risk?

Tarkiis began to talk. His five companions, uncaring now and no longer watchful, simply relaxed, withdrew somewhat to his rear, lit small tubes of paper from their pouches and inhaled deeply. Interesting. They'd "turned us off," so that for them we'd ceased to exist. So much for what they truly thought of us as opposed to the pleasures of their own company.

Tarkiis, the would-be overlord, then spoke oddly, as if by rote; as if he were reciting something but with little knowledge of the content. "We are your forefathers," he shouted, so that spittle formed at the corners of his mouth. "We are from that world which your elders fled in cowardice in the long ago to then degenerate and to become as animals upon this world, the second of your sun-star, Fletis. We've come to claim you. Not as our equals, but as beasts who once were men. In the far future, perhaps, your children will become again what they once were. In the meantime we are here to guarantee that you'll sink no further in degeneracy than the level on which we've found you."

He continued on and on in this vein. And even as he talked he seemed unaware that those he spoke to hadn't the slightest idea as to what he was talking about beyond the fact that he intended ruling them against their will. Moreover, his wanton killing had already revealed the lack of even a barbaric morality within himself and his warriors.

And finally, his dialogue suggested that he actually had but a limited understanding of anything. Indeed, *it was as if he'd but recently been briefed on the very history he was expounding;* and even that, superficially, from a book of fiction.

Twilight was now hard upon us, and he chose to cut his speech short to demand abruptly that a dozen Marackians meet with him on the morrow, including the royal family, at which time he'd appoint new administrators and establish a new set of laws.

I could not help but note that when he'd mentioned the royal family, his eyes had fixed hard on Murie, while she glared back at him. . . .

Then two wealthy merchants of Glagmaron City, quick to sense an absolute shift in the power base, thrust themselves forward to beg Tarkiis that they be allowed to speak. On their knees, in obvious obeisance, they both then put their heads to the ground.

The risk was great. The merchants did show courage. The possibility of gold and power is often the catalyst to change a flimple to a gerd. Tarkiis's brow blackened, at first, so that the merchants trembled. Then, curious, he agreed.

The leader of the two raised his head. "I am Rol-Tabis, lord of lords," he began unctiously. "And this is Bar Tabis, my brother. 'Tis that we and our friends have long believed that there were other gods beyond those we've been forced to serve. The proof's now here, in *yourselves*! In your skyship. We but ask, lord, to be the first to serve you."

To show their ardor the two men touched their foreheads to the dirt again. Rol-Tabis continued. "We but wish too, great lord, to be but a small part of your glory and to aid in the administration of this land which is now yours. And we do assure you that you'll find many like us who, with our help, see to it that all you wish will be carried out."

At which they again lowered their heads to the ground and were silent.

Tarkiis's immediate reaction was to laugh wildly, contemptuously, and to call to his compatriots. These bestirred themselves from their conversation to glance down at the object of his hilarity. One, still holding his blaster, pointed the weapon at Rol-Tabis. But Tarkiis stayed his hand, saying while still laughing, "Let be, Marques. If we're to set up a game of rewards and punishments, why then I'd say that these two deserve the first reward. As for punishment, why that we can always give. Nay! They've set an example. We'll see how it turns out."

He then ordered them to their feet, saying, "Attend on me tomorrow. And woe be to all the rest of you," he threatened, "if you come not to my conference. Hey! Why, I'll even drink to you in the liquor of the land. You there!" He pointed to a young student warrior who sat his mount next to Rawl. "Toss me that canteen at your beast's saddle."

The student did so, lips tight compressed. If he'd had a choice, I knew, he'd be flinging his fal-dirk straight to the monster's heart. He flung the canteen instead.

Tarkiis caught it adeptly; uncapped it, put it to his lips and drank. He immediately spat the contents out shouting, "Faugggh! What filth is this you give me?"

He hurled it back. But Rawl leaned in front of the young student to snatch it from the air and, in full view of the angered Tarkiis, to mumble a few words over it. Shouting boldly, "Try it again, my lord, I've taken the edge off it," he tossed it back.

Tarkiis tipped the canteen to his mouth, swallowed. A grin of pleasure split his handsome features. The gog-milk had been changed to *sviss*, the finest of Fregisian brandy. He said to Rawl, his eyes flat. "You'll come to my hearing too. Now leave. All of you. And when I open this lock at high noon tomorrow, I expect our field to be cleansed of all this filth." He pointed with a limp hand to the bloodied swaths of men and beasts. "Now, go!"

And we went. . . .

But even as we withdrew, I saw that the two brothers had

held back to exchange a few more hurried words with Tarkiis, who then dismissed them again, contemptuously.

We trotted white-lipped toward the castle. Curious, I asked Rawl the simple question: "Why?"

"Why what?"

"That business with the gog-milk."

He shrugged. "I meant to try them, Collin; to see if the bastard knew of our magick."

"And?"

"Well, he does. 'Tis obvious, else he'd have said something."

"And if he knows?"

"Why then, 'tis useless. Moreover, what we have, he'll have too—but ten times over."

"Nay, old comrade," I chuckled happily. "It just may be that 'tis the other way around. For I'm thinking that he not only knows nothing of our magick, but likewise knows nothing of how his own ship works. To him (like yourself, I could have added), the two facts are one and the same. You've saved Marack, sir! Not," I exclaimed immediately to his instant whoop, "that it'll be that easy. Indeed, there'll be sufficient blood before the final act to satisfy even you. I promise it!"

Returning through the main gates, I looked one last time toward the east to see the Tabis brothers already on the hill road and riding madly toward Glagmaron City. There would always be Tabis brothers, I mused. Without such opportunists, egocentrics, psychotics and the like, society, as we know it, would indeed mature in but half the time. . . . They disappeared in the swift moving shadows of night. And, as if it were ordained, great storm clouds rushed in again from the east, their rolling shapes all rent with slashing lightning.

To hell with the Tabis brothers!

We'd cross that bridge when we had to. We had now to snatch victory from defeat, and this with the scantest of weaponry and from under the very noses of our insane would-be overlords. Who, I wondered, in all the galaxy, had ever faced such odds? There sat a warship with a hole-punch-warp potential upon our jousting field. It surely had a crew of as many as forty to sixty heavily armed, in the truest sense of the word, Alphian warriors. Across the Cyr River at a distance of three miles—and there was a most definite connection between the two—was the blue sphere, silent, *brooding*. As the sun set its color had changed from electric to slate-gray, to scabrous, so that it seemed to be dying. I prayed that such was the case.

Those from the city below had returned to the city, bringing their tale of terror. Those from the castle, excepting for the privy council, were sent about their business. They went fearfully, for the image of the ship and its death-dealing shafts of light was ever with them. They would linger long over sup for the escape it afforded.

The guards on the walls, with full knowledge of what had happened, were now finely alert to any action from the ship or sphere.

We went directly to the king's small council hall. Food, drink and other sundries were ordered up. A large fire was lighted against the beginning storm. More candles were brought to replace the nubs of yesternight.

After silently downing the first drink of our individual choice—there was no gaiety—we settled to the business at hand. Gen-Rondin summed up at length what had happened. He even had praise for me, for my having cautioned prudence so that our council, king, and indeed most of our castle lords still lived to, hopefully, fight another day. "As to what we've learned from all this," he concluded dolorously, "well that remains to be seen. Do you wish to speak at this point, Sire?" he asked, turning to the king as was the custom.

Caronne was wise enough to know his limitations. "I defer to all of you," he replied calmly. "The wisdom of kings is derived from those with whom he surrounds himself. If he's of a frivolous bent, 'tis reflected in his council. Such kingdoms seldom survive their rulers. 'Tis my hope that *I've* chosen well. We are in your hands."

Fel-Holdt arose to play devil's advocate. He said bluntly, "I deem that skyship to be impregnable. What say you all to this?"

They glumly agreed.

"Since this truth also applies to the other, the blue sphere," he continued, "we've no choice but to send our royal family to a hidden place until we can find a way to deal with this spawn of ghast. Why say you?"

Again they agreed.

But Caronne arose to reject any idea of sanctuary. "My place," he announced flatly, "is here! At the great battle of Dunguring, I left our castle to lead Marack's armies against the enemy. But that was an all-or-nothing engagement. When our Lord Commander, together with our Collin, then sought out the Dark One in his dread land of Om and destroyed him, I was forced by circumstances to guard our center, just here, against those of *you* who'd become mind-possessed.

"So must this be again. While the king lives and is at Glagmaron Castle, though he be in the deepest dungeon, then Marack, too, is not dead. If I am slain here, why then I'm also martyred, as is our country, likewise. In any case, if I live and am here and am oppressed, opposition can then be rallied. . . . I'll leave the particulars for such a strategy for those best equipped for it. Collin!" he called sharply. "What say you to this riddle within a riddle? Those from the skyship say they are our ancestors, the very ones you've described as having been destroyed on that other beauteous world; while we, or our fathers were being magicked here, across the heavens. Are they our ancestors? And if so, what shall we do now? I've an observation, if you will: If these are indeed the sons of our forebear; of those who destroyed their world in the long ago, I can now understand how it could be. For I say to you all that whatever they are or were, they are no longer such. 'Tis *they* who have degenerated. And 'tis *we* who have grown!"

He'd put his finger on it! Proving the Adjusters' principle that leadership bestows upon all leaders some modicum of knowledge that they'd otherwise not have. Though such is not always the case, it was most certainly proven here, with this king of Marack. . . .

I arose. "Sire and lords," I called, "to claim such ancestry is one thing; to prove it another. I've seen what you've seen. And I say that our king speaks truly: that in the flesh this may be so. But in their conduct, which opposes all that we hold dear, it is truly they who have degenerated."

I got a burst of applause for that. "However," I continued when the acclaim died, "the problem we must deal with now is to find a solution to the whole, else we and all that we know will perish."

I then paused to draw a deep breath and say dramatically, "We have a weapon, sirs, that these usurpers do not. It is weaker, true. But!" and I raised a hand to stay their instant enthusiasm, "if it is properly organized it can help to win the day. This weapon is the magick possessed by our witches, warlocks and sorcerers. But, and I repeat, it must be *organized* to be effective.

"It is in this respect, then," I continued, "that I now ask permission to leave this very night with such of my student warriors as will accompany me, and with sufficient lords of this council, inclusive of our master strategist, Fel-Holdt, to rally the northern kingdoms against the enemy. We should find no problem in this last, my lords, since the remaining enemy ships will most certainly have landed at Corchoon, in Kelb; Janblink, in Great Ortmund; Rheen, in Ferlach, and at Saks in Gheese.

"I also ask that our Princess Murie Nigaard be allowed to accompany me, her betrothed. For it would not be wise to leave both the king and the princess in the hands of our enemy."

I'd meant to continue, but Murie arose to yell: "Hey, Collin! Though 'tis true that you'll be my lord, 'tis also true that I'll remain your princess. And so 'tis I, sir, who'll have the final say here. Now do you list me well and do not take me wrong. . . . Those from the skyship are men and should therefore be dealt with as such by you and our Lord Fel-Holdt, in *your* way. I, in the meantime, will deal with them in *mine*! There are many ways to win a battle, sirs. The stakes are high. I therefore choose to stay and with my person to delay them, to buy time to organize this struggle. And that, Collin, is the way it will be."

I was struck momentarily dumb!

It was the one thing I'd not expected to hear. Indeed, so conditioned had I become to full possession of that nubile and delightfully rewarding body that any suggestion as to its real ownership and real purpose had simply been written out of my thinking. In effect, and completely unknown even to myself, I'd long since lost any measure of balance and maturity in that most delicate of areas—jealousy!

The effect now was an instant redness to cloud my eyes and to rage inside my head so that I called out, "But my lady, you fantasize, at best. One cannot control these creatures. Indeed, 'twould be presumptuous to attempt to—considering the risk."

With the redness had come a series of indelible strobes, each of them showing Murie with Tarkiis. And each of them, born of my own quite wicked imagination, was so graphically specific as to make me literally grind my teeth in impotent fury. It was *uncanny*! Especially, since there was still a part of me that recognized the schizoid nature of my thoughts. In all my thirty years I'd never felt a streak of jealousy in the accepted sense; nor had I ever lost my—as Hooli would say, in Terran archaic—cool. Why now, the small sane part of me wondered, this nonsense, this paradigm of childish pique?

And there she stood, my fairy-tale princess, and in the exact stance that so epitomized her total personality: hands on hips, booted legs apart, and with her elvish eyes hard on me, challenging. She ended the quite weird tableau herself by simply bouncing her golden bangs, frowning and saying easily: "Hey, Collin. *I* think I can!"

Her words were a flatted sword smacking my chest.

My reply was choked; I was actually trying to swallow my words before I said them, because I *knew* better. My saner side lost. I heard myself saying foolishly, "Murie. Hear me. I'll not allow it!"

To which she replied between clenched teeth. "My lord. You *will* allow it!"

There are a myriad of shibboleths, procedural methods in protocol, customs, rites, whatever, and all of them within the accepted mores of any developing society. . . . I now stood mutely within that absolutely silent hall, for I knew full well that in Marack, I'd just broken every one.

I drew a deep breath, focused *in* and seized hard upon myself. I held for seconds, creating the proper rhythm until the red left and my heart stilled. I then said quietly to all that silence, "Sire. My Princess. My lords. I ask your pardon and deeply apologize to all of you. Our Princess of Marack is right and I am wrong. It is, sirs, that I'd thought too much upon my own needs and too little on the problem at hand. So let it be. I will now, if you wish, withdraw myself as the leader of this project, or continue, as this council will decide. One way or the other, I remain at Marack's service."

The silence persisted. To my rear Rawl coughed, deliberately or nervously. It came as the loudest crash of thunder.

The king himself arose finally to hold each of the fifty with his eyes and say—and there was some amusement in his voice—"Well now, so much for youth. If we've learned nought tonight but that our Collin, too, is human, we're still the gainer. Yet, the time grows short, Sir Lenti; as you yourself have warned us (he'd called me by my Marackian name). We await, therefore, a continuance of your discourse."

I nodded, breathed deep again and continued as if nothing had happened. "We will go first," I told them, "to Gortfin Castle. For, if I recall correctly, it is there that the Lady Elioseen, greatest of witches, sorcerers, warlocks and the like in all the north, is still imprisoned. I'm even reminded that 'twas she who spiritied myself, my comrade, Sir Rawl Fergis, and her niece, the Princess Murie Nigaard, from the Glagmaron highroad to Castle Gortfin in those far days before Dunguring; beginning thusly, the war of Marack against Kelb and the Dark One's hordes from below the River-Sea.

"I've heard nought of her since Durguring, 'cepting that she'd been put in the care of six of her kind, for only that many, enjoined, could stay her power. I propose, my lords, to use Elioseen's magick now in the interest of all Fregis. If the price we pay is her freedom, why then it should be little enough in the face of what we might lose without it. . . . What say you all? I think 'tis the proper path—that we work with the Lady Elioseen, on the one hand to organize all Fregis's magick against these sky men, and on the other, to reorganize our own disbanded forces to oppose in every way the new evil that's come upon us.

"In this regard," I warned them, "there'll be many like the merchants of this afternoon, who'll turn against us for power and gold. Such men work quickly to prove themselves to their new masters. In the case of the merchants and the others they hinted at, it could be only hours before they have armed men in the field against us. Which means that we must move to nip *that* in the bud, and instantly."

Per-Looris interrupted, his voice barely a whisper. "Collin," he said. " 'Tis obvious, regarding our Lady Elioseen, that you know not whereof you speak. Her power was in some ways greater than that of the Dark One. You must understand that other than the twenty-thousand troops, there were *twelve*, not six of us who went against her at Gortfin. And I assure you, sir, we'd still not have won except for a surge of great power from an unknown source. 'Twas because of that alone that we won and she lost. To free her now, young lord, whatever her pledges, is to risk a darkness to easily rival that of Tarkiis."

I smiled sadly. "Nay, good sorcerer. You may know your Elioseen. But *I* know such as Tarkiis well. I doubt she could equal him with all her tricks. Now I'll ask you sir: Is there a witch or warlock, *aside* from the Lady Elioseen, who can do what she did: deliver the princess, myself, Rawl and the good Dame Malion across two hundred miles of space with but the snap of a finger?"

"There is not."

"Yet 'tis precisely *that* magick that we'll need. My Lords." I turned to face the council. "There's an old saying: Better the devil we know than the one we don't. I've never seen His Majesty's sister; never talked to her. I deem it appropriate now that I do so. I'm bound to think that at heart she's Marackian and that she will recognize our mutual peril. As for after, well sirs, I cannot begin to match her powers here. But I can *exile* her to where her *words* can wreak no harm on anyone."

The king seized his head in both hands and groaned. "She's my sister, Collin. I swear, I've never sought her death."

"Nor would I seek it," I told him quickly. "There are other worlds, my lord, like this one—as our princess, Per-Looris and the others can now attest. She could be happy there."

"So be it then. How say the rest of you?" He lifted his head to show a face quite gray and weary.

They agreed and we discussed it some more until it was generally understood what we would do and how we'd do it. We then pledged solemnly that no single word of what we'd decided would pass our lips outside this chamber—on pain of death!

We were to leave immediately after sup, which was beginning that very minute, with tureen-laden platters being marched in from the kitchens. A thing to remember: though the sky is collapsing around him, a true Fregisian will never refuse a proffered meal; nor will he allow extraneous happenings to interfere in his pleasure in it. We'd even begun to relax somewhat. For now at least we had some idea what we would do; no real plan, true. But it was something to believe in. Moreover, I'd kept a few aces up my sleeve which could speed things up considerably, if I could get them moving.

My prime concern was the sphere, not the ship. I half believed that with a modicum of luck we could take the ship. The sphere, however, was something else. The sphere had destroyed a starship, *and a starship was indestructible*!

Murie had joined me for sup. She sat close, sad-eyed and quiet, while most around us, in defiance of the morrow, had even become a bit merry. She'd been that way, I'd noted, since the name of our Lady Elioseen had first been introduced. I tried to comfort her, touched her when I could, along with other surreptitious intimacies. At first I'd thought she had second thoughts as to staying. But when she could stand it no longer what I suspected to be the true reason, surfaced . . . She said hoarsely, "My Lord. What have you heard; what do you *know* of my aunt, the Lady Elioseen?"

"Very little," I said lightly, though I knew what everyone else knew—that Elioseen was one of Marack's true beauties.

Keeping a straight face, I refilled our glasses and raised mine to pledge Rawl who was seated across the table. He raised his own glumly. The reason? Caroween had agreed to stay with Murie. "For the same purpose," she'd told my shieldman. "Our cause demands it. I, too, am a princess, and will soon be queen in Great Ortmund. Tactics, my good father told me, are but the tools of the trade. 'Tis strategy that's the art. What's best for Marack," she reasoned, "is therefore best for Ortmund."

He couldn't argue with that; indeed, that wasn't what was troubling him. The strategy was his *bête noir*. For she had yet to define it clearly. . . .

Murie, thinking my thoughts had wandered, pinched me to get my attention, as was her way. "My aunt," she informed me, "is more than a sorceress. She's an *enchantress*, too. . . . 'Tis said that all men who see her love her."

I raised my eyebrows, perversely happy to see that she was as jealous as I had been. And, I thought smugly, with less reason! Well now, my love, I mused inwardly, here indeed is a game that two can play. To her, I said, "Well mayhap she'll find me not so vulnerable."

"Just *mayhap*?"

"Hey, Murie. I'd be even less so had I a certain dimpled

tummy within reach to distract me." I placed a probing hand beneath the table and walked my fingers all around upon the delightfully velvet covered object in question.

From habit, she squirmed deliciously, though a deep frown had touched her forehead. Still she made no move to thrust me away. She said intensely, "I know her, Collin!"

"How could you not. She's your aunt." I let my eyes wander again to show disinterest.

"My father's a full twenty-five years her senior, Collin. She's your age. 'Tis said that her birth was a miracle of Wimbely. Her mother died of it."

"That young? And with such power? It makes no sense, my love. I'd accept an aging facsimile of our good Per-Looris. But at age *thirty*, and the greatest worker of magic in all the north?"

I too frowned. All games aside, I wondered, had the Dark One had a hand in it? There was something here that I didn't like at all. . . .

"She was born with it, so 'tis said."

Fel-Holdt signaled then that the time of departure was near. He'd sent two daring young warriors down the castle's number one secret passage—it surfaced at the foot of the cliffs on the west road circling Glagmaron city. Their task: to contact the wardens of the king's dottle herds to the north. We'd need four dottles per rider, for we would each ride straight through to Gortfin, a distance of over two hundred miles. There would be a picked company of two hundred swordsmen and fifty of my best student-warriors. Fel-Holdt, by this time, would have also selected some two dozen lords and knights who were bone-loyal to the king and skilled in all manner of leadership. The lords and swordsmen, plus half of my students, would ride with Fel-Holdt; the rest with me.

Therefore the need of two hundred and fifty dottles on the river-road to take our people *around* the city to the herds; while I and mine rode directly through it to attract the attention of whatever forces our merchants would have had time to amass. I'd told the others that any attempt by the merchants would be perfunctory at best; designed more to capture one or two of ours as both a present and a source of information to Tarkiis. They would send maybe twenty or thirty; this, to attack what they would presume to be but a dozen or so couriers—and I had a plan to upset even that.

Fel-Holdt's signal had meant that his men would soon be starting out, which meant that my group too should get ready.

A burst of hard rain literally churned the slabs in the outer courtyard, like a great waterfall. Lackeys came running to curtain the windows with heavy tarps. All around us the candles guttered as if touched by the whispers of corpse-men.

Murie was saying, with a certain ill-hidden testiness, "Well, then. I doubt not but that you're looking forward to a new conquest."

"That *I'll* be looking? By the gods," I said meanly in reply, " 'tis not I who suggests that you dally here with that buff-furred, murderous manikin. You think to bend him to your wishes? You've thought wrong. He'll eat you up, my lady, and that's a fact."

Damn! I was talking again when I should be listening. What, I wondered, had happened to my Adjuster training? A single elvish eye looked up to measure me; this, from where her cheek touched her chest. She said demurely, moving queen to check, "Well then, my love, the joust will not lack for pleasant moments, will it? I'll tell you now that few women in all Marack would reject advances from so comely a person."

I went instantly cold and stiff, the wrong defense against such teasing. She felt it instantly. I countered. "You are my love, Murie. But I'll play no games with you. Do what you will when I am gone; in the name, as you put it, of 'saving Marack.' But spare me the details. I've no stomach for them. In the meantime, I'll check out your Lady Elioseen."

One can be cruel in striking back where cruelty's been used. It's a game wherein people who truly love can rend each other bones-bare, and often do. A basic maturity's supposed to intervene before things get critical. But there's always a time factor. And that's what we didn't have—time!

"By the gods, you'll not!"

"And you?"

Her small chin went up defiantly. "I'm Marack's princess. I play no games, sir. I but do what I must. No one in all our council but you has said me nay."

"Murie," I groaned in exasperation, "no one in the king's council will *ever* say you nay."

She grew pale at my intimation. "I now know for sure that you're not of Marack, my lord—or *Kyrie Fern*, as those strange people called you on that skyship. But I remain what I am, heiress to the throne of Marack. What I do is expected, whether I wish it or not. *I have no choice*!"

I nodded, white-lipped, saying by rote: "My lady," and arising to bow toward the king who was using the moment to return to his chambers and the ailing queen whom the day had in no way treated kindly.

The time had passed more quickly than I'd imagined. It's like that when serious things are afoot. I recall battles that seemed to last all day, but in reality took but fifteen minutes. Many of our fifty had already sought their homes in the city below, or their wives in their castle apartments. The rains had eased, only to come roaring down again. The Lord Fel-Holdt bent to my shoulders, saying, "Collin, I've word that my first man has reached the road below. The dottles are arrived and waiting."

I asked curiously, for he'd spoken again of the major escape passage from Glagmaron's great granite pile: "How long will it take you—to reach the road?"

"Well, 'tis narrow, poorly kept, serpentine; it winds a thousand feet to go but three hundred. I've some two hundred and fifty men to get from here to there. The torch smoke's a problem too. We'll use but three, with each man hooked to the belt in front of him. That way, they can at least breathe. So, I'd say at least forty-five minutes, Collin."

I said quickly, "Then we're off, too, my lord. If nothing's astir, there'll be no problem. We'll meet you within an hour on the east road to Gleglyn. If otherwise," I laughed, "well, we'll still meet you, in hell—or Gortfin."

Fel-Holdt hesitated. His craggy face and aged, blue-purple eyes—and they'd somehow lost their color as a man's fur does when he grows old—were alert to danger. "Then you do think," he queried, "that our merchants will be awaiting?"

"I do."

"Is it wise that you personally oppose them? Others could as easily do the job."

"True. But they'll not expect me. And for that very reason we'll shout the fact of my presence to the heavens. A cry, as it were, to all freemen of the city and to all of Marack, too, that the Collin has escaped. . . . Believe me, my lord, if that oaf, Tarkiis, had done his business tonight, we'd all be either dead or taken. The fact that he didn't shows that he knows little if anything of the affairs of *true* men. It is my hope that he'll never have time to learn. In the meantime, to focus him on us gives respite to the people, whom we will organize while we organize Marack's magick!"

Fel-Holdt laughed quietly. "I've oft' deemed it, my lord, that *your* magick is more of the intellect than of 'words.' Tonight you prove me right. We'll be on our way, sir, to await you on the Gleglyn road. . . ."

Gen-Rondin had come up, as had Lors Sernas, Rawl and the huge Sir Dosh. Rondin, a strong man who believed in action, said simply, "The rain looks like it'll last, Collin. What say you?"

"Why 'go'!" I replied. "Full armor and gear. Let's to it!"

We shook hands then with those who would ride with Fel-Holdt and went our separate ways. Murie and Caroween had, in the meantime, gone to fetch cloaks in their chambers.

And so it began. . . .

Of all the partings on the stone slabs of Glagmaron Castle's great courtyard, I think that was the saddest. Murie and Caroween joined us as the twelve students who would ride with us brought up the dottles. Gen-Rondin brought the four lord-ambassadors of Kelb, Ferlach, Gheese and Great Ortmund. Sir Dosh's five swordsmen-knights were given to Caroween as her guard; each of the ambassadors had a handful of his own men.

At a nod from me, Gen-Rondin led the others off to the shelter of the portcullis arc. Indeed the rain was such that between the main castle entrance and the gatehouse they simply disappeared. The portcullis arc was invisible, lost in the mist of water.

Rawl, less stubborn than I, was able to forgive his Valkyrie redhead and to wrap her in his two strong arms for sundry "rubbings and pattings," as Great Ap the Vuun would say, in disgust. Such, however, was not the case with Murie and me. We but went through the motions. Still, embracing as we did in the light of the burning torches, we were an appealing, romantic sight to certain castle scullery maids who watched us from a doorway. One even cried into her apron.

Pushing me from her, Murie said solemnly, "You are my love, Collin. We should not part in anger, especially since we don't know when we'll meet again."

I pulled her roughly back to nip an ear and murmur, "It need not be this way at all. Come with me, Murie."

"I cannot and I will not." She leaned her slight weight against my furs and armor. "Nor will I be cozened into it. I know the power of my aunt, and of your potential, sir, as a breeding gerd. I've also seen the power of those skymen in *your* eyes. The road back for us will be hard, indeed."

"Trust me, Murie."

"Trust you!" Tears brimmed her eyes. "The gods damn you, Collin. I do *not* trust you. With your jealousy, you'll wreak a harm to ruin us all."

"And yours?"

" 'Tis natural with women, but harmless."

I thought to spin her a web just one more time. I couldn't help it. I even presumed that what I did was right; that I was properly smoothing things over. "Murie," I told her, " 'tis true. I was jealous, for nothing like this has happened to me before. But I now see it your way. You *are* the princess. You'll *be* the queen. You must do what you do for Marack. I, my lady, have simply asked that you spare me the details, and there's nothing wrong with that."

"You *bastard*!"

"Murie. Again you take it wrong."

"Oh? You know that I'll do nothing with that perfumed *thing* unless I have to. But you, my sweetest lord. Why you, at this very moment are bound to play our Elioseen's game and then to blame the very deed on me. Oh, I read you, Collin. I read you like a candled egg!"

She made to pull away. Our dottles, disturbed by her anger, whoood softly. In the near-distance, Dosh and some of the student-warriors caused their own mounts to prance and called out to calm them. Rawl, that feather-topped gallant—he'd dressed for show instead of battle, saying that he doubted much that any damn yarn-seller would stir himself on such a night—actually hummed now while whirling his carrot-top in a lively pavane to the further tune of a brace of rainspouts.

I held Murie tight. She relaxed and held me too, but finally said, "Leave, Collin, before we say things we can't take back. I love you, my lord, and that's my final word."

"I love you too, Murie." I bent to kiss her one last time; upon which she sank her small white teeth into my lower lip and hissed, "If you do it, I'll know. Never mind how, but I will. And by the gods, sir, I'll seek you out and have you flayed and stuffed, you hear?"

I laughed aloud. I couldn't help it. "What if I said the same to you?"

"Why, I'd say you mocked me." She then burst into tears, slapped my face hard, kissed me again, collected Caroween from the cavorting Sir Fergis and disappeared through the great opened doors of the main hall. All she needed was Hooli on her shoulders to convey her ultimate anger.

We crossed the bridge in a shaft of silvered moonlight from Capil the larger of Camelot-Fergis's two satellites. The clouds seemed to have parted for just that little scene, ghostly dottles; ghostly riders. Then the rains came again in timely gusts to hide our presence. Somehow the dottles *knew* that noise of any kind was taboo this night. We skirted the sky-ship in a great round-about curve before hitting the hill road. At the junction to Glagmaron, Ferlach and Saks to the south and Klimpinge to the west, we bid godspeed to the two southern ambassadors and their men. I adjured them one last time to ask of Chitar and Draslich, the respective kings of those countries, that they offer no resistance and that they send their best warlocks post-haste to Gortfin Castle. Resistance, I said, will surely come. But it must be organized. . . . And if somehow or other this could not be done; if the leading lords of these two kingdoms had fought and been slain by Alphians from their respective ships, then the ambassadors were to do what they could in getting their sorcerers to aid us.

Glagmaron city was sound asleep. It was not a walled city. Only the entry roads were guarded with post houses and warriors from a central garrison. Rawl, myself and the lord, Gen-Rondin, rode at first to the fore, and purposefully. We wanted the word to spread on the morrow that certain lords had fled the castle. We knew we would be counted. We were fewer than twenty. That twenty would be seen while the two hundred and fifty of Marack's finest swordsmen, led by Fel-Holdt and Al Tils, would not. It was but a small part of our game.

We rode on, saluting at least two groupings of a dozen or

so of the night watch in the town's depths. All these king's men, of course, were now alerted as to what had happened earlier with the skyship and the aliens on the tourney field. They were wary, nervous, offering us their swords and begging to go with us. Gen-Rondin told them to hide their weapons and to be ready, for we *would* return!

I then sent six of my best student warriors to the fore for bait. Two more padded on silent dottle paws at a few hundred feet to their rear. We followed on at another hundred or so.

And then it came, what I'd expected, and in a small square toward the west road. As our six crossed it, better than two dozen armed men attacked from the side streets—and should I mention that the rain had stopped again? Since my six were prepared for it, none were taken. But the assault was fierce so that we actually heard the clash of swords before we heard the yells of "A Collin! A Collin!" from the central two who were meant to warn us. . . .

Even as we arose in our stirrups to unsheathe our great-swords, I was yelling, "Let just three escape to carry the message—Kill the rest now, else we'll be forced to kill them tomorrow or the day following."

Within seconds we'd smashed into them. Only four of my six students remained, their backs against the wall of a guild's harness shop. Their dottles, from which they'd either jumped or been pulled, awaited the outcome at the arch of the square exit. Five bodies were strewn from the fountain to where they now fought. The two of their own who'd been lost were precisely there. The street-fighters, hired to do the merchants' job, were pressing in so strongly that had we not arrived ours would have been dispatched, and soon, by fal-dirks alone.

There was nothing gallant about what we did. They hadn't a chance. No Fregisian warrior is merciless. Though he loves a fight, he loves it with an opponent who can in part match him, else where's the glory. We killed them quickly, and it wasn't pretty. I cut one great hulk to the sternum and took the screaming heads of two others. The Lord Gen-Rondin, methodically, as if at a training post, lopped off heads and arms and laid open beer-swill bellies to the spine. Sir Dosh did likewise. Rawl pinned but one man to the wall, then wiped his bloody weapon on the man's jacket and sat his mount in arrant distaste of the whole thing. Lors Sernas joined with my students who, after each had killed his man, pursued the others down two winding streets, roaring their war cry: "A Collin! A Collin!" to attract the proper attention. They returned shortly with the word that, as per orders, but three had escaped. The rest were dead. . . .

At two miles beyond the city we drew up to face five silent figures seated on their dottles and barring the road. Fel-Holdt and Al Tils were with them, the remainder of our two hundred and fifty being hidden to either side. I told them what had happened. Leathern bags of sviss were then tossed from hand to hand and we drank deeply. For some reason, however, I was not in a mood for chit-chat, so I nodded perfunctorily; Fel-Holdt marshaled our forces and we continued on toward Gortfin.

It was still at two hundred miles to the east. We'd ride straight through with but a single, four-hour dottle browsing period; this, after a nine-hour stint on the road. To force a dottle to run one second beyond the nine hours was impossible. If you persisted the dottle would simply lie down, look up sadly, and refuse to move until you either let him alone or he died. And no one, but *no* one, had ever done that to a gentle dottle in living memory. They would run at their heartbeat speed of twenty miles per hour. After the browsing period they would do it for another nine hours, and another nine, and another and could conceivably keep it up until old age cancelled them out. All of this being predicated, of course, upon Camelot-Fregis's twenty-six hour axial spin. . . .

We'd started out at ten p.m. It was eleven now. With the first nine hours, plus four, it would then be but eleven a.m. when we started out again; and this was only one hour's riding to go. In essence we'd arrive at Gortfin within the hour before lunch. Good timing, I thought, especially since we all would have slept through the browsing period and would therefore be fresh as newborn babes. . . .

To a Fregisian nine hours in a dottle's saddle is no big deal. They, like the dottles, can seemingly go on forever. But not me. I had a problem. I had twice the strength of a Fregisian but only half the stamina. My inability to withstand the rigors of dottle riding had long been known as "the Collin's curse."

Nothing had changed. The contradiction remained. At the

ride's end, when we'd pulled off to a great meadow dotted with deciduous trees, I simply collapsed, swearing, amidst a wave of muted laughter. They'd chosen a good spot for me, beneath a broadleaf tree by a sparkling stream. The grass smelled sweet, clean. The hum of stingless bees and myriad other insects was softly pervasive. I slipped immediately into the night's sleep I'd never had.

I awakened just once, with a deep sense of peace, lethargy and complete relaxation. It was when I slept again that what I hoped would happen did happen.

Hooli came!

His coming was also relaxing. I could even see myself as if I were awake and watching him; with my hands behind my head and leaning back against the bole of the great shade tree. His coming was always a delight, really—for the way that he did it. This time, alerted to the event by some primitive triggering device, I know beforehand he'd be there. It was like opening one's eyes in a darkened theater and with the knowledge that the actor would arrive very soon to begin his monologue.

I was alert, though asleep; seeing, but with closed eyes. I but awaited the sound of a voice whose tone and content would be my own.

He seemed at first like a dot somewhere off to the left. Then a bigger dot. And then, at a certain point, his skating figure evolved into an ancient Terran internal-combustion vehicle, with himself in the driver's seat. It was a sleek two-seater with wire wheels, pointed rear end and a long, low, hood-covered engine. The difference between his facsimile, however, and the real McCoy, was that his was custom-made to size, *his* size!

He slid to a stop before me with a screeching of brakes and a couple of *whoom, whooms* from the motor. He got out to leisurely peel heavy gloves from his paws, a dust coat from his body and huge goggles from his eyes. This left him in mortar-board cap, tweed suit of the late nineteen-hundreds and wire glasses with heart-shaped lenses. He busied himself at first with a meerschaum pipe, filling and lighting it, and then blowing exaggerated clouds of smoke. He then deigned to notice me, saying, as was his style: "Hey, buddy! What's happening!"

"Shit!"

"Oh? That's no way to greet a friend." He sat down in midair and snapped his gaiters.

"So? You're wearing Holmes's suit, and that's his pipe. But you're in the wrong generation. That vehicle—well, they used to call it a bear-something. . . ."

"Stutz, buddy. Stutz. Your collagen's screwed up. They were the rage in your great, great, great, great, great, great, etc., etc., etc., granddaddy's time."

I shook my head. "Why do you do this?"

"Takes your mind off problems; helps to put 'em in perspective."

"Your perspective, not mine."

"Oh?" He stood up, tossed his glasses to nowhere, fixed a monocle to one eye and grinned a rodent grin. "Did you like my death scene?"

"What death scene?"

"*Camille.* On the good ship *Deneb.*"

"You little bastard. Why?"

"To get your attention, buddy—without scaring the bloody crappola out of you."

"You had my attention. You were yelling like a goddamned banshee."

"*Your* attention span's not all that good, Collin. I had to *fix* it."

"How did you know what would happen?"

"I was trailing the sphere through the gateway."

"But why didn't you tell me? All you did was warn. The *Deneb* could have escaped, Hooli. There was no damn reason for all those men to die."

"The *Deneb* could *not* have escaped."

"Because you say so?"

"Because I say so—believe me, buddy."

I swallowed. "Tell me about the sphere."

He blew a perfect smoke ring, watched it roll. He said, "Well, I went through the gateway to check things out, and there it was."

"What?"

"The goddamned Dark One's *uncle.* Idiot! What do you think that sphere is, a soap bubble?"

I had to ask. "Where are you now, Hooli?"

"This side, Collin, but barely."

"What the hell does that mean?"

"Just what I said. I'm sort of stuck betwixt and between. A

mental matter-to-contra-terrene-conversion's not all that easy."

"Yet you're here, now, and were in Glagmaron Castle too, with your butterfly-firefly stunt. How do you do it, ace?"

He grinned. "It just takes more time; and there's a different time factor here too. It sort of draws you out, like on a taffy wheel."

"Hooli," I asked hoarsely, "if you can, why not close that damned gateway, now!"

He sang: "Forever is a long longgg time—" then said softly, distractedly, "It hurts, buddy."

I sighed and shrugged mentally. "Okay. You're here for a reason and I'm wasting time. What is it, Hooli? What should I know?"

"Don't mess with the sphere, else it'll make a *nova* out of the two Fomalhauts."

"*Jesu's* ass! What else?"

"More of the same. You're on the right track. But don't, I repeat, *don't* involve the sphere in any way, else we're dead, buddy; this, until I get there."

"How do I not involve the sphere, Pooh-bear? It's the heart of the matter."

"Just do what you're doing, the magick and all that. Oh. And don't attempt to snatch an Alphian ship to go after the sphere either. You do and we're dead. Same thing. Hear?"

"Hooli?"

"Believe me, buddy."

I took a deep breath. "What's on the other side?"

"A three-planet system; all useless. The sun's verging on *nova*. The expansion factor's what killed the planets. That's what I was doing, checking it out."

"Where does the sphere get its power?"

"From the pre-nova. It's on the order of your *Sirius*. The physics are fantastic. The power's drawn incrementally. But any break between point 'A' and point 'B', and that's the end. The sphere goes; the sun goes; the gateway goes; the Fomalhauts go; but not exactly in that order."

His voice inside my head was fading fast. I mentally yelled, "The Alphians, Hooli! Tell me about the Alphians!"

"Dangerous. Murderous." His voice came weakly, while the Stutz-Bearcat began to fade and his body too sort of whisped off leaving only the head and the shoebutton eyes from which somehow the monocle had disappeared. One of them winked at me as his voice now came from far off—"They're like children, Collin—a gang of know-nothing brats; machine-taught. Collin! I beg you. Don't attack the ships!"

I screamed mentally: "Hooli! Take care!"

There came a sort of murmuring answer of "I love you, buddy." It was like a soughing of wind in great pines.

I awoke to Rawl at my shoulder, shaking me. He had an odd expression on his face, a curious light in his eyes. Beyond him was Gen-Rondin and Sernas, the first, grinning, as if he'd caught me, the much-touted Collin, in a weak moment; the second slightly more sympathetic.

"A nightmare," Rawl explained his shaking. "We'd thought for sure that the Dark One had returned from the grave to claim you."

I sat up, shook the fog from my mind. "The dooky-stew, last night," I said. "Or maybe the new wine. Nothing that that stream over there won't cure. Join me, comrades."

And they did. For, as oft' pointed out, Fregisians are the cleanest humanoids in the galaxy; a cause for wondering, really, why they care so little for the sea.

The summer current was strong, still in spate; the water cold. Fully refreshed and back on the little river's bank again, we were toweling briskly when Rogas, one of the best of my student-warriors, called softly and pointed toward the southern horizon.

We looked. A skyship floated low in the far distance. And even as we watched a great fire broke out beneath it, as if a mighty grove, or *town*, had been touched by invisible—from where we were, that is—laser beams.

I looked to the others. "What would you call that?"

"My lord," Rogas spoke up. "I was born on the Kelbian border. I know somewhat of this country. Over there is the village of Hedas and beyond it an old castle, once owned by the heggle, Costin. He's now a land-poor knight and spends most of his time drinking in Gleglyn. 'Tis not the village that's burning, sir, but the castle."

"Ah huh!" I grunted. I was already reaching for my sword belt to press the communication's stud. It was the first time that I had ever done this in the direct presence of Fregisians.

"Come in Kriloy," I called mentally, staring into the distance. "Come in." I said it over and over again while the castle burned and the others stared just as silently at me.

"That you, Kyrie?" He'd finally made it. Again his voice sounded sleepy. I could even hear him yawn.

"Who else?" I answered curtly. "Were you asleep?"

"Yep. Not much to do."

"What about the transmitter?"

"Dead end."

"Gog-shit! There's no such thing as a dead end. On top of that, mister, those damned ships have been landing everywhere. No warning from you; no *nothing*. They hit Glagmaron last night. How the hell long have you been asleep?"

He attempted to mumble an excuse. I wouldn't let him finish. "Here's a straight order," I said. "You're to move the scoutship out *now*! Keep it in 'null' plus 'five.' That's the distortion level, in case you've forgotten. You'll be as invisible as you are now. And, since you'll be making the run on the mag-lines, the sensors can't get you either. Now hear me! You'll fly that ship to the best spot you can find which will be closest to Gortfin Castle.

"It's all mapped on the quadrants; automatic on the lines. Just feed in the data, buddy, from A to B. And if you can't do that, why then follow east from Glagmaron City to Gleglyn town and continue for a hundred and fifty miles on the Corchoon road to Kelb. There'll be a turnoff at that point. Gortfin's to the north at about twenty miles. Lots of mountains; heavy forest. When you land put the ship on total 'null'—extended. But first call me. You got it?"

"Yep. What's it all about?"

"Just do it. You'll find out when you get there."

I relaxed, turned to the others. "Let's get to Gortfin. I've a hunch your forefathers from the skyships will be trying to knock out all the castles wherever they find them. They can control the cities and towns; the villages too. But any castle not connected with a town or village will be fair game. They're not about to allow any points of resistance, if they can prevent it. Let's ride!"

Gortfin Castle, surrounded by mountains, had just four approaches; not roads in the accepted sense, but rather cart paths, and damned poor ones at that. Each approach was heavily guarded. Situated on the border with Kelb, Gortfin had always been a redoubt against invasion from that country and had supported at all times a sizable garrison. Until, and after, its possession by the Lady Elioseen, it was *the* secondary center for all Marack's armies.

The army, however, had generally been demobilized after the fall of Hish in Om and the end of wars. The garrison was now but two hundred and fifty strong.

We came storming up the south canyon road at just before high noon. Flying the colors of the royal house, we had clear passage. The bridge was down, the great gates were opened, and the portcullis had been lifted. In the immense military courtyard warrior-lackeys came running from all directions to take our happily whoooing dottles and to guide our swordsmen to the extensive barracks rooms below and to the north.

Myself, the Lord Commander Fel-Holdt, Lord Jos-Viins, commander of the castle for the king, Gen-Rondin, Rawl, Sernas and the rest of Fel-Holdt's chosen leaders, marched straight from the saddle to the council rooms.

I called to Jos Viins, a wily old battler, with a hundred scars to prove it, "We'll have Elioseen up here immediately, sir; and I do mean 'immediately'! And double the guard at once on all roads and paths. All who come in our direction, for *any* reason, are to be seized. We'll give them 'guest' rooms in the caverns below."

"As prisoners, my lord Collin?"

"For the moment, yes."

We seated ourselves around the great central table; a beauteous thing of inlaid ivory and turquoise for which the area was known. Wines, ale and sviss came instantly, as did tankards and cups which we filled and raised to each other when our cloaks had been flung to the benches lining the walls.

The clouds, I knew, had retreated to the west. Glagmaron was apparently still being rained on, while we at Gortfin felt sunlight through every window.

I glanced to Fel-Holdt and nodded, a sign that I would continue in what had to be done. It was a courtesy to his age and position, really, since it was agreed that I would lead in this. He nodded acquiescence.

I turned again to Jos Viins, "My lord," I said. " 'Tis best too that those wizards, witches, and the like, who also guard our lady, be called up with her."

He signaled a page-herald to his side. "There are twelve altogether," he informed us. "They work in shifts."

I laughed. "The more the merrier since we'll need all the power we can get, and now!"

Viins asked, "My lords, 'tis obvious there's an urgency here. Are we to be informed as to its nature?"

I glanced at Gen-Rondin. He arose to brief them in as few words as were needed. As heavy tureens of steaming gog stew arrived, Jos Viins, his tone somewhat querulous, said, "You must understand, my lords, that we may have some trouble with our lady. She seldom sees anyone before the fourteenth hour."

Fel-Holdt said sternly, "Sir. The urgency's been explained. She'll see us *now*, if your men have to drag her here."

"Collin!" He turned to me in horror. "She's the king's sister."

"Sir," I replied. "I hold his majesty's baton. For our purpose she's what she is, a prisoner in this castle. If she were not here, she'd otherwise be dead. Order her up, now!"

He looked to Fel-Holdt, his officers, and to my stalwarts. They gazed stonily back at him. Fel-Holdt said flatly, "Get on with it, man. The peril mounts with each wasted moment."

Though angered, I thought to ease Jos Viin's position somewhat. "What we do," I told him, "is not done in pique, believe me. 'Tis done for Marack."

The frown slowly left his face as he studied mine. He said abruptly, "I'll get her myself, Collin."

"You may tell her," I called to his retreating back, "that she will lunch with us. . . ."

It was a true summer's day. The council hall, a smaller replica of the one at Glagmaron, complete with banners, flags, tapestries and the like, was filled with golden dust motes, bird calls from without and the softest of mountain breezes.

She arrived with Jos Viins, two ladies-in-waiting, her twelve "keepers"—eight sorcerers or warlocks and four witches, all looking stern and solemn—and a full squadron of men-at-arms. Seeing her this first time, I knew at once that her beauty had been but hinted at. . . . She was golden-furred like my Murie, but there the resemblance ended. For there was no brightness of eye, nor did she have that certain nubile athletic quality, or the pert sauciness and downright arrogance my princess so often displayed. She was, indeed, the very opposite in form and feature.

Willowy, languid, she was slender to the point of being wraithlike. Her femininity of form, her poise, the studied gaze of her eyes—all of it whispered, I knew, to each man who saw her, of beds and bedrooms and intimate pleasures. Her appeal, in part, was that she seemingly promised a personal surrender to any man whose gaze she captured. She was *the* supplicant female to the dominant male, and there wasn't a one of us who didn't feel that *he* was the male in question. The correctness of this was apparent in the smug expressions of my comrades.

Still, we weren't fools. We'd been briefed as to her propensities and any Marackian beyond the age of twenty knows somewhat of the wiles of the tender-prey. The truth of the matter is that of all those in the room, *I* was the most vulnerable; if for no other reason than that I was truly *curious.* I also came from a galaxy of worlds wherein sex, as such, when the situation permitted, was in no way a social crime. Indeed, to such inconstancy one could expect but the faintest of raised eyebrows from one's mate of the moment.

As for my own jealousy? Well, nine months on Fregis-Camelot and in the company of such an inspiring honey-pot as Murie would cause regression in the prime graduate of a Sididion stud farm. Such was my fate. . . .

Fel-Holdt gestured that she be seated. She did, at the far end of the table; this, with her three ladies, all quite young and overly conscious of the importance of their charge. Plates, platters and cups of wine were rushed to them. Elioseen, ignoring it all, sat straight in her chair. In her eyes the promise of love had faded—to be replaced by the power of a patrician's hauteur.

I wasted no time. Hungry, I talked while I ate, a warrior's habit not frowned upon.

"My Lady Elioseen," I began, "I am he who is called the Collin, and you know our Lord Commander, Fel-Holdt, and the king, your brother's judge, the Lord Gen-Rondin. . . . We are here," I said, while dipping myself a second helping of gog stew "to ask your aid for Marack, the north, and indeed, for all this great and beauteous world of ours."

I paused deliberately, ostensibly to test the temperature of the stew. She seized the moment as I knew she would. Her instant smile was appealing, her voice pure silver, the tones all crystal clear like the tinkling of a bell. "Why," she asked, "should I help you in any way who have imprisoned me, a daughter of kings, against my will and against the laws of this land?"

"Because if you do not," I smiled and waved my spoon, "why then we will all die and it is as simple as that."

"Death," she countered, "is not always the enemy. I ask you again: Why should I help you, my jailers?"

I sighed, put my spoon down and stared straight into her eyes. "Enough," I said, "of protocol. We've a thing to do right now, my lady, else even this argument will be over quicker than you can imagine. The peril's here, now, *this instant*! I therefore ask that you do two things immediately. One: if 'tis within your power, and of course with the aid of these twelve good sorcerers and witches, that storm clouds be made to come from all the horizons to cover this castle from the borders of Kelb to the town of Gleglyn, and to the north and south for an equal distance. Two: that magick be made so that when these clouds retreat again, for natural causes, our castle will continue to be invisible from a height of the highest tree in all this area. Moreover, this last condition, if we are to survive, must be maintained for an indefinite period of time. Do you understand me, my lady?"

She looked at me long and coolly, said finally, "I understand you. But I still ask for an explanation. I've been cozened before, sir, whether you believe it or no."

"All right. 'Tis like this, my lady: Within the next two hours an enemy from the sky, seeking this castle and finding it, will strike it with a hellish fire so that it and all the land around will be destroyed, utterly. Believe me. I speak the truth, if for no other reason than to spur you to the task. Moreover, though the span is two hours, we could be hit in the next five minutes. As to bargains, my lady, and I speak for the throne of Marack, well we'll discuss them *after* the fact of the clouds and the invisibility. *Now* do you understand me?"

She laughed. She actually laughed. And the laughter was real. She put her wine cup to her lips for the smallest of sips and said while rising to her feet, "What I've heard about you, Collin, my lord, seems proven true. What you say seems true too. I know this, for I can see your mind, sir. And, since I've no desire to die either, as apart from saving Marack and the world, we'll just draw those clouds for you, to hide us from this beast. As for invisibility; well, sir, that will come later, when we talk again."

I raised my cup in salute, saying, "Let's to it then, and quickly." Our Marackians raised theirs in courtesy. "But remember," I told her, "we cannot have it storm forever, my lady."

She stopped her movement away from the table. "Oh? And why not?"

"Because," I smiled, "this new enemy, who unfortunately is not a beast, but rather men like ourselves, is not stupid. 'Tis now the end of spring; the beginning of summer. Soon there'll be no clouds to draw from. 'Twould seem strange then to those who fly through the heavens in great ships to see below them one large fat cloud in one fell spot, which stays and stays and stays. . . ."

"Great ships, my lord? *Men* who fly through the heavens?"

"Afterwards," I promised. "We've no time now, remember?" The bait extended—and taken, I arose to accompany her and the twelve who'd followed at her nod, plus Commander Jos Viins, his men-at-arms and her ladies.

For privacy, she chose a small anteroom off a corridor of the council hall. Rawl came too, and Gen-Rondin who was deeply interested in such things. Sernas and Dosh joined for our comradeship. Fel-Holdt wisely remained with the other lords, to keep them company and to keep them quiet.

In courtesy to our *coven*, we stayed at one end of the anteroom with Jos Viins and his troupe.

A simple huddle as to the word-sounds needed, their number and continuity, and they began. It took but a second or so to enjoin the chorus properly. Once unleashed however, each word from each mouth became but a single, powerfully intoned word-sound with no meaning beyond its proven *effect*. This single sound, when enjoined with others in a continuity—I counted nine in all—became *the* incantation of the moment, the Magick of Camelot-Fregis!

But was it truly magick? Is there such a thing? Goolbic, the great sorcerer of the north has written—and he was the first to discover the supposed basis for it all—that: " *'Tis a thinge of sounde alone. And if one do not saye the wordes aloude, the witchery will come to nought.*"

And, too, for each word or incantation there were counter-spells. If one, for example, did not want the rain clouds, counter words could be intoned. The winner would be he whose incantation was the most perfect and the most impermissive of other sounds. This concept of exact tonal inflections, or word-sounds, as activating specific areas of the planet's magnetic field for a designated purpose, had its origins in the early policies of the Dark One. He'd given it to the priests of the religion he'd created for the people in the south—the better to hold them in thralldom.

Osmosis-wise, however, the "magick" had crept north, jumped the River Sea and come into the possession of northern priests. The *gestalt* effect of five thousand years of practice was such that the practitioners of the north, priests, warlocks, witches and the like, had surpassed in many ways the priests of the south.

Through a tedious process of trial and error, this "Magick of Camelot-Fregis" had become a viable, growing thing. Word-sounds were collected; their effects observed and tabulated. . . . Hooli, of course, was my informant as to how all of this had come about. Had I accepted his rather simple explanation? Not quite. My situation, however, was that I had either little or no time for the study of abstract problems, or used that time in more pleasurable ways when I did have it. I'd hoped some day to take the question of Camelot's magick to the *Deneb*'s computers. Now even that door was closed.

One of the four witches was a peasant housewife, the others maiden ladies, daughters of this lord or that who'd not been asked in marriage. They seemed so taken with their work that I had no doubts that in the affairs of love their magick had long won out where society, Marackian style, had failed them. The sorcerers were mostly middle-aged men; three of them priests of Ormon, Wimbely and Harris. One, a young knight called Sir Sobstice, confessed to me later that the "stuff" actually came easy to him. He boasted too that he was quite good at quoits.

Noting that a door from the anteroom opened directly to the courtyard, I stepped through it and moved quickly to a ground-floor window to observe the action further. Again I pressed the belt-stud for Kriloy, felt the node embedded at the base of my skull grow warm and called mentally, "Come in, bastard."

His reply came instantly. "I'm right above you."

"Why the hell haven't you contacted me?"

"Had a blip on the screen. Still got it. Could be the Glagmaron ship. It's directly north of us; about twenty miles."

"You son-of-a-bitch! You in null plus? Because if you're not and they've got a sensor on you, I'm gonna feed you to the goddamn kaatis—that's a Camelot grizzly."

"I'm in. Don't worry."

"What's your barometer read?"

"The bottom just fell out. You wouldn't believe how fast those clouds are coming on."

"I'd believe," I said. "Get the ship down quick, else you'll be coming in on infrared. One last thing. You were supposed to contact me. You didn't. Now listen up. Once more, for whatever reason, and you've had it. You're out of the ship and into the forest, bare-assed and on your own. You hear me?"

He laughed. "Hey, Kyrieee!"

"Hey, gog-shit. We're in a life-or-death deal. You do your part, or I'll do you. That's it. No more talk. Now bring it in."

"I'm in."

"Where?"

"North of the castle, maybe five hundred yards. There's a big meadow, gogs, baby gogs, dottle-mounts and the like. There's a big granite boulder. You can't miss it. I'm a few yards to the west."

"You phased out?"

"Of course."

"Good. Now keep trying to track down the other four ships. When you nail 'em, get a sensor on 'em and keep it there. Work the grid-screen, the coordinates. Stay *awake*! Also—and this is the number-one priority—keep trying for the power tap and the tie to the galactic grid. That's it. *Ciao*!"

"Okay. And Kyrie?"

"What?"

"Bless you."

He sounded contrite. An A-plus. I said, "I'm coming over tomorrow morning," and turned him off.

At which point a first gust of wind hit me square in the face. Accompanying raindrops were as big as marbles. In seconds I was again forced into the anteroom to avoid a downpour that hit the great flagstones of the courtyard with the force of a waterfall.

"In the name of bloody Ormon!" I roared in some alarm at the monotonously chanting *coven.* "Cease! Stop! There's only so much water *in* those damn clouds. When it's gone we'll again be visible. Slow it to a drizzle, I beg of you. As a matter of fact, all we really need is the clouds. . . ."

And they did slow it, with the Lady Elioseen advising the others how best to proceed and dividing them into groups of three to spell each other at the quite hypnotic task. Then, her patrician lips touched with a soft and silent laughter, she advanced to take my arm possessively and triumphantly lead the return to the council room and the interrupted lunch.

The ambassadors of Kelb and Great Ortmund, having been sent on their way at the end of the dottle browsing period, still had a hundred miles or so to go; or so I figured. With a difference of but twenty to fifty miles at best, all four ambassadors had each to go but three hundred miles from Glagmaron to reach their respective capitals. I figured they'd *all* arrive within the twentieth hour. Considering, however, I had no choice but to check the situation myself. This being the case, I'd arranged that they be in a place of their choice on the morrow where I'd meet them and be given the particulars as to what had happened; providing, of course, they were still alive.

In no way had they questioned my ability to get there. They were "Collin veterans," space veterans, now; for they'd been in at the death of the *Deneb*, plus a few other singular oddments about which they could now boast to their grandchildren. That they had only the foggiest idea as to what had happened was also the guarantee that they'd risk their fate in *my* hands.

The afternoon was spent in further council with Elioseen, the twelve sorcerers and witches, Jos Viins, Fel-Holdt and the Lords of Marack. All access roads were now heavily posted with a double guard; this, since we now had twice the strength of the usual garrison. Agreeing generally on the tactics to be used in events we expected to unfold, we had little else to do but await whatever information I'd bring back on the morrow.

Taking Fel-Holdt to one side, I suggested that I meet with

Elioseen privately. "I must converse with her under relaxed circumstances; for her sake," I told him. "I would win her wholeheartedly to our cause." He frowned darkly, upon which I glared just as darkly as his obvious assumption. He shrugged then, smiled icily and agreed. It was understood, of course, that her ladies would be present.

I had a strong presentiment that even the aged Fel-Holdt was a mite jealous that Elioseen would meet with me this way. A better word would be—envy.

After a late supper to the continued accompaniment of lashing rain, wind and hail—this last the size of ping-pong balls—most of our party wanted nothing else but to retire to their quarters with a pint or two of ale. The pervasive sound of it all was hellish, like the soughing of a great death-wind through all the forests surrounding Gortfin.

In Elioseen's apartments the four witches too had remained, prepared to intervene should she attempt any shenanigans. I was shown to a comfortable upholstered chair, with ottoman, and served with a decanter of good wine and a silvered chalice. Our Lady, after changing into something more befitting the intimacy of her rooms, chose an equally comfortable divan and had a decanter and chalice to match my own. We made small talk and toasted each other with raised cups, while her ladies laid a fire on a stone hearth a short distance away.

I sighed contentedly, free for the moment from the images of Murie and that bastard Tarkiis that lurked hauntingly just on the edge of my vision. . . . The atmosphere was conducive to precisely what I intended. "My Lady," I began seriously; this, as she adjusted the flimsy gossamer robe about her sheath-slip, which was also anything but opaque. "I deem it in the best interest of all that you be told what we know about what is happening and why. The more so since you've lent us your aid for which I'm sure the king, your brother, will eventually thank you personally."

I paused to breathe deeply. Her body beneath the thin stuff seemed absolutely naked, though I could not believe she'd attempt to seduce me. The thin stuff of her robe and sheath lay on her flesh in such a way as to emphasize every curve and hollow. She exuded sex, literally; and knowing, ignored the fact except where it was reflected in *my* eyes.

Even the gold fur with its silvered tints on back, arms and thighs (Fregisians are devoid of fur on face, breast, belly, and on down to the area of the inner thigh; there is no pubic hair), shone with an almost transparent rosy fire. Her hair, no bouncing, shoulder-length, page-boy—was a shimmering veil.

I sensed strongly, however, that though she knew all this quite well, even delighted in its overall effect on others, it was still not a deliberate design for the conquest of males. *She liked herself*! Her care and dress were therefore for herself alone, and to hell with what others might sense or feel.

She brushed back the aureole from about her head and waited, bemused, for me to continue.

I told her everything, bluntly and without embellishment. At the beginning she was, at best, curious. As the tale developed, she bent to it, alert, all senses open. Then, at the end, when I described the Alphian's arrival and the aftermath of death and destruction, I knew that I'd captured her attention fully and in a way that nothing had done since she'd been taken captive and the Dark One driven from Marack.

Ending it abruptly, I refilled my glass, drank deeply and waited. . . .

"So," she said after awhile. Her large eyes were pensive, staring to nowhere, then to me, then to nowhere again. "Why then, sir, I'm bound to think that all you say is true. For never have I heard such things from any living being; nor read them either."

The blue-purple eyes grew suddenly larger still. Her parted lips showed the pinkest of tongues playing over snow-white teeth. She sighed, said suddenly, "You are without a doubt, my lord, *the* Collin, as I've imagined you to be. For, indeed, I've wondered who you were, really, and from where you *really* came. Had I known—" and her accompanying, contemplative laughter was both silver-sweet and deadly—"when I had you in my dungeon, what you'd eventually do, what you *could* do to me and the dreams I'd dreamed, why, sir, I'd have brought the very stones of this poor keep down on your head rather than see you flee." She laughed again. "But now, I'm most pleasantly glad I didn't."

"I, too, am 'pleasantly glad' my lady," I told her softly. "And I do hope that things will never revert to what they were 'twixt you and me. Indeed, I beg of you now, as one who'd be your friend, that you do not dwell upon the past. I assure you, too, that all that you sought can still be gained in other ways; if not here, then in other places. Power, my lady, is but a passing fancy. There are machines that can destroy both you and me and this world too, and all the stars! They were not created to do this, however, and so are, in fact, controlled. In essence, power misused, from whatever source, is power wasted. Power misused in the enslavement of intelligent life in any form is an abomination. Unfortunately, life in *all* its forms must learn this for itself, else it will not truly mature. The road up the evolutionary ladder is therefore in no way smooth.

"And so? What would you, my lady? I've told you of the stars. Would you go to them? I'll show you how. I doubt me that you're so small as to wish only to reign somewhere as queen and ruler. 'Tis a waste of the years for a thinking person such as you. And if that be true, and it is, then why bother? Listen to me, Elioseen, for I swear to you that there are some who are meant by accident or the trickeries of history and conditioning to do these things—*and some who are not*! The only true law of life is to *respect* life!"

A slight glitter had come to her eyes, perceptible but faint. Her left hand reached out across her body to take up her cup. In so doing it touched her waist and belly ever so lightly, lingered to caress her flesh for seconds in a strange intimacy with self. It was as if she needed no mate, no partner, but was all things to herself and *with* herself, alone! I knew then that she truly loved herself in a way unknown to others. It seemed also, in this last respect, that she viewed her body as being completely apart from her mind, self, id-ego. A thought touched my mind. By the gods, she seemed like *Hooli*, the host-occupant of a chalice welded to her will. My reaction was instant revulsion. But, no! It wasn't true and I knew it and was strangely glad for the knowledge.

"Well now," she was saying softly, her voice as one with a night breeze that blew the curtains and smelled redolent with more rain, "I do believe my lord Collin, that you've lectured me."

I smiled. "I have."

She shrugged so that the diaphanous robe slipped to expose a naked shoulder and finely moulded breast. She ignored the nakedness as my Murie would when bathing in a stream. " 'Tis that I've never been spoken to in exactly this way, sir. I find it interesting, compelling even. You must know that our lords of Marack, what with their Ormon, Wimbely and Harris, know little and care less for such philosophy."

"But your sorcerers do."

"Do they?"

"I'm minded on one. They called him Goolbie."

She sat up, startled. "You knew *him*?"

"Nay. I saw only his body. He was slain, you know, by your compatriot."

"My compatriot?"

"Aye. The Kaleen. The Dark One."

She frowned. "I did not know this."

"Why *did* you join with him?"

"Because this is a fool's world. He would have changed it."

"Had you much talk with him?"

"I did. We spoke of many things. I could have learned a great deal. He wanted," she told me, remembering, "only to leave here, to return to his home. Why?" she asked directly but with no rancor, "did you kill him?"

I frowned. "My lady, if I had not killed him, he would have destroyed this world, and much more besides."

"I do not understand."

"His magick," I said, in words she *could* understand, "was flawed. What he sought to do would have unleashed powers beyond his control." I repeated again, "Your beauteous world would have died. I killed him. Your world lives as do you and all your people. They are free now, within the context of their social order. That too will change, my lady. The process, however, is exceedingly slow; unacceptable to such as yourself. And rightly so. I will now tell you something else which you must hear. When I'm finished, you'll be given a choice to tell me yes or no." I then told her flatly who I was, where I'd come from and what I was doing on Camelot-Fregis. I doubt that she understood but a fraction of the particulars. But she did grasp the whole, as I knew she would. And that was the thing!

"My lady," I confessed, "only the coming of this new peril and the destruction of our ship allows me to speak as I do. And I say, with no intent to flatter, but with open honesty, that only to you and a handful of others have I revealed what I have. What then do I want of you, for obviously I do want something. 'Tis simply this: that you follow me in all things until this deadly game is ended—one way or the other! After? Well, then, you may take your choice of the roads I offer you. . . . You may go to the stars if you wish, and return, too; or, you may stay here freely. The last is offered because if you refuse the stars, though that possibility will always remain open, I cannot believe that you would do so for the old 'negative' reasons. The very idea of such should by then be as alien to you as they are to us. Again—do you understand me, my lady?"

She deliberately ignored everything I'd said to ask, "How old are you, Collin?"

"Thirty."

She smiled. "And you'd wed my niece, that bouncy-haired little vixen; that epitome of insufferable female arrogance. Why, sir, they tell me that she's killed a hundred men or so; that she lives by the sword, with *you*—when she's not exercising the royal prerogative. Now how, indeed, does that meld with the philosophy you preach?"

I smiled right back at her. "If you're suggesting that she in no way compares with you in intellect, why yes, you're right. But there's no contradiction there. You remain the same in terms of values. They are simply expressed in different life styles, different needs. I speak of *basics*, my lady. In that area you're alike as two peas in a pod. Aside from that, you're worlds apart. As to her sword-work, why she's killed a hundred *enemies*, my lady, who'd have killed her had she not nicked them first. Moreover, she did this in battle for her country, for her life, for her people, against enslavement."

"But with such relish, my lord, such enthusiasm. A princess of the royal house?"

"Why not? Because no princess heretofore has done so?"

"Perhaps." Her smile had returned. She studied me.

"What then of myself?"

" 'Tis known that you've been in blood up to your neck, so they say. But you're a man, sir; indeed, you'll be queen's consort. You are and should be honored for your prowess."

I laughed. "One then is honored, the other condemned—and for the same thing. Moreover, a point could be made that I have four times the strength of Murie Nigaard, yet still I'm praised where she is not—*though she takes four times the risks*. Nay, my lady, within the context of what we've done, 'tis she who should be admired, acclaimed. I, frankly, would ask for no other at my side in onset or melee, unless, perhaps, it were my lord, Sir Fergis. . . ."

Elioseen said, "You are loyal, my lord, above all else. I do envy my niece." She managed a smile then so that her beauty seemed suddenly as bright sunshine through tempestuous clouds.

I asked curiously, "How old are *you*, my lady?"

"The same as you. You've said," she returned to the question, "that after, if we win, I'll have my freedom either to stay or go, as you put it, to the stars. But that in any event, I *will* be free."

"That is true."

"Then I ask that you free me now, for I can no longer stand the presence of my jailers. You read me well, sir, and I know it and accept your judgment and your charge. For that very reason then, you must know that I die a little bit each day, and will surely die completely soon. I am a woman, my lord"—and here she stared at me long and intimately—"but I am also more than that. I'm a person, too, a *human*, as you so strangely put it, who needs her privacy above all else. I beg of you again: Release me *now*. Clear me this room so that I may breathe air that no one else has breathed. I would be free *now*, my lord!"

"Of myself too?"

"Yes. . . ."

"Elioseen," I told her softly, " 'Tis said that since time began women have cozened men and vice versa, and that this is inevitable and that one or the other will always prevail. . . . I tell you now that such is *not* the case. Where you will go—to the stars if you choose—it is not like that. There's an easy equality, a respect for life between the sexes. The differences remain, but the war is over." I reached out, took her hand and enfolded it in the warmth of both of mine. "There's indeed been a truce," I told her solemnly, "that will last for as long as time. 'Tis the truce that I offer you now, the one of trust. And there's an end to it. You are free, my lady—in every way."

I arose to bow briefly. I then called to her companions, "From now on," I told them, "you will obey the orders of our Lady Elioseen, sister to Marack's king. She is free. She will tell you if she wishes you to continue here or no." I turned to our sorceress. "I will call upon you after noon tomorrow, for we've much to do. I'll try to come between two and five. I'd know better except that I must be away and then return, and there are always problems. Forgive me then, if I'm delayed. I can say only that what I do is important. Indeed, I'd ask you now to think also on that trick of yours wherein you lifted myself, our princess, the good Dame Malion and Sir Rawl Fergis from the high road southwest of Glagmaron. We may need it all too soon. . . . I'll leave you now and I'll ask our comrades, the sorcerers and witches too to withdraw." I bowed again with the formal sweep, swirl and dip, from the hips. "My lady!"

She arose, tall and slender, to bow her golden head in turn and whisper softly, "My lord."

I'd been in my quarters but fifteen minutes, just long enough to divest myself of boots and light armor, when the node at the base of my skull began its buzzing. I pressed the belt stud to say wearily, "Okay. What's up?"

Kriloy yelled excitedly, "I finally did it. I rigged an energy tap for the scoutship's transmitter." His words came thick and fast, all jumbled with the odd admixture of euphoria and fear. The contriteness remained too, a point in his favor. But the fear we didn't need, not with the job ahead.

He was yelling, "But it's all screwed up. Get this: I put a crosstie on the secondary phaser-converter outlet from the CT geodyne fusion power-packs; you know, the outlet *constant*, for heat, light, servo-mechanos, etc. Well the linkage was shaky at best, which scared the hell out of me because the question was not so much whether it would work or not, but what would happen if it did. Well it *worked*! And the measure of output was exactly the amount I'd tapped for intro into the transmitter power-pack—except no input showed on the banks. Output from the CT pack, yes. But no input to the transmitter pack. In effect, Kyrie, old comrade, there's a drain somewhere. The question is where? I say *drain* because there's no buildup anywhere along the line, just output flow—*enough to send the scoutship to Alpha and back*, which means that the flow will have a life expectancy of at best, two weeks. Then we're dead all around. It's crazy, Kyrie, spooky, too. I've been at it all afternoon."

"Why the hell haven't you called me?"

"I wanted to get it right."

"Yet you were afraid you'd blow us off the map, and you still didn't call. . . ."

"Well for bubu's sake. . . ."

"Kriloy. This isn't fourth-year 'show and tell'. How do I

convince you that we've no time for ego trips? So what did you finally do?"

"I shut it down and unhooked it."

"Well hook it up again and stay with it. You're on to something. And since there's no buildup, the flow's got to go somewhere. If anything happens, call me. And I mean *anything*. And no more twenty-hour naps. And keep your damned sensors open for movement. You get a line on something, lock in on it. Rig an alarm system to wake you, if and when it happens. You hear?"

"Okay. Out, Kyrie. Bless you."

"Well, bless you, too. But what I said still holds. You screw up again and I'll give you to the kaatis."

So he must have loused it up somehow. Christo! There was simply no such thing as a registered flow of CT energy going nowhere. . . . Then suddenly, as if Hooli himself were whispering it in my ear, I remembered his earlier warning on the energy tap maintained by the sphere—the one extending *through* the gateway to the pre-nova. If the sphere could maintain such an obviously impossible tap, then why not . . . why not? Holy, bloody Og manifest! It had suddenly hit me. My heart literally skipped two beats at the implication. That I was aware that all matter beyond the gateway was anti-matter, goes without saying. That the mass of the sphere was itself quite possibly anti-matter had just never entered my head. I'd had no reason to think about it within any meaningful context. But now? Well, if it was anti-matter it could only exist in this universe with a shield to protect it; ergo, the need for such a fantastic tap. The sphere, I'd figured to be about a quarter of the size of the *Deneb*. That's a lot of mass. If the shield weakened, was destroyed, why then all of Marack would be blown right off the northern continent!

Gods! No wonder Hooli had begged me not to attack it.

Except that though Hooli never lied, he had a way of not quite telling the truth either. Usually I found myself manipulated by him. In effect, though we worked, fought for the same ends, I seemed forever to be doing the job *his* way, despite my own plans.

Blast and *damn* Hooli!

Succumbing to a wave of doubt, I wondered: did I dare even believe the little son-of-a-bitch was caught somewhere within the gateway? Was it a maneuver, perhaps, so I'd bear the full burden of tackling the Alphians, i.e., win the *secondary* war, whereupon *he* would come in with some trick to knock off the sphere after warning me to stay the hell away from it?

Which led to another question. *Did* the sphere actually have a tap on a pre-nova sun in another universe; which could only suggest that the sphere itself was anti-matter? Ho! Ho! Ho!, I mused. *Nyet*! No tap, no CT sphere, no threat of massive fission and the blowing of Marack off the map—and no reason for me not to attack it either, *if* I could capture one or more of the ships. But there was still the quasi-conundrum: Hooli *never* lied. He'd actually *said* there was an energy tap of the great fission mass of the pre-nova; and this, by the sphere, through the gateway. *Damn* the little bastard! What had he omitted, or had he? If his purpose was simply to immobilize me, he was succeeding. As it stood, I dared not attack the damned thing. If I did, and called it wrong, why then it would be me, Kyrie Fern, a *Senior Foundation Adjuster*, who'd be blowing Marack to smithereens. Except that I wouldn't know that. I wouldn't know anything. . . .

A great jumble of questions hit me then; the ones I'd wanted to ask him before he'd conked out with his "poor Hooli on the rack" scene. What, indeed, was the sphere other than being the vehicle of, as he put it, "the Dark One's uncle"? Was this an actual invasion, a repeat of the original attempt by life forms of that other universe as represented by the original Dark One?

If so, from whence came the Alphians? Why were their ships not *contra-terrene*? Where had they been these five thousand years? Moreover, what, precisely, was their connection with the sphere?

One thing I knew from personal observation and training: they came from no ongoing civilization; no milieu of a developing social order. I figured them for incubator types; not cloned but bred—for a purpose. Hooli had guessed that I knew: ergo, his warning. . . . Damn again!

My head hurt. I was tired. To hell with it. We were still faced with the deadliest kind of peril. I had either to believe him and win with his way and with his ends, which were basically our ends, or to disbelieve, *ignore* him—and do it my way, and risk, perhaps, the destruction of the Fomalhaut systems!

But hadn't he said, too, that what was happening to him—being stretched, as if on an antiquated taffy-wheel—hurt? He'd never admitted to such a thing before and he'd been in some tough situations. That, too, had been a direct statement—and Hooli *never* lied!

We left early the next morning. There had been no changes, no "discoveries" aboard the scout ship. It was still raining. I chose Rawl, Sir Dosh and Lors Sernas to accompany me; in full armor beneath simple woolen cloaks.

Since the irresponsible Kriloy had slept through the coming to ground of both the Alphian and the blue sphere at Glagmaron, we had no idea where or *if* the other ships had landed. There being but five altogether, it was quite possible that one or more had chosen the continent and the cities of Om. We'd soon find out.

Once above the cloud bank, I saw with relief that in terms of protection it stretched northwest to as far as Gleglyn, and southeast to beyond Corchoon and Janblink, the capitals of Kelb and Great Ortmund, respectively. Whatever the cloud's original mass, it had been added to so that it covered the greater part of the northern continent. Such, apparently, was the power of Elioseen's incantation. Her *coven* had drawn clouds from as far east as the great sea, and from as far south as the Selig Isles.

At the drive controls, I took the scoutship directly to the westerly capital of Reen in the kingdom of Ferlach. On arrival, we were quick to note that whatever our expectations, the facts were more terrible still. The great castle above the port city had been reduced to a few hellish acres of blasted stones and burning ruins. The city itself was half-destroyed, mostly deserted, with but here and there a band of citizens attempting to flee with their belongings. There'd been little looting. The buildings hit had been gutted. Indeed, wherever laser beams and heat-positers had touched there was nothing but black swaths of destruction. Secondary fires raged everywhere.

The area of the port with its great breakwater and lighthouse was a lake of twisted, burning wreckage. The masts of sunken coasters stood like twisted antennae above the waters. Here and there were the bright blue and red bottoms of swamped fishing craft. The debris of Ferlach's merchant and naval fleets filled all the harbor.

Above, on the castle's tournament field was the evil bulk of the Alphian invader. Nothing moved around it. The terrain had died the death of the castle. Indeed, it was as if the ship had returned to *Alpha.* For the very earth around it, red and black like that of the mother planet, was lifeless—and *glowing.*

Below the castle, I saw a grouping of a half-dozen Alphians in silvered armor astride saddled dottles, picking their way down the destroyed road toward the city. They apparently wished to observe the effects of their work at close hand.

Swinging back, under the invisibility distortion factor of "null" plus "five," and following the road east at tree-top level, we came to a small encampment. It was off the road, hidden from both traffic and the skies by the thick branches of deciduous forest trees. *I* knew it was there by the accompanying presence of small troops of riders coming and going. Hovering, and with my contacts focused at ten mags, I could also discern the oak-tree banners of Ferlach's royal house flaunted bravely before a single tent.

I landed the ship in a vale some hundreds of yards from the encampment. As we approached it on foot, advancing boldly between the heavy fern-clothed trunks of great trees, we began to hear a whistling from all around us. We interpreted the distant answering calls and the absence of zinging arrows as an agreement to let us pass.

Nearing the tent we discerned a huge figure in bronzed armor, together with a half-dozen others similarly clad, awaiting us. At fifty feet, for the tent was centered in a small clearing, the bronzed figure roared in a voice to blast the eardrums: "If that's you, my lord Collin, then by the gods, I deem you ill-advised to come here, and that's a fact. Approach me slowly and stand when I say, for I've little patience with those who'll tell me now, *after the fact,* of plots and plans to snatch victory from defeat. Do you understand me, sir? You've come too late—for all I've ever loved in life are dead!"

He'd spotted my colors, a sprig of violets on a field of gold. As an Adjuster, there was but one way I could meet this bombast. I dared to risk it. I had no choice. Without breaking my stride, though slowing just the slightest, I shouted back, "By Ormon's breath, sire, do you think you're alone in suffering, you damned gerd's head? Must I match you loss for loss? A goodly portion of the flower of Marack lies dead upon our tourney field. Moreover, I see *you've* escaped to fight again while *our royal house is taken by the very scum you hide from.*"

"DAMN you, Collin!"

He was Draslich, King of Ferlach, and he would *not* be spoken to that way. He took a step forward amidst the sound of swords being unsheathed all around us, including those of my own stalwarts who, with bared blades, now positioned themselves instantly to my left, rear and right.

". . . And *daammmn* you, Draslich!" I matched him in voice, "for greeting a brother thusly, who's always held you dear; 'een though he's come to do exactly what you've said: to plot a vengeance, sir, against these murdering cowards that'll live when all our seas are dry. Now tell me: Do you have a drink for an old comrade, to wet his throat—or will you turn me away?"

My roar had been such, I think, as to cause even the forest birds to grow quiet. There were at least a hundred men in that camp. All stood as if carved from stone.

Draslich sneered, his voice still grating. "You prate of hiding, sir. Why, then, I see you're free—as is our Lord of Fergis and yon largish oaf who seems in form and feature like my good friend Breen Hoggle-Fitz."

Rawl, flat-faced, clashed sword against shield to acknowledge recognition. Sir Dosh, glowering, did likewise. From Sernas we heard but the faintest of chuckles.

Aikon Draslich, King of Ferlach, was indeed a huge man. His shoulder-length mane of black hair and curling beard matched the rampant, ebon fur of his troll-like body. He continued, raving, damning me and all my forebears. His curses were one prolonged blast. I let him go on, get it out of his system, satisfied that when he'd finished, we'd have that drink.

The tirade ending finally, he asked me sarcastically how I'd gotten here *this* time, referring to what he supposed was my "magick." I replied, smiling: "Why, the same as before, sire." He cursed again.

"So may we now approach?" I asked.

"Approach and be damned to you."

We did, after sheathing our swords, and were grudgingly invited to enter the tent.

There was but a single table and a scattering of chairs, all seized from peasant homes in the vicinity. Draslich poured ale all around. Among his six lords, I espied one whom I had known as a brave fighter at Dunguring. He was Pers-Gaan, an admiral of the fleet, a tall red-fur with smiling eyes. I raised my cup to him. He pledged me in turn. I said to the king, "You called it right of our companion here. He's Breen's son, Sir Altin Dosh."

He grunted in ritual: "A son of Breen is a son of Ferlach. But who's that other fellow? He looks more ring-eared pirate than northerner, to me."

I grinned. "Allow me, sirs: Our Lord Lors Sernas, Ambassador to Marack from dread *Hish* in *Om*!"

Draslich's eyes flashed. The six lords drew the circles of Ormon upon each breast and calloused hands reached again for swords hafts. Such was still the effect of the very name of *Om*.

"Why is he here?" Draslich demanded.

"Why, for his courage, sire. And why not?" I challenged. "That war's long over. And in it he fought well for Ormon, as well as his own god, Hoom-Tet." They hissed at that. "His sword is now pledged to Marack," I continued. "*Against the sky men!*"

At that point the aged Gaati, king's sorcerer to Ferlach, entered with two others of his kind. He whispered to Draslich, "I came as quickly as I could, sire." He nodded a gracious greeting to all of us.

"No need," Draslich muttered. "But stay. Your thinking has power beyond your magick."

Riding on Gaati's shoulder was the Royal Ferlachian Pug-Boo, Mool!

I then described all that had happened at Glagmaron and why we'd fled to Gortfin and why we were here: to begin the organization of a planet-wide resistance.

The king snorted his contempt, emptied his flagon, filled it and shouted, "What resistance? How do you fight sky lords when they command the very lightnings? What values courage in the face of *that*? I know. I know." He raised a hand. "That you've a certain wizardry of your own. But how"—and I suddenly noticed the very ghost of a smile in his slitted eyes—"indeed, can we fight such as have destroyed our city, slaughtered my knights, sank our fleet, left not a stone unturned of what was once a mighty keep—and this," he thundered again, "without ever so much as dirtying their silver robes?"

Allowing a twinkle to appear in my contacts, I answered wryly, "Why, sire, I'll admit it'll not be easy;" upon which Draslich and his knights all roared their laughter and shook their heads at such pithy defiance in the face of what they *knew* was total disaster.

I asked seriously. "How *did* you escape, sirs? I've a mind to know."

Draslich, calmed, settled to it. "When the thing landed," he began, " 'twas like at your Glagmaron; just before twilight. The greater part of the garrison under our lord-commander, Gen-Kols, went out to have a look. I then heard a yelling from the walls, and all the trumpets and the drums; this, at almost the very moment they were blown apart as if from the blow of the fist of a thousand-foot giant. Looking from the south tower we saw the entire garrison slain in a rain of fire and bolts of lightning. The tourney field became a smoking, reddish pit of *ghast*. Then, even as the east wing of the castle was destroyed by the same great hammer blows, we, my lords"—and Draslich fixed us all with a challenging eye—"were already fleeing through the 'passageways.' Now, Sir Collin, I adjure you, by Ormon's breath, if you've a plan—beyond your parlor tricks of 'glowing in the dark'—why then, sir, we'll hear you out."

At the mention of parlor tricks, I could not help but note the wide grins on the faces of all the Ferlachians. They had good memories.

Still I persisted. "And your city?"

"You've seen it. 'Tis half destroyed. The sky men have called an assembly for this morning. They intend, so 'tis said, to set up new rules under a new religion. Ormon, they say, is overthrown. They'll now be our gods as well as our executioners."

"How do you know this?"

"Stragglers. Yesterday sky men went to the city, killed some, rounded up others and told them to gather today to hear their orders. Moreover," he smiled grimly, "we've sent men back too, and have others watching. Now tell us your plans, Collin."

"There aren't any," I confessed. "And I'd be a liar if I said different. Hopefully we'll develop some; based on yourself, Chitar of Gheese, Laratis of Kelb, and the privy council of

Great Ortmund in the absence of their soon-to-be-crowned queen, the Lady Caroween Hoggle-Fitz. In this last respect all ambassadors of these countries were sent home from Glagmaron immediately after the Alphian's arrival to tell of what had happened and the action we had taken. Which raises the question: where is Kal-Tiers, your ambassador?"

"Ah, ha!" Draslich exclaimed. "This explains it. A man of ours reported last night of bodies upon the road, among them the heraldry of Kal-Tiers. We'd refused to believe it was the ambassador, for there was no proof. The face and parts of the body were incinerated by the sky men's weapons. . . ."

We all traced the sign of Ormon on our breasts.

Draslich went on. "If you've no plans, what then are your proposals?"

I grinned. "That you give us Gaati, for a start, and we'll be on our way."

The king's brow grew black again. "You dare. . . ."

"I must. We need Gaati. You've three wizards here, all of them competent. Moreover, we'll return Gaati within forty-eight hours."

Draslich fumed. He half arose from his seat. "You've got your bloody nerve, Collin. You'd take the only real weapon I have left to me."

"When he returns," I explained, "he'll have the plan."

Draslich, still fuming; angered, too, at his personal impotence, smashed his fist upon the table and shouted, "All *right*! Take him. What choice have we except death and slavery? We'll be your men, Sir Collin, for the length of time it takes to work the miracle—and no longer. Give me your hand, sir."

I did, and he shook it and flung it back.

I smiled. "My lord. One thing I'll tell you: these sky men with their new religion will now set out to recruit levies of warriors, knights and false lords to their service, all to control the populace. This being true, I suggest that you begin too, to gather your levies. Send trusted men to all villages and towns to rally the staunchest to your standards. Tell them that all is *not* lost; that Marack is taking the field and that warriors from all the north are rallying. You may tell them too that we *will* strike. And that when we do, 'twill be done with the protection of *all* the magick of the north, inclusive of Marack's *Collin*!"

Their eyes gleamed as I spoke. Their hands inadvertently

sought the hafts of their swords. Their indrawn breath was a sibilant hissing that boded no good for any Alphian. I sensed too that if there was ever to be a victory, it would be *no quarter*—without a doubt!

"Do you speak the truth, Sir Collin?" Draslich's plea was almost pathetic, so difficult was the bridge from despair to hope.

"When have I lied? I may get you all killed, and there's no gainsaying that. But I do *not* play games."

"Well then," he said, while arising to fill our flagons one more time, "let's drink to it." He was a reborn, bright-eyed *Lazarus*; poised, even confident.

Our toasts were hearty, adrenaline-charged, reflecting a new spirit. It was as if they'd heard the uncompromising trumpets of fresh armies charging to the rescue of stalwarts at bay on a thrice-stricken field. In essence, I'd deliberately psyched both them and ourselves in a way to spite the devil. And this against an enemy who, in the face of any reality, could easily slay us all—and with perfect equanimity.

The Ferlachian sea admiral said in more sober tones, "You are ever the dark bird, Sir Collin. But I would hope that just once, when and if you come again, 'twill be for wassail and in a time when peace will reign, for all of us." He then made the intricate swirl and dip, the protocol bow of all great lords.

Rawl, ever alert to a chance for whimsy, said owlishly, "Our Collin would say *yea* to that, for 'tis his choice, too."

Gaati, the aged wraith-like sorcerer, smiled, asked curiously, "Do you oppose peace, sir?"

"Nay, good sorcerer. 'Tis that I'm more alive in war and thus find pleasure in our Collin's contradictions. If he had his way, sirs, there'd be no war at all; not even the simple exchange of blows for the possession of this bridge or that ford, or even small raids for the joy of it. *If he had his way there'd be no tournaments either*! Think on that when you frown on our Collin for the fact that his fate is ever opposite to his wishes so that he seems, by personal design, as the center of every storm. . . . That storms exist, is fact. They are our fated burden. But I, sirs, would have it no other way. 'Tis why I ride with him!"

He got a round of enthusiastic applause; some from outside the tent where others had gathered to listen.

Draslich, pursuing the small-talk for the pleasure of it,

asked courteously of Sir Dosh, "And you, sir. Do you too think this way?"

Dosh, his thoughts elsewhere as usual, shook himself, as would a trained gerd who hears a bell. He batted his bulbous eyes, harrumphed a few times and then said testily, pompously, "Well now, my lords, I hold to the theme that a gog will linger where a kaati will not browse." He emptied his cup and stared around him, challengingly.

The statement of course required no answer except, perhaps, the observation that a kaati is carnivorous. . . .

Draslich, puzzled, still had sense enough to turn to Lors Sernas as an escape from Dosh, or so he thought. He asked of Sernas: "And what of you, my lord of Hish? What think you of our Collin's predilections?"

That blazing worthy—his surcoat was a riotous garden of color so that his heraldry of two castles was lost in a myriad of painted flowers—exclaimed loudly: "Why, good king, *I* follow our Collin for his humor; for the fact that he's a dancing master that I can learn from, and because he's the greatest wizard in all the kingdoms. Why, sirs, if you had been where I have been and seen what I have seen: jewels, my lords, precious beyond all belief . . ." He shook himself. "But as to war, sirs, know this: *I* fight not for transient glory. 'Tis an illusion, best ignored. *I* fight for love alone and to stay alive to enjoy pleasures of the flesh. I also delight in the savoring of foods, liquors, wines and the feel of satins, silks and velvets on my skin. In Hoom-Tet's love, sirs, I am a true sybarite. I am enamored of perfumes, poetry and lewd murals; or nakedness in all its forms. But most of all I do treasure the soft and willing bodies and limbs and parts of women—*all* women, young and old! As Hoom-Tet, our jolly master, has so succinctly put it: 'When all that's gone, what else is left?' So, sirs. Hear me well. *I* fight only for to stay alive and love. To our Collin then!" he shouted, carried away by the wicked pictures of his mind. "To our most gracious Collin, whom our sweet-bellied, fat-assed Hoom-Tet truly favors!"

Bloody Mohammed-Og! I looked around. All but Sernas were staring at me, aghast. I'd no choice but to ignore it all. I nodded sternly. They smiled mechanically and raised their cups, while making the sign of Ormon on their breasts. . . .

Draslich alone chose to whisper, and he too had a sense of

humor— "By the Gods, my lord, you do keep strange sword companions."

It was most certainly time to go, else all I'd won would soon be lost. I arose, saying, "We must leave now, sire and my lords, and go to Gheese—and with your sorcerer, Gaati, do you permit it."

"How could I not?" Draslich still chuckled inwardly. We all bowed to each other. But then, as Gaati plucked the Pug-Boo, Mool from his shoulder to hand him to one of his fellows, I swear I saw the little eyes widen for just a second, long enough to catch and hold my gaze. A small pink tongue came out to swing loosely back and forth. The eyes crossed. The little round head went tick-tock, from one side to the other, as would a metronome in a counter motion to the tongue. It lasted just two seconds. But Hooli had had his fun. He'd announced his presence too. . . .

Damn him!

"Screw you." I yelled mentally, uncontrollably. "You're playing games, you little bastard, while they're scraping the rest of us off the walls. I hope you're caught in a hype-warp, frigging taffy-machine. I hope to bloody hell that they stretch you from here to *Antares*. I hope. . . ." But Draslich and Gaati were staring at me strangely. To hell with it. I'd see him later—maybe.

The port city of Saks in Gheese still stood; so did its castle. There was no sign of destruction anywhere. Still, on the tourney field to the south of the castle's low hill, was a *third* Alphian ship. It all seemed so peaceful, we could almost imagine that King Peres Chitar had been allowed to surrender himself and the people without the usual show of mindless destruction.

Again we came to ground in a small clearing in the forest area to the north; right next to a herd of browsing dottles. We whistled them over, saddled the first four in the line-up (we kept saddles aboard the scoutship), nodded good-bye again to Kriloy and Gaati, phased out the ship and headed toward the city.

In each case our residing ambassador had given us a meeting site. To be on the safe side, it was always outside the city's walls. In Gheese, the spot was a combo boathouse-inn in a small cove where a sparkling stream came down to meet the river-sea. The surrounding trees were alive with tic-tic birds, blue-bottomed pity-docks and something akin to a daytime nightingale. Its warbling was fantastic. The cove, we learned shortly, was the personal property of our Gheesian ambassador, the grossly fat, Tils-Alden of Saks. It being as well protected from winter gales as was Saks' harbor, he'd coaxed a small fishing fleet to use it; taking a percentage of their catch as pay. The inn too was ostensibly for them. Actually it was all for Tils-Alden who was a gourmet lover of seafood. . . .

He was there now, a most punctual man, having a late breakfast or early lunch of ale, bok-bread, flatfish and a huge platter of mixed scallops, clams, oysters and certain unfamiliar mollusks. Seeing us, he arose, beaming to cry, "My lords, the sight of you must lead me to believe that all is well." His round face was awash with fish and ale, his mouth overly full of oysters. He waved a spoon, said, "Sit! Sit! Join me!" Then he choked, gasped, grabbed his throat and tried to swallow—which he should not have done. I immediately seized him and began to pound his back, thinking that we'd come too far to have our man die now of a surfeit of oysters. At a point where his face had turned blue, I was fortunate to hit the right spot. He hawked, spit, and regurgitated a great gollop of something. He then said weakly but promptly, "As I was saying, sirs; be pleased to join me." He sighed deeply and drew a number of pleasurable, happy breaths.

We needed no second invitation. Indeed, we fell to instantly, each finishing a platter of this and that in short order. Fat Tils-Alden, picked up where he'd left off. His mouth filled again, he asked us what was happening.

I told our story. "Yon clouds," I finished, "are but the edge of a blanket that extends to far Great Ortmund. So you can see, we're well protected, sir. But what of yourselves? 'Tis why I'm here, remember?"

He chewed mightily, waved his spoon again—and cautiously swallowed. He then gulped, cleared his throat. " 'Tis both good and bad," he exclaimed. "Example: The alien ship landed a full twenty-six hours *after* the one at Glagmaron. I was thus able to warn our good king Chitar a full hour before the fact. Our cunning Chitar—and he's oft' been likened to the flimpl-dot who can snatch the best of a meat pie from your mouth without your knowing—did two things immediately. He left the castle with his knights and moved to a scattering of farm houses about three miles from the city; he sent heralds to warn all citizens that such a ship would land and that they were to go nowhere near it on pain of death. Well acquainted with our leader's wisdom, no one has gone within a thousand yards of the Alphians. And they in turn have done nothing as yet but to come out of their ship to stare around.

"They seem oddly reluctant," Tils-Alden chuckled, "to go anywhere near the castle; this, though the bridge is down, the gates yawn widely, and all-in-all, it's deserted. I warrant, my lords, that if they're like those at your keep of Glagmaron, they are then so stupid as to know not what to do."

He'd put his finger on the Alphians' weakness, though I avoided the implication. I asked instead: "Do you have a message for me, sir?"

"None, except that we be told what is happening elsewhere and what you plan as a consequence. Chitar says, too, that you must understand that he *knows* the peril here; that this stalemate cannot last forever, and that he awaits your suggestions."

And so I told him of our meeting with Draslich, King Chitar's old enemy and "friend", and what I thought Chitar should do to supplement our common effort. "Above all," I insisted, "keep doing what you're dong. The enemy's bound to react eventually. I do advise that your city be evacuated; still, I'm sure that your king will know what to do for he knows his people better than I. As for ourselves, well sir, we wish the loan of your revered Plati, King Chitar's sorcerer. I'll take him with me now, for a conference, and return him within two days."

"Ah!" Our fat friend shook his head and sighed a corpulent sigh, redolent of basted fowls, pickled gog's feet and flatfish soup. "Plati's dead, my lord; died of an ague while I was with you in Marack."

I winced. He'd made it sound as if I was somehow responsible.

"Well, then," I told him strongly, "in the absence of Plati, we'd like someone else with equal competence."

"It'll take a couple of hours to reach the king, my lord."

"Why, so?"

"He's to the south. We're to the north—and we'd have to go round-about."

I arose, signaling my comrades to do likewise. "My lord," I told Tils-Alden, "be pleased to inform my old friend, Chitar, that I'll be here tomorrow between the eighth and tenth hours to pick up the sorcerer of his choosing, whom I'll return on the following day. Advise him of the urgency here—and give him my best regards."

"I'll do that, my lord. Rest assured. And my lord?"

I slowed my step toward the door.

He said hesitantly, "I've a baked tug-fish of some twenty pounds. 'Tis a rarity and the taste is delicious. 'Tis like no other. Take it with you, sir—as a gift from me."

I smiled and begged off. Not that we couldn't use a twenty pound tug-fish. It was the look in his eyes—as if the gift was really his right leg, basted and logged in turnip juice, and cool'd in its own jelly. I hadn't the heart. "But I do thank you deeply," I told him. "Another time."

He gratefully returned to his flatfish and mollusks.

Within minutes of the release of our dottles who, as always, were reluctant to go, we were cruising low over the Kelbian capital of Corchoon.

As in Ferlach, the castle was totally destroyed and the city had suffered considerably. Landing, we met our ambassador, Rariko, at the appointed spot, together with the young king's sorcerer, Dretus. Dretus, I must confess, looked like the very devil himself. He was a pinto, for one thing, his fur being black, white and strawberry. He was also the only red-eyed man I'd ever seen on Camelot-Fregis. Moreover, he seemed more warlock than sorcerer. And there *is* a difference.

The pattern in Kelb was the same as that of Glagmaron and Ferlach: a new order; a new religion, and with the Alphians as the new gods. Only one thing was different. The young king, Laratis, who'd fought the *dead-alives* so bravely in the second attack of the Dark One, had been slain with his new queen and all the lords of his privy council. The people were desolate.

We took the red-eyed wizard and left the ambassador, Rariko, to organize what resistance he could. Sensing an urgency I'd not felt until now, I ordered, too, that all professional practitioners and teachers of magick proceed along the highroad toward Glagmaron city. Somewhere on that road we would stop them all. A few would be taken to Gortfin, the remainder sent on to Glagmaron, or back to Corehoon—where they could still be used.

It was well after high noon when we settled to ground just a few hundred yards from the opened south gates of Janblink City. Unlike the capitals of the previous kingdoms, inclusive of Glagmaron, Janblink was walled. Warehouses, stables and great dottle pens pressed solidly against the expanse of towering stone. In time of war they'd be the first to suffer the fires and swords of a besieging army.

The ambassador from Great Ortmund had promised either to meet me personally at the first dottle pen to the west of the gate, or to send his substitutes. They were to watch for four unmounted knights in brown cloaks. We'd left the now quite impatient Kriloy, with the *two* sorcerers, in the lee of a small hill—safe from all prying eyes.

On a hill to the north of the city was great Castle Janblink. And precisely on its military-tournament field was the *last* of the five Alphian warships.

We plodded our way around the hill and down the road to the clutter of wooden buildings under the walls. Dosh had walked stumbling, with mouth agape and eyes bulging. He'd almost fallen a number of times and had to be rescued, such was his intensity.

Young Alten Dosh was no stranger either to Janblink City or Castle; indeed, he'd been raised there when his father. the Lord Breen Hoggle-Fitz, was warlord of all Ortmund's armies under the false king, Feglyn. When Feglyn had made his pact with the Dark One, Breen had immediately raised the flag of revolt from his own city of Durst. Four of his sons were killed in the ensuing battles as well as many hundreds of his household. Excepting Caroween and Dosh, his remaining children had later been captured and executed. Dosh, the youngest, had supposedly been killed at Dunguring where he'd gone to join his father who was then supporting Marack, Ferlach and Gheese against the Dark One's hordes who'd come swarming across the river-sea. . . . An exceptionally hard thump to the pate—and it would have had to be that, considering—and young Dosh was out of it; only to revive as a mindless nitwit. Where he went then, or how he managed to survive until his memory returned to him, will always be a mystery. But then, just a month before, he'd appeared at Glagmaron, tattered, barefoot, but still insufferably proud, the very image of his father, to demand to see his sister and to claim the Ortmundian name and heritage.

With Feglyn slain, Breen, the father, was to have been named king at the late summer harvest. His death gave the crown to his daughter, Caroween. Dosh, being youngest, made no claims; nor could he have. The right of succession in all of Fregis is to the eldest child, male or female. Caroween would *be* the queen.

Which was perfectly all right with Sir Dosh since, despite his pomposity, a certain religious fanaticism and an ingrained belief that he was superior by blood to most around him, he was, in contradiction, easy-going, generous to a fault—and without guile.

"You know, of course, my lord," he plucked my sleeve and questioned as we walked, "that I am knowledgeable as to Janblink's secret passages. I often played in them when a boy."

"We're not here for such deeds today," I told him. "My intent's to chat with a few who'll meet us, then get out."

His eyes glittered. "But we will return, Collin, right?"

I murmured, "Indeed we will."

At the dottle pens, and being nosed lovingly from between the pen-rails by a dozen or so of the beasts—they were apparently quite bored with the pens and sought a friend to free them from such dullness—we found no one as yet to greet us. We petted and soothed the dottles to pass the time, while their fat fannies wagged in doggy happiness and their tails flailed the air like hairy windmills.

We continued to wait, the four of us, or rather the three of us since Sernas chose against my discipline to wander after a pie-maid and to take advantage of her burdensome tray and her knapsack to maneuver her against the great wheel of a potter's wagon. At that point, while we watched entranced, he began skillfully to stroke an unprotesting buttock, being amusingly indecisive the while as to which pie to purchase. Not that the maid resented either his advances of his use of her time. Oh, no! Indeed, even after the sly devil had kissed her soundly and fiercely gripped the captured buttock as if he'd purchased that too, and then left to rejoin us—her eyes had followed him hungrily.

Rawl, breathing heavily in my ear, said enviously, "By Ormon's ass, Collin, that raunchy bastard has but to seize their parts and they fall to their knees in adulation. I swear, I don't understand it."

"He knows," I said softly, "the secrets of womankind; that they indeed prefer such direct action; that they are in no way built for pedestals."

Sernas, overhearing as he approached, said bluntly, "Our Collin's right. 'Tis a fact that Hoom-Tet teaches. All women are fated to be loved, my lords. They desire it, live for it; are *built* for it. To waste time with the silliness of wooing, poetry reading and the like is, in Hoom-Tet's eyes, plain stupid. Shoot for the target; waste not a second. That's the ticket. As our gracious wise one so blithely puts it: 'A pat on the ass of a queen will win a crown where all else fails.' Be not laggards in love, sirs. Moreover—"

"My Lord Sernas," Rawl interrupted sourly, "I've learned to dislike you less as the months go by. Don't press your luck, sir."

Sernas turned instantly to me with a twinkle in his eye and said, "Ah, ha! Did you hear that, my lord? He's at it again. Pure jealousy, sir. And he *knows* I'll not be challenged, lest it be for the immediate rights to a willing crotch which, when you get down to it, is never his to defend or offer. Why, my lord—"

"Have done, Sir Omnian," I snapped—and I, frankly, was a little tired of his obsessions— "Save your strength for the cause we fight for. No peasants are allowed in brothels, sir. And that's what you'll be, at *best*, if our enemy has his way."

Sernas grinned and shrugged. His skin rivaled a gerd's in thickness. Nothing could touch him. With a lightning-like display of his skill with the fal-dirk—it was *his* weapon, and fittingly so—he quartered the pie and offered us each a portion.

Since the pastry was of meat and not of fruit, I deemed it quite poisonous and shrugged it away. He grinned again, winked, and ate the full portion in one greedy gobble. My stalwarts did likewise with theirs, leaving not even a crumb for the diving, chattering tic-tics. . . .

Sir Dosh, in the meantime, had been eyeing a group of a dozen or so men-at-arms led by a husky young knight with a round, stupid face, small eyes and a pronounced scar from temple to chin. He announced suddenly, "I know that bastard. Indeed, if my memory serves me, 'tis ***I*** who am the cause of his ugliness."

He was about to say more, but I wanted no trouble. "Then turn away," I told him. "Don't let him see you."

Dosh did better than that. He removed himself from our group for about thirty paces and gave his attention to the dottles. If the worst should happen there would then be no connection with us, unless he chose to make one.

I'd noted that the scarred knight and his dozen all wore patches of white on their shoulder harnesses. They passed us *and* Dosh in a jingle of steel, going on toward the main gate of the pens where another large group of citizens had gathered. At that moment, too, a foursome in cloaks of dark blue, as opposed to our brown, came directly toward us. They paused just once on the way, ostensibly to appraise the dottles. Then, when they were within but a few feet of us, a stocky man, cowled until that moment, threw the cloak back to reveal himself as Gen Disti, Ortmund's ambassador, from whom we'd parted the previous noon.

"My lords," he said without hesitation, "since I deem it that you came here by other ways than dottle-back, I'll assume also that you know our enemy is here."

"We do. Have you brought the king's sorcerer?"

Disti nodded to the oldest of his group. "We bring you Per-Teens, one of our best."

"What is the situation?"

"The same as Marack's, but with less bloodshed. They killed a hundred or so at random to prove they could do it, then awed the townsfolk with their magick—the *magick* of their weapons; this, with a few destroyed homes and buildings. They then announced themselves as being our new gods. And that's it. They held a meeting this very morning. Declarations have been posted. The temples of the Trinity were invaded, the priests and wizards killed. As of now the temples are being renovated by guildsmen as ordered by the enemy. Their leader's a man remarkably like the lord Tarkiis."

His tones were so casual that I became alarmed. I asked sharply: "Do the people take this so easy then?"

He frowned, actually glared at me. "They've been without a leader for some time, Collin." He was forced to shout the words so as to be heard above a sudden caterwaul of fighting dottles—and was then forced to a quick whisper when the fighting ceased. "Before that they had only Feglyn and the

Dark One. True, they loved Breen Hoggle-Fitz. But Fitz is dead—and his daughter? Well who really knows?"

"Lord Disti," I said firmly, "the fact that 'tis you who are here rather than a guard of the sky-men to take us suggests that you at least are loyal. That you've brought your sorcerer proves it. Still, the reaction, as you describe it, is disturbing."

I then told them all that had happened. Disti agreed to begin the same sort of operation, the rallying of those loyal to Ormon as well as to Great Ortmund; the immediate preparation to participate in whatever we deemed necessary—and the sending of additional sorcerers and witches *toward* Glagmaron.

"Fear not, Collin," he told me firmly. "You'll find the Ortmundians at your side in the end."

I nodded a reserved satisfaction, saying, "I'll return *this* good sorcerer within forty-eight hours with our conclusions as to what to do. . . ."

And then what I'd least expected happened!

Riding through the city gates and with the citizenry falling back in panic in all directions so as to make way and keep a goodly distance from them, there came two quite resplendent Alphians on prancing dottles.

Their spotless white and silken jumpsuits repelled dirt. They glowed as I had never done. They were beautiful; too beautiful. They were indeed "angels." Some of the crowd were already beginning to kneel. Those beyond us, at the main dottle gate, also began to disperse in fear of the sky-men's passing. The young knight and his men-at-arms turned back to us, and came on to offer themselves to their masters.

"My lord," Gen-Disto said quietly, "we knew nought of this, and now we are undone. Still, we will die with you. That I swear."

I ignored him. There was no time. I could kill both the Alphians with the belt-laser. But again, if I did I'd draw attention to myself; *bring the sphere, too,* into the arena. One way or the other all would be lost—except?

"My Lord Sernas," I said softly, and he stared as paralyzed as my companions, "would you risk a chance at the love of humankind for all eternity?"

He answered, "Why surely, and do you mean *love* the way *I* mean it?"

I slipped my fal-dirk into his hand. "You now have two," I told him. "When they," I nodded, "are within ten paces, I want these blades embedded securely in their throats. Understood?"

Sernas had gone cold sober. His face paled. The elvish light in his eyes had dimmed. He said calmly, "I died once, Collin. Do not think that I'm unaware that 'twas your magick and that of 'the little brown one' that returned my life to me. Just pray now, with me, to Hoom-Tet, that my hands be steady."

"You know I will," I told him.

The squadron of men-at-arms was just then passing Sir Dosh. The Alphians were *thirty* feet away. Dosh, alert to what was happening, decided on his own on a tactic which proved him, at least to me, a true son of his father. He stepped out boldly as the last man passed him. Hands on hips he shouted to the young knight: "Well! By bloody ghast, you snot-nosed bastard. I knew I'd seen you before. You're Tostan, that burnt my father's keep when none of our name were there to defend it. I thought I'd killed you, turd. But no mind. *I'll do it now!*"

A man of absolute action, he'd drawn his greatsword, thrown his shield to the front and, as the last word passed his lips, drove a whistling blow to Tostan's head that would have sent it flying had he connected.

"Hold to the front!" Tostan roared after his dozen, who still came on toward us and the Alphians.

They halted, turned, saw their commander attacked and moved instantly to attack the attacker. Dosh, whirling with the weight of his own heavy blade, followed through on squat Tostan, took an arm, and sliced through cloth and metal to cut the man half-way to the spine. Not stopping there, he fell to one knee and caught the first of his attackers on his shield-front; arose, threw the man over his head to crack his neck and then literally skewered the next swordsman to reach him.

We, in the meantime, were not idle. The Alphians were almost upon us. I said simply: "Now!" to Sernas who let fly with the proper deliberation so that only the sound of a double, sibilant hiss and the twin *thunk* of steel in flesh disrupted the already growing chaos around us.

They fell from the dottles, the welling blood in their

throats choking their cries. Their heels beat a drumfire tattoo on the hardened ground. I was upon them, instantly, to rip the belts and weapons from their bodies. These I tossed to the aged Gen-Disto, saying, "Hold them."

I think it was the pent-up frustration of all that had happened that then caused us to unleash the fury we did. It could also have been because I raised the cry of "No quarter." I had by accident, when handing the weapons to Disto, glanced to the skies—and saw that the clouds had receded toward the west. *Great patches of blue were suddenly and dangerously visible.*

"No quarter!" I'd roared instantly, sizing up the situation. "There's no time!"

And we were on the remnants of the dozen in a lashing whirl-wind of steel, a kind of berserker drive that would normally be beneath us. I smashed the first man to the ground with my shield's edge alone, drove my sword's tip straight through the skull of another. The back-sweep of my blade took the head of a third, almost by accident, so that it flew still screaming from the torso.

Rawl, disdaining his shield for mere men-at-arms, was into them with both hands on his sword's haft. Roaring: "Marack! Collin! Marack! Collin!" he killed four men in as many seconds. Sernas, I must say, was no laggard when it came to bloody in-fighting. Inspired by his deed with the fal-dirks as well as the company he now kept, he skillfully dropped to one knee and whirled his greatsword to sweep the feet from off the legs of a veritable giant of a sergeant—he also used both hands—then arose to catch a second man beneath the arm, the chink in the hauberk, as it were. He drove to the very heart—and was inundated by a fountain of blood that drenched his flowered surcoat.

I, in the meantime, had broken the last man's neck with my shield's edge. I quick spun to seize the captured Alphian weapons from Gen-Disto, upon which he and his companions, minus the sorcerer who remained with me, raced for the dubious protection of the crowd now gathering in the arch of the city gates.

Dosh had wasted no time either. He'd run ahead to open the gates of the dottle pens, holding the beasts 'till we got there. We mounted them bareback, one by one as they were freed, then raced with all speed toward the hill and our ship.

At the site, I quick phased the craft from its luxury of invisibility, while Rawl, Dosh and Sernas whacked the dottles' broad fannies to chase them off, and the five of us passed through the small port to confront the awestricken Kriloy and the two amazed sorcerers, Gaati and the red-eyed Dretus.

"Take it up!" I yelled to Kriloy. "Quick! I want it over the areaway to the south gates, *now*!"

Within sixty seconds I'd fathomed the simple structure of the laser and blaster guns, pressed the right studs and was rewarded with both freed power-packs in my hands. They were the same, interchangeable. I applied a monitor-gauge to both, pressed the input stud to my belt-packs and saw what I'd expected take place—a noticeable rise in my pack, a noticeable drain in those from the two Alphian weapons. I figured that at full drain it would take perhaps a half-hour to immobilize the packs completely. I then subjected the guns to a series of three-dimensional, electron photography shots and that was it. I could barely contain my joy. I'd planned some sort of a commando strike to seize a gun. It would have had to have been done. But not now. We'd done it! By the gods, I thought—a windfall from old Ormon, himself—the war was one third won!

I took over the drive, gave the weapons to Kriloy. "Send 'em out the eject, right in front of the gates, ya hear? I want them to be found, quick!"

Seconds later—while I hovered, a fifty-foot air-distortion to those by the gates below, Kriloy yelled, "Bombs away!" and I knew that the guns would soon be back in Alphian hands.

We were home free!

Except for the fast disappearing, double-damned clouds. . . .

From Janblink to Gortfin, the distance is just two hundred miles. Another five minutes and we were there. The cloud cover was weaker than over Janblink city. Indeed, in all the north, though clouds remained, they were now piled in great, miles-high cumulous formations of white. Blue sky was everywhere. The rains *and* our protection had definitely ceased.

But now, below us, was a sight to do my heart good. In all the green vales and on all the mountain tops of the little Alpine range, there was no sign whatsoever of the somber pile of great Gortfin Castle. It was simply gone. Vanished. Disappeared!

I breathed a sigh of relief and uncorked a bottle of Velas, while the rest stared bug-eyed at what they undoubtedly viewed as the ultimate magick!

"Blast, Kyrie," Kriloy exclaimed in awe. "Where's the damn castle?"

I'd had as yet neither the desire nor the patience to apprise him of the problem. I'd figured that he'd know it soon enough. The rest of my band seemed equally in the dark since Rawl and Dosh had listened but idly to our exchange with Elioseen, and the lecherous Sernas, not at all.

I played the topo-computer coordinates with my fingers. The exact contour block appeared to parallel the visuals. Pointing, I said to Kriloy, "There it is. Don't you recognize it?"

I'd directed him to an oddly flat and barren hilltop, behind which was a great meadow with herds of browsing gogs intermingling with many dottles. The hill was between two lush valleys which arose on either side to small mountains covered with conifers. Streams were at the bottom of the valleys as well as a few hunters' huts and the houses of woodsmen. "Recognize the north meadow?" I asked Kriloy.

His eyes widened, stared. "Bloody Jesu-Og! But what happened to the castle?"

"Not a thing. Just set her down."

He did. And I swear it was like going through *warp*. One second, nothing; the next—when we'd descended past the level of the tallest tree—a brilliant flash, *and there was Gortfin Castle in all its medieval, dark-ages splendor*. On the meadow, I noted for the first time, there were a number of cavorting dottle babies, colts. It was foaling time for dottles. The mares, if one could call them such, stared proudly and waved their fannies.

I hustled everyone out of the ship, except Kriloy, that is. I made to leave myself, but he yelled, pleading: "Hey, Kyrieee! Sheeh. You've got to cue me in. Here you come staggering back to the ship like a gang of butchers fresh from the abatoir. Gortfin Castle disappears. We find it again. Hell, man. You *got* to let me know what's happening."

"I'll get back to you. I promise," I yelled. "Work on that energy flow . . . And close the port, NOW!"

He slammed the entry door inward. I phased it out; this, to

the puzzlement of a couple of hoary dottle wardens. Our little band went running toward Gortfin's northern gate. . . .

Greeted in the great hall by Fel-Holdt, Rondin and Jos-Viins, I briefed them quickly as to what had happened and we retired to the lower rooms of the *chirurgeons*, Marack's court doctors, who accompany every army and who are a part of every populated community. We luxuriated in the great heated pool, served by cane conduits from which water flowed throughout the castle, pumped by crude devices from the streams below. Afterward, we were massaged with perfumed medicinal oils and left, to a relaxed catnap.

I'd also sent a quick message to Elioseen that we would meet in council at the sixteenth hour. Marack's lords had shown no concern that I'd freed her. Indeed, the opposite was true. There was a new feeling of relaxation, of well-being, even, at the news; a consensus, I took it, that I'd done the right thing. She'd informed them too of her success with Gortfin's invisibility. Another reason, I concluded, for that relaxed state of mind. Without a doubt, we were on the road to recovery, in spirit at least, from the initial trauma of helplessness in the face of an omnipotent enemy.

But Elioseen refused to wait for our council. My messenger returned with a note from her requesting my urgent attendance in her old rooms in the castle's west wing. Waking Rawl, who forever slept with the innocence of a five-year-old, we retired to my apartment, dressed in clean linens and such and followed the guide to our lady's chambers.

" 'Tis that I thought that you should see for yourself what is happening now in Glagmaron," she told me solemnly in greeting. "I would not have been able to bridge the gap 'twixt here and there," she confessed, while leading me by the hand through a number of inner chambers to a final large one which seemed like an ancient Terran cabalist's retreat, "had I not had the help of our wizards. One's power wanes, you know, when it's not used."

The twelve members of the coven awaited us; joined now by the sorcerers, Gaati, Dretus and Per-Teens. They reflected Elioseen's solemnity and concern.

There were great burning tapers everywhere. Some gave off

incense; others seemed capable of noxious fumes. Bottles, boxes and charts lined the east wall. Tables were strewn with black firepots, retorts and all the stuff of the witches' art. More. Signs and words of magic were all-pervasive, on the great tapestries, the walls; painted upon the floor in great circles wherein power, I'm sure, was supposedly gathered—and re-released. Some tables were strewn with charts and spells. One side of the room was a library, with tight rolls of papyrus and heavy tombs of vellum; all of it hand-printed. . . .

I was struck with a sudden trepidation. It was as if something, until now hidden, were peeping out at me from behind a darksome curtain. . . . How much of all this, I wondered, was malarkey—and how much of it practical, the real McCoy? And more frightening still: Was the answer to Camelot's magick to be truely found, as Hooli had said—in word sounds to distrupt and use the converging lines of the planet's magnetic field? For the first time, I actually questioned Hooli's description of how it was all supposed to work. I questioned it more when Elioseen led the twelve (minus the three, who'd yet to be worked into her schema), to a table where sat a flat pan about two feet in diameter and an inch or so in depth. It was filled with liquid mercury.

She paused reflectively, placed me and Rawl to one side but in close view of the silvered surface and then arranged the others. She then conducted them, literally, as if she were the maestro and they the orchestra, in a word incantation. . . .

It sounded almost *Gregorian*. And it was in three parts. The first made of the pan of mercury a window to whatever Elioseen wanted to see. The second created a zeroing-in effect on a particular area of Glagmaron City. The third provided the *audio*—gave voice and sound to what was happening there. The three incantations seemed actually *directional*; apart from each other and even insulated, *sound-wise*, from each other. I simply couldn't believe what was happening; though, in one way or another it had been with me for all of my days on Camelot-Fregis.

The chorus began; we saw the city. The second chorus intervened in volume; the *eye* of the liquid mirror zoomed in as would a scanner so that we were actually on a corner of the city's central plaza, or square, facing the temple of worship to the gods, Ormon, Wimbely and Harris. Statues of the three, as well as of a goodly number of their apostles, had been pulled down. They lay broken; chunks of marble, legs, arms, heads and torsos strewn about like so many plaster rejects. In the square's center a bonfire roared. Around it danced hundreds of people, while the fire itself was fed by icons, tapestries and "books of faith" hauled from within the temple. Squads of warriors were posted around all the entries to the streets leading away from the square. They wore the *white* tab upon their swords' harnesses, where they crossed above their hearts. Knights were with them; I recognized a goodly number. . . . And in all the streets, being held back by the men-at-arms, were throngs of weeping citizens.

We watched as the doors of the temple opened to allow the exit of a half-dozen Alphians, followed at a respectful distance by a troop of Marack's lords, knights and merchants, all dressed in their most costly robes. A *white tag* was now pinned to the breast of each. The Alphians paused at the top of the steps. A line of what appeared to be "neophytes of the new religion" was then allowed to advance from one of the side streets. They knelt in six rows below the Alphians; upon which a single sky-lord unsheathed the sword from off his back and walked down the lines to touch each supplicant upon the shoulder and thereby bestow some favor or office upon him. The Alphian, in his splendor, seemed like the "Angel of Death," which he proved ultimately to be. For another single line of Marackian lords and knights was then thrust forward from a side street. Their arms bound, they were forced to their knees and made to wait while the same Alphian with his shining sword walked slowly behind them to deliberately strike off each shrieking head as he went.

The bodies were thrown hastily into waiting wagons, only to have their places taken by another line, and yet another; the last being made up of students, some of whom I had known and liked.

The executions continued, with now and then a change in executioners so that each Alphian had his chance to show his sword work. . . .

Then Elioscen spoke softly to her coven. The directional group changed tonal inflections but slighty—and the scene shifted—lifted from the square to soar up and away to a sylvan glade to the south of the castle. Two tents were pitched. A picket line of saddle dottles browsed unhappily on what they could reach from their strangely, to them, confined circumstances. No one *ever* tied a dottle to anything. Penned them up, yes. Stabled them, yes. But *tied*? Absolutely not!

There were at least a dozen Alphians present, and with them a dozen or so of the prettiest daughters of Marack's court. Our magick mirror enlarged upon the scene so that we saw Tarkiis and Marquest, his adjutant, in all their splendor. Seated next to the two of them were Murie and Caroween. Unlike the sad dottles, our two lovelies were not tied and seemed in no way to be unhappy. . . .

I heard Murie say—and her voice came strangely slurred as if from under water—"Well, my lord, what think you of our courtesy now? Does it compare well with your far land?"

He leaned across from where he lay quite close to her, against huge pillows beneath a tree's protecting limbs. "Nothing compares to our fair land, as you call it. For we have no 'land' as such. We simply have what we need; what we want. For all we can imagine is given us by the elder gods of whom we're a part. Example: *This* scene. If we think it and want it, we can have it."

Murie was in no way nonplussed by this answer. She actually teased: "If you think *me*, can you then have a *me* for your own?" Her accompanying smile, the small fingers that traced a line down his arm, nigh drove me to hurl the mirror to the floor. But the watchful eyes of Elioseen cautioned and forced my control.

Tarkiis replied, "Since I could never imagine *you*, I could not create you. We know of the two sexes. But in my land there is only one, ourselves, such as you see. We confess," he smiled mechanically, "that we are strangely touched by you. 'Tis an example of the atavistic urge, no doubt, about which we've been told."

"Would you give way to it?"

"We do what we wish to do."

"Do you know how?"

In a sense she was making a fool of him, if the concept fit at all, and if he'd but known it. But in no way did this observation lessen my rage.

Tarkiis replied, "What's there to know? All animals and most lower life, for that matter, couple in some way. If I thought it would be pleasurable, I would use you to do it."

"But how will you know if you don't?" Murie asked softly. Her voice was husky, her lips just inches from his own, her eyes wide, staring steadily into his. Gods! For Tarkiis not to react was a damned insult. I'd kill the bastard twice—for the contradiction.

And Caroween: I could not help but see that that bold vixen, for whatever purpose, was pressed against her accompanying Alphian lord and was actually walking her slender fingers up the silvery stuff of his pantaloons to his thigh top. A vague glitter shone in her eyes. The newness of what he was obviously experiencing caused him to shudder inadvertently.

Murie said, and her voice was huskier still, "Would you do it now, my lord—if I asked?"

Tarkiis said, "If *you* asked? I don't understand. It is not for *you* to ask anything. You are here, my lady, because I wish it. All of yours remain alive, as does this world, because *we* wish it. We have a task to perform here. That is all. If there are accompanying things of pleasure that are as yet unknown to us, and if you are somehow a part of that, I'll surely use you. But not, my lady, because *you* ask."

Murie, without batting an eye and with the same boldness displayed by Caroween, placed a hand directly on him and began a caress, ever so softly. . . .

He frowned, watching the hand. His eyes became troubled.

And the mirror went dead and cold.

Elioseen said—and it had been her raised hand that had stopped the chorus and thus the mirror—"Be angry, sirs, with what you have seen in the square and elsewhere, but not with your ladies. I think I know what they're attempting to do, and it's not for you or me to judge them. Earlier on there was a chant in the square that the 'Collin' was dead; this to a question and a statement of defiance by a student who was promptly taken. . . . Whatever. You now know what is happening. The sky lords move fast; too fast, perhaps. Indeed, I fear me, Collin, that even now we may be too late."

My ears were ringing. My body literally thrummed with the tension of what I had seen. My brain seemed to boil with a fever of rage and unbridled hatred. I'd become an animal, the kind that the likes of Tarkiis could not easily dismiss. I fought for control, feeling the hot sweat over all my body. My eyes, *sans* contacts, would have looked like the pits of hell.

My shieldman stood with fists clenched and eyes unblinking while blood from his bitten lips rolled down his chin. Whatever happened, I knew that Tarkiis would never survive the both of us. I grasped Rawl's shoulder, saying softly to Elioseen, "Mayhap you're right, my lady. But, on the other hand, we just might be able to change it back. I'll ask you for just one thing: Can you repeat what you did once before when you plucked myself, the Princess Murie Nigaard and two others from the kings' road and brought us here to Gortfin?"

"Possibly."

"This time, my lady, we must reverse the process and with as many as ten. The destination is the square in Glagmaron city. Moreover, you must be able to maintain contact and to bring us back on signal. Again: Can you do it?"

This time her reply was slow in coming. She said finally, "There was a time when I'd say yes, and instantly. But I can't guarantee it, Collin. To send you, yes; I think so. But to maintain contact, as you call it—and return you safely—the risk would be great. . . ."

"My lady," Rawl Fergis said hoarsely before I could speak, "I know our Collin. We'll take that risk, e'en though it be just the two of us. Prepare your magick!"

Her eyes flew to me. I nodded, asked simply, "When?"

"When do you wish it?"

"As my comrade said. Now."

"I need an hour."

"We'll be here then. My lady." I bowed my head and led off toward the exits. . . .

There was still an hour or so of daylight. We held our meeting in the council room, told all that had happened in more detail, how it was in the other kingdoms and the like. A few additional sorcerers and teachers had arrived from Glagmaron. They served to substantiate what Rawl, myself and the Lady Elioseen had seen. They emphasized further that in all of Glagmaron and the towns and villages around it, it was thought that the Collin, Sir Rawl Fergis and the battle commander, the Lord Fel-Holdt of Svoss, had been slain. It was also told that the Pug-Boos had left the land, were nowhere to be found. . . .

"One more reason for us to prove them liars with our presence," I announced. I then told the council what I intended doing and asked the aid of Dosh and Sernas. Sir Dosh raised a pained eyebrow that his name should even be mentioned, since where I went, he went. He even arose to announce—for he had need of a certain bravo image—that he, personally, would rebuild Ormon's temple with the heads of the apostates who'd pulled it down.

Sernas but rolled his eyes and nodded while keeping up a running patter of foolishments with one of Elioseen's ladies who, oddly enough, found his company—he'd plunked himself down beside her unasked—quite entertaining.

There wasn't a knight or lord who didn't volunteer. But Fel-Holdt, knowing our limitations *and* the risks as stated by Elioseen, allowed only Gen-Rondin plus three student warriors of my choice to accompany us.

Our now avowed objective? To slay all in the temple in the name of the Trinity, the Royal House and the "very much alive Collin," as representing the Lord-Commandor Fel-Holdt—*in the field with the core of Marack's reborn armies!*

Fel-Holdt, the ever-practical, asked bluntly if I thought Sernas's trick with the fal-dirks would suffice to cancel the weaponry of the sky-lords as they'd done at Janblink City. "My lord," I told him, "there are more ways than one to skin a flimpl. Trust me. . . ."

I then excused myself and left the meeting for some extracurricular business. In the great hall I buzzed Kriloy and ordered him outside to await a guide and guards who'd take him to the castle. . . . On his arrival, I told him that it would be he on the morrow who'd pick up the Gheesian sorcerer and that it would be *he* who'd return them all to their respective kingdoms on the day after; this, depending on whether our raid came a cropper and we were either taken or killed.

We'd seated ourselves on a divan in that marvelous "hall of lords," which he, I'll add, looked at with wonder, even awe. It was his first time outside the ship and inside a Camelotian-Fregisian stronghold. He was deeply impressed.

A carafe of sviss and cups had been brought and placed before us on a small table. His guide *and* guards awaited him at some distance.

He didn't take to it well at all. I'd known he wouldn't. Kriloy, to me, had become a complete surprise. On the single occasion when I'd belabored him for what he hadn't done, I'd been oppressed with a feeling of alienation; that I was failing completely to get through to him. A Kriloy aboard the *Deneb* was one thing. There, he was within his own element, a part of it all, as it were. But a Kriloy on Fregis, with me, was something else. The death of the *Deneb* had been the catalyst, I think. Now, with the others dead, I was no longer Kyrie Fern to him, but rather a Fregisian—a Marackian Overlord. To Kriloy my fur was as real as it was to Murie; so were my blue-purple eyes. To him, the fact that in the spans of nine months I'd killed more men than he would ever personally know was just unacceptable. He simply could no longer relate to me as Kyrie Fern, Senior Adjuster of the Galactic Foundation Center. Whatever his studies at the academy, *I* was now an alien, even a monster, perhaps.

Thinking about it, I was inclined to agree with him. The old cliché that "a man has to do what a man has to do," held true. In self-pity I even allowed my eyes to brim.

When I told him what was happening, explained it to him in detail, he asked soberly, "Well, what becomes of me if you're killed, Kyrie?"

I replied just as soberly: "Well, you can take my place for one thing. Or, you can keep trying to break through to the Foundation for a rescue. You can even try for Holbein. There's a small base there. Take you twenty years without warp, and even then I doubt if you'd make it. Gotta have full tanks. Lastly, you could just hole up; get yourself a sex partner for those dull evenings and pray that all the crap that's coming down, won't; or at least that it won't touch you."

"You think the Foundation will check out the missing *Deneb*?"

"Certainly. But slowly and cautiously. You don't move into the area of a starship's destruction in the usual way, Kriloy. Remember the *skuuls*? It'll take a few years, maybe five, ten."

"Why does it have to be you?" He couldn't help himself.

"Well take a good look at me, buddy. I'm what I think *you* think I am. I could walk away from all this easily. But I'd die of a broken heart if I did. I'm reminded of one of our old Terran poets, Burns, I think. He had something that began with: 'If ye ha' been where I ha' been,' and like that. But you, Kriloy, will never be where I have been, because it's all in the past. Anyhow, buddy, the players are still out there. And it's the last act, the final curtain. It's like *Ragnarok*; the *Götterdämmerung*! There's something happening, too, that I can't put my finger on, like the old 'play within a play.' Whatever. Mysteries have a way of disclosing themselves in time. In this last act, we'll either make it or we won't. . . . The only role you can play is the one you're playing. You wanna be a hero? Find the drain. Correct it. Break in on the goddamn grid and tell 'em to get their bloody asses over here. That way, buddy, if either of us wins, we'll both win. Think about that. There ain't no other way. . . ."

He said, quoting: "So let it be written, so let it be done." The half-puzzled frown still touched the pale forehead. He said, "It's beginning to gel. I even had a pang of sympathy."

I laughed. "Heyyyy! That's progress. Keep trying for the matrix. If I don't buzz you at eight tomorrow, then come out of that skyship in a hurry and present yourself to Fel-Holdt to take my place—or else run for it; whichever you please."

The frown had deepened. A few beads of sweat had appeared. "Don't lose any sleep, Kyrie. I'll know what to do before that screwing Fomalhaut starts waking your fauna. Don't worry."

"Me worry?" I grinned. "Forget it." I then whistled up his guide and the two men-at-arms to walk him to the ship. It was now dark outside. "So the kaatis won't get you," I called after him.

We'd stripped, bathed, oiled ourselves lightly with a curative substance with antiseptic qualities, put on fresh linen long shirts, light-padded jupons, hauberks, plates and our best surcoats. This time the world would fully note just who we were. I allowed my three students to wear my colors, the sprig of violets against a field of gold. Rawl's three scarlet bars on an azure field was now known to all the north; so too was the Dernim tulip of Sir Dosh. His father had carried it with valor from one end of Fregis to the other. The book and sword of Rondin against a white field was splendiferous, to say the least. An odd heraldry, his family had always been either judges or warriors, and so the logo. . . . And then, of course, there was the thick-lipped and lecherous Lors Sernas. *His* blazonry would be long remembered when all of ours were dust. For the north had no paint pots to equal the brilliantly permanent colors of his shield and surcoat.

We gathered quietly in Elioseen's great room of witchery.

She'd limited the viewers to ten, what with all the sorcerers, witches and warlocks present, and most of them involved. Fel-Holdt and Jos Viins led the viewers, ten knights and lords. They were forced to stand well back from where I and my eight were positioned. There was only candlelight to see by—an eerie atmosphere. The smell of incense was thick around us. The signs on all the walls, the floor, the tapestries now seemed familiar, like ancient tombs I'd seen of the protective pentagrams of Earth's warlocks in that far-ago time. Again I wondered, where *did* the science begin and the fol-de-rol leave off?

The chanting began. Word sounds well spaced; each vowel hard and fully pronounced. Within seconds I felt the tingling I'd experienced in that far time of nine months before when the then "wicked Elioseen" had seized Murie and me from the king's road to begin the saga. . . .

Suddenly then it was as if we were encased in a silvered, transluscent bubble. There was no sound, nothing; indeed, all was an instant ebon-black so that I thought that perhaps we'd died. But I had not lost consciousness, nor had any of my comrades. This time, to interrupt the great thrumming that had set all our muscles to quivering to its tune, there came a simple brilliant flash of light, and there we were, *at the very center of the square and directly before the great temple.*

A celebration was taking place; the aftermath of the day's destruction and killing. The scene was riotous. Great tuns and tubs of wine, beer and sviss had been laid out on long tables. Food, too, was everywhere with, at the square's four cardinal points, whole gogs being turned on roasting spits over huge fires. Before the series of steps leading to the temple's entrance was a double line of as many as two dozen men-at-arms. Behind them, still on the flat entry space before the doors, were two chairs in which sat two Alphians. They, apparently, were the appointed "watchers" for the evening.

As could be expected, our coming elicited some surprise. I pressed the ion control at my belt, fingered it instantly to a low radiation so that the high-sulfur content of Fregis's steel would thus be activated. We began to glow, phosphorescently, with a beautiful golden aura. We then quickly formed a rough circle with myself at point and marched in cadence to stand directly before the double line of warriors and the two seated Alphians. . . . I surreptitiously pressed the stud at my belt to effect the power-pack drain of our enemies' blaster and laser guns.

The roar of the crowd ceased. The ensuing quiet moved like a tactile encompassing wave, rolling out from those around us to the furthermost limits of the square. Even the roisterers on the side streets were affected. The Alphians arose, walked gracefully to the edge of the dais to peer down at our small ring of swords.

One of the roisterers, a huge bearded warrior with the white tab on his harness, chose to step forward to touch Rawl's shield with his own drawn sword and roar: "Say your name, fellow, for I think I recognize that shieldfront." Then he blanched, crying, "By the fallen gods, 'tis Sir Fergis, the king's nephew. And there's the *Collin*. And the Justice, Gen-Rondin! You're dead, all of you," he shouted in drunken terror. "You should have stayed so." He tripped then and fell and had to be restored to his feet by his comrades.

Ignoring him, I yelled up to the Alphians, "Hey, now. Sky-men. Here's a man who says we're dead. What say you to that? Indeed, who is there among you murdering scum who can say *he* killed the Collin, or any one of us? I call you liars, cowards. Would you be gods? I'll show you the way. Come taste my steel you sons of bitches; the road to immortality lies through these shields, these swords."

Nothing.

I called insultingly again: "I see you wear greatswords across your backs. I challenge you to use them, and tell you now that if you do, in fair fight, that I alone, or with but one of my companions, will strike your heads from off your bodies and feed your entrails to the beasts. What say you, sirs?" I called cheerfully. I drew my well-honed beauty from its sheath, advanced two paces, whirled it twice around my head—and waited.

Nothing.

One of the Alphians now rested a hand upon the butt of his blaster, but that was all. If he'd tried to use it, Sernas and one of my students, also a devil with the fal-dirk, would have driven two blades hilt-deep in his throat. . . . As of the moment, I played for time; time for my belt to drain the power-packs of their weapons. I figured we'd need twenty minutes, at least.

And then, at a signal from the Alphian leader, two husky Marackian sergeants stepped forward. I recognized them as castle teachers, swordmasters. I called lightly, "Stand back, sirs. 'Tis not your lives I want, despite your treason. 'Tis that scum that hides behind you. Throw down your weapons."

But they came on, so we met them square, with a sparkling kaleidoscope of blade-work plus but the slightest movements of the shield. Five seconds and I had the first one. An arm severed and my blade straight between his teeth so that it stuck out a hand's breadth from his skull's base. The grim Rawl Fergis had simply couched his shield beneath a rain of frenzied blows and then casually, but with tremendous strength, thrust his heavy point right up through the double fold of hauberk; through the living heart and out the shoulder. . . .

The gasps of horror, even from that semi-drunken mob, at such a feat swept out to the streets and beyond.

"Was that, sirs, a blow from a ghost?" I shouted. "How many more will die, oh lords of the sky, before you who dare call yourselves our *gods,* will take our challenge?"

The white-clad almost angelic figure of the Alphian who'd toyed with his blaster now moved quickly to draw. But his eyes were on *me* as I'd known they would be; indeed, it was another reason for my yelling. Two whistling silvered streaks, as close together as to be almost indistinguishable, hissed past my ear to appear as fal-dirks, buried to the very hilt in the Alphian's throat. He dropped the blaster. His hands flew up. His instant high-pitched scream was that of a child who's run a splinter into his finger. Bright blood fountained out over the double line of men-at-arms.

A gasp arose from the crowd.

"Well, now," I yelled again, my voice even louder, "we are not ghosts. But our gods *are* mortal. They bleed as we and can be killed as we. . . . But you, my most cautious and cowardly dubot," I called to the last Alphian, "have still not answered my challenge. I ask it again. Come down, sir, and show us how you'd use that sword you so brazenly wear upon your back."

Silence.

I'd half expected it would be this way; indeed, I'd had doubts he even understood the niceties of the "challenge" with its cultural implications. To wear a sword is one thing; to know how to use it does not necessarily mean that one is acquainted with its social lore.

Still he hesitated, but for different reasons. He'd had his

chance and failed. He could have drawn when the first man drew and thrown himself for protection behind his wall of warriors and from there wasted the lot of us. Now he stood alone and exposed. To reach for either laser or blaster now, or to yell for his men to attack, was simply to invite not one or even two fal-dirks in his throat—but *seven*!

I took the first step myself, called sternly, "Hey, you Marackian dolts, 'tis I, your Collin. And I ask that you stand aside while I slice the liver from this mewling zotl. If you do not, I'll have yours first and then his. I've challenged him properly. You've no right to interfere."

Conditioned to protocol, they murmured and began to make a path. But I didn't have to mount those steps. The Alphian had made up his mind. He came down them.

Tall, he was my height. Beautifully muscled, he was built like me, like Rawl, Rondin, Dosh—like any Fregisian fighting man. His eyes were clear and bright; his expression calm, confident. One thing was instantly apparent. He was *not* afraid!

The double row of warriors closed behind him as he stepped down upon the first slate slabs of the square below the steps. Great torches, ablaze before the temple's entrance and in mounted sconces all around us, illumined a large area before the temple. The scarce-breathing crowd kept well back from my intimidating seven. As the Alphian drew his greatsword, I handed my shield to Rawl. The sky-lord had no shield. In all fairness, therefore, I could not use my own. Because of who I was, I'd no choice but to be responsible to the mores of the land; even in the face of those Marackians who'd betrayed us.

Need I say that my heart was pounding? It surely was! I had no fear of the man's swordsmanship. It was his *sword* that scared me. It glowed as did our armor, with a yellow, golden shimmer. Why? Was it what it seemed to be, just a sharpened, metal weapon? I'd soon find out. We began to circle, to measure each other. Beyond him, ghostlike, more warriors with the white tab filtered through to join the lines before the temple. The task, I knew would not be easy.

But then, we'd never expected it to be so.

There is a triple art to the fighting with two hands on a sword's haft. The first is the art of the true *greatsword*, that clumsy, giant bar of heavy steel reputedly used by the Terran Arthur in his time. The second is the art of the somewhat smaller greatsword, but still a *greatsword,* as it continues to be used on Fregis. The last is the art of the double-handed sword which is neither great nor small; as it had been used in the long ago by Terra's famed samurai. . . . I was a master of all three!

I hoped to learn his style before I killed him and, at the same time, to show my stalwarts what they too could expect. These last watched tense, their breathing deep and studied, as they prepared for violent action. Indeed, in the light of the many torches their eyes were already red-rimmed.

He attacked, silently, fiercely, skillfully. It was like no other attack I'd ever experienced. Whatever the true weight of his light armor, to him it mattered no more than the woolen hose, shirt and shoon of a dancing master. And that is exactly what he was, a dancing master. . . . Though I was a better swordsman than he, it was still all I could do to fend his blows; indeed, the single thing that saved me was that he'd been wholly unaware of my strength. Moreover, I quickly concluded that our average Marackian swordsman was also stronger.

I would let the advantage work for me.

At one point he sliced through the mesh of my hauberk to cut my left arm; upon which my foot slipped. Laughing wildly like a ten-year-old, he rushed in for the kill. I rolled easily away from the sweep of his blade—and slipped again, but this time, *deliberately*. Again he came in, blade held back as an extension of the length of his arm. Since I was half down, the sweep of it, if he'd connected, would have taken my head. But my slip being a feint, I was fully in control. I arose suddenly up and directly *into* his swing, caught it at my waist and on my own close-held blade, then literally threw myself against his off-balance body—and pinned him to the stone of the square with the heavy point of my own weapon. The crowd roared, but I didn't know whether their yells were for me or against me. No matter. I knew what I had to do, if for no other reason than to establish firmly in the minds of all that the true arms of Marack were in the field, that the sky-lords would be opposed. I held up a hand to silence them, to focus their attention on me, on my sword—and on the creature at the other end of it. Achieving my ends in part, I gave the Alphian the coup de grace with a quick reflex thrust.

Cruel? Unworthy of an Adjuster? Right on both counts. But I was a Fregisian now, a true son of Camelot-Fregis and a prince consort of Marack. And this screaming *thing,* this lab-created animal had, just a few short days before, killed hundreds of ours, ruthlessly; for no purpose other than to show that he could do it.

Unfortunately, Marackians have strong loyalties even to their own errors, including the act of treason. The lines of men-at-arms above us—and there were four now instead of two—swarmed yelling down the last steps to avenge their lords and to save themselves, if possible. I'd hardly time to grab the enemy's laser and blaster guns and to shove them into my belt, when they were on us.

With rare exceptions, battles fought on Camelot-Fregis are crystal-clear in my memory. Especially the fight for the temple of the Trinity of Ormon, Wimbely and Harris.

They were sixty to our eight. I'd expected such odds; known, too, that despite them, what with our prowess, we were still quite evenly matched. The Alphians, the source of my greatest concern, had been slain. The thing now was to prevent ourselves from being overwhelmed by the press of numbers. We would strike for the proverbial "high-ground," the dais itself, and quick!

Our tight circle had become a phalanxed diamond. As they rushed down upon us, we each went to one knee, caught their plunging bodies full on our shields and came up to fling them over our heads and into the watching crowds around us. We utilized, in this way, the full force of their own momentum. We also chopped legs, thighs and groins, while smashing forward and up through the melee of writhing, screaming bodies.

The dais was forty feet from the slabs of the square. With myself at point and Rawl and Gen-Rondin to either side, we achieved it in as many seconds. In the final sword-swinging, raging surge of steel—and in a veritable spindrift of sweat and gore—we killed at least a dozen and left twice that many hors de combat. When we'd attained the top we turned on them. . . . And it was precisely then, with hardly a pause for breath, that we wreaked such bloody havoc among them as to destroy completely what combativeness they still retained.

It must be understood that those who attacked us were men-at-arms, whereas we, excepting our student-warriors, were among the finest swordsmen in all the north.

With the main flurry over, we rested our weight on our swords and gazed down through the bloody mists to the enemy's remnant thirty. The scene was a chaos of bodies, severed limbs and bloodied stones. The oily smoke from the torches plus a red glow from the incense pots made of it all a blazing inferno. The crowds of gaping watchers beyond the prime circle of light had become gargoyles, distorted, grotesque, half-beasts and humans. For those with weak stomachs, it was a collage of purest nightmare.

And, too, the crowd, no longer contained by the men-at-arms who'd joined the original twenty-four, pressed even beyond the still laden tables to stare hypnotically at those blood-drenched stairs. The dead Alphians, their fallen, would-be "death angels" for the new god, *Diis*, still glowed with a faint and shimmering aura akin to our own. Two of my students, Rogas and Kodder, went to them and took their swords. No hand was raised to prevent them.

Then, and I'd asked that it be timed this way should we succeed, there appeared on the dais, indeed, in our very midst, a three-statue ensemble, life-sized, also glowing. It was of Ormon, Wimbely and Harris—courtesy of our lady-enchantress, Elioseen.

A groan swept the ranks of the would-be turncoats. Some fell to their knees in terror. Others, fearful, made the sign of Ormon upon their breasts. There were still a few, however, who looked around them cannily for what might now come from the other side. They could not believe that the sky-lords would take such a defeat so easily. . . .

Then a chant began; came rolling across the square. At first a whisper, it swelled, grew: "Ormon! Marack! Ormon!—Marack!"

I at once shouted above this new obeisance to the white-faced throng beneath me, and especially to those thirty who still clung to their arms. "If you love life," I told them, "then throw down your arms and address yourselves immediately to Marack and to Ormon's grace." The crowd did, but the thirty swordsmen who'd accepted the white tab refused. Though trembling, they were still Fregisian warriors and they could not, for their honor's sake.

It made no difference. Indeed, it was already too late. One by one they were seized, beaten; knives thrust to their bodies—and this by the very sycophants of the erstwhile Diis and his sky-lords.

Some had appeared, however, who were not sycophants. From two side streets and rallying, apparently, to the voices that had shouted that the Collin and the Lord. Gen-Rondin. the king's judge, were leading warriors against the debasers of Marack's gods, there came at least two hundred swordsmen, warriors, armed students, simple people, ready to place themselves at our sides, though they'd not known of our small victory.

They split the wavering crowd like so much jelly, to arrive below us and to shout: "Collin! Rondin! Collin! Rondin! Marack! Marack!" and to kill instantly any who so much as looked at them cross-eyed, or dared to curse them.

But it had to end, and quick. Sooner or later, and more likely sooner, our Tarkiis would certainly get wind of what had happened and descend upon the city.

And so I yelled once more for their attention. "Hold!" I cried. "I speak now to all of you, whether you be followers of the new god, or of the gods of Marack and Marack's king. Know this: The war of Marack and of Ormon, Wimbely and Harris against the sky-lords, has just begun. We of Marack will win this war. But the enemy's still strong. I ask you all therefore to gather your belongings and to flee this city now. Warn your friends and neighbors to do likewise. The enemy will most certainly return to wreak such vengeance and destruction as to leave the house of neither friend nor foe still standing . . . Leave therefore. Leave now for the countryside. For those who would fight this enemy, why then I ask that you organize yourselves in bands and companies and under your chosen knights and lords. *Do not seek us!* When you are organized, we'll come to you. I promise it! Now. I repeat. They'll be coming shortly. We cannot prevent this. But we will return! And when we do, why I say to you that these sky-lords will be destroyed once and for all. . . . *Put your trust in Ormon and Marack, who have never betrayed you!*"

And they cheered us, *all* of them. There were *no* supporters of the Alphians now. Already, on the crowd's fringes, people were running for the street exits to carry out our bidding.

I then handed my sword and shield to Rawl, asked that he step back from me a bit, raised both my fists over my head—and gave the prearranged signal to Elioseen.

At once our three students disappeared, to the ooohs and aaahs of the throng. I raised my fists again. Lors Sernas and Gen-Rondin vanished in a burst of golden light. Again I raised my hands, and Sir Dosh was but a cloud of dust motes against the now billowing smoke from the untended torches. I then threw an arm around my sword-companion's shoulders, gave one last wave—and fell into the blackness of an abyss which was uncomfortable, to say the least.

I remained in the witches room of Elioseen just long enough for her to check Glagmaron Castle to see if Tarkiis was aware as to what had happened in the temple square. He wasn't. Like the D.O. before him, he lacked perceptive abilities, had no experiences from which to draw and, having been conditioned to the limitations of arrogance, his ability to analyze anything was but a mishmash of non sequiturs: He was all-powerful; therefore none could stand against him; therefore none would ever try, etc., etc.

I thought then to have a look in on the king and Melylys too, but Elioseen would have none of it. She told me abruptly, and with some heat, that it was obvious that I had little or no understanding of the price paid to do what she had done. She showed me—in the persons of those who'd participated in the three covens. They were listless, hardly conscious and with a wan and deathlike visage. It was as if the very life itself had been drained from them. And no wonder, when you think on it. They had participated in a matter-to-energy conversion process and back again; had even been forced to hold to their original package throughout the period, with all that that meant in complexities. In essence, it was not just the *sound* and its various tonal, vibratory qualities that did the job with the magnetic field. Another energy source was first needed to impose the sound at the right places and in a proper continuity—and to *keep* it there. This could only come from the humanoid body itself. . . . I had a lot to learn. I apologized sincerely.

But all the while in the witches room, I'd felt strangely weary myself. It was a tiredness not shared by my comrades. They remained boisterous, loud and ebullient in our victory.

I mentioned my condition to Rawl, saying, "Hey, old comrade, I'm strangely weary. When we've been released from the baths and the ministrations of our good chirurgeons, I'd ask you as a favor to see to it that I'm left alone to sleep through 'till tomorrow morning—unless, of course, the enemy's burning the castle around our ears."

He looked at me with a frowning concern. "I'm minded you're cut." he said, "from that damned sky-lord's blade, too. We'd best call Elioseen, for there may have been magick in it."

I shrugged. "Nay. If 'twas from that blade, it would have taken me completely long before now."

But his eyes grew dark. The concern remained. He said curtly, "I'll call her anyway."

"See to it," I changed the subject, "that our own 'sky-lord' from our little ship is accompanied on his rounds tomorrow by perhaps yourself and Sernas. And do not worry him too much," I winked, "for, as you must know, he's not of Fregis, and is somewhat fearful of our ways."

He grimaced at my mention of Sernas but agreed. He did, however, ask me of Kriloy which normally he would not do, respecting my private matters. He knew, I think, that I was really sick. . . . I explained what I could, finished with the suggestion that if anything did happen to me, he was to watch over Kriloy. "Because," as I put it, "that poor lad's a flatfish without an ocean. . . ."

It was in the room of the chirurgeons that I lost consciousness. I scarce remember even being there. All I can honestly swear to is that for some time I was aware only of dreams, one following another in time and space so that all that had ever happened to me again passed before my eyes. There then seemed to be a *gray* period. The dreams became fewer and mixed up; nothing ever really began or ended. And suddenly, with an accompanying chill to my sleeping spine, there was just nothing at all; only a twilight landscape that stretched away forever. It was a plain of sand, low loess hills at a distance of a mile, or maybe a thousand miles, then nothing. . . . Finally, even that grew faint, opaque.

It was then, I think, that I knew I had left my body, but not quite. It was something, perhaps, like Hooli's predicament of being betwixt and between. I was actually experiencing the act of dying, and knew it. It was not all that unpleasant. Indeed, the only shadow of unpleasantness was when Hooli showed up. . . .

This time his sense of humor was absolutely macabre, gauche. And since he forever chose to associate what he did, his various guises, his aping of this supposed character or that, his speech (with my voice), its idiom and the like, he was way off base. Indeed, he was even a might tacky, as it were.

He came strolling across the sand plain in a monk's black robe and carrying a monstrous scythe. He was Death, coming to get me. The apparition was so ghastly, so utterly terrifying under the circumstances—and mind you, I didn't actually know it was Hooli—that he could easily have pushed me the final few millimeters over the edge. I was saved by the fact that at the very last moment I spotted the mortarboard on top of his cowl. Moreover, as he drew closer still, I was able to see inside the cowl and to note with some relief that he also had on his purple, heart-shaped glasses. He slowed, did a buck-and-wing, switched to a knee-knocking dance, and halted. Leaning directly into my line of vision, he yelled: "Heeeeeeyyyyy, Buuuuddyyy! What's happenin'?"

I took a deep breath. "You know what's happening, you little bastard, or you wouldn't be here."

"Not true."

"It *is* true."

"Well," he asked, his little black eyes beaming behind his shades, "where do you think you are right now?"

"Where else? Gortfin."

"Mais non, mon petit." Hooli shook his little fat head sorrowfully. "But you soon will be." He reached out a small paw to touch me. He had the power, amongst other things, to rearrange every cell in one's body; he could make you brand new again, from top to bottom—cure you of every disease.

I couldn't feel the actual touch. What I did feel was an instant, allover shock, plus the ensuing calm of a burgeoning peace and well-being. Moreover, I had the sudden presentiment that an approaching doom had somehow been avoided. I felt solid things again, such as a current of air against my face; the bulk of pillows behind my neck, head and shoulders; the warmth of bed furs and the actual *flow* of that sweet air into and out of my lungs.

Beyond Hooli in his cowl and robe, I could now see a shadowy square of latticed window through which the rays of Fomalhaut I poured in beams of a million dancing dust motes.

"Well," I told him, intending to answer his first question, "here's what's happening. You ask a question, you get an answer. The way I see it, up to a few minutes ago, *I* was dead and on my way to that great 'black hole' in Cygnus III, to be refloobled and returned as a Farkelian white ape. As of now, however, and as anyone can plainly see, I've been returned to Gortfin Castle, courtesy of one, Hooli, the Universal Adjuster.

"Now don't go away," I pleaded—he'd begun to fade somewhat. "And don't wake me either, brown-bag. We've still some talking to do."

"Fire away."

He grew solid again while struggling out of the clumsy robe and cowl; careful to hold his mortarboard so it wouldn't be crumpled in the process. His scythe had wavered and disappeared completely, a reaction, I think, to my unhappy reaction at the sight of it. Stripped of the robe, he now wore beach shorts, a webbed tank top and open-toed booties.

"First question: When last we talked, you were supposedly caught in the gateway—in some four-dimensional taffy-stretch. Yet the Ferlachian Pug-Boo, Mool, distinctly winked at me with your eyes. What have you to say to that, plus the obvious fact that you are out of the gateway now?"

"Why, *obvious*? How would you know, doo-doo-head?"

"*Was* that you?" I ignored his attempt at dissimulation. "Or must I conclude that the host occupants of Jindil, Chuuk, Dahkti, Pawbi and Mool are back again?" I'd named the various Boos of the northern kingdoms.

He said solemnly, "Rephrase the question."

"Gog-shit!"

"Oh, my!"

"Hooli. This is no goddamn time for games."

"How right you are. How'd you like to be sent back across the Styx right now, buddy-boy? I can do it, you know."

"How?"

"By just leaving you alone. Something'll get you then, or my name ain't Aunt Jemima."

"But you couldn't do that. You're an Adjuster, too, remember? You can't take life above molluscs and anemones."

"Nothing in the book says I have to give it. You were already dead, Collin. Me? I saved you, with three ounces of 'ol Doc Mandelbaum's 'live-forever-cocktail.' You want me to restopper the bottle? I can do it."

"Screw you, Hooli."

We stared at each other. He said suddenly, lightly, changing the subject. "It was the sword that did it, you know."

"You mean the cut?"

"I mean the sword in the cut. The alloy's a grabber. It breaks down just a bit at the touch of some kinds of humanoid blood—your kind, not Alphian or Fregisian types. It screws up the hemoglobin. You had instant leukemia, buddy."

"Gods!" I shook my head in both thanks and exasperation at my little Florence Nightingale. "What do I owe you?"

"How's about a big wet kiss?"

I started to laugh, then stopped. He'd done it again, shunted me off into some backwash area of nonsense and repartee. "Okay," I said meanly, "if that wasn't you winking through Mool's eyes, then where were you when we did battle with the Alphians, and how *did* you escape the gateway?"

He countered sadly, "You know I'm not permitted to fight, to kill. You know, too, that if my powers were used in any way, especially in the sphere's proximity, that *it* would know. And if it did, buddy, well, as I've said: that's it, the end of the ball game. Besides," and his little eyes twinkled, "you didn't need me anyway."

"Yeah," I said grudgingly. "Perhaps not for fighting. But I do need to know what's happening. However many victories we win, me and the Marackians, that screwing blue marble could still have the final word. I need to know its true strength, Hooli; what it is and how it operates. You have the answers. I don't. And, Hooli, that's a situation with which I damn well can't be satisfied."

"Well *be* satisfied, bird-brain," he answered coldly, in tones he'd never used before. "It's out of your hands, I'm telling you, so don't make waves. Just keep doing what you're doing." A sudden conciliatory grin swept across his round little face, for I think he knew that he'd come on a mite too strong. He said, "It's the big one, buddy. I mean it. So please, cool it. Stay the hell out of it."

"And who's going to end it? You?"

"I can't answer that."

"You mean you won't."

"All right, Kyrie, I'll tell you this much: It can go two ways; one way, I'll call you in; the other way, no. I love you, Kyrie."

"Thanks for nothing. In the meantime you've set me up to believe that the sphere is anti-matter. Is it?"

"No comment, except I didn't set you up."

"What of the energy tap through the gateway to the pre-nova sun?"

"No comment."

"Okay, tell me about the Alphians."

He countered my question with a question. "What have you deduced?"

I sighed. "That they are not clones; that they are most likely lab-birthed from male and female humanoid sperm and ova, that they have but a limited knowledge of themselves; that they lack even the slightest understanding of any theory about the socio-economic aspects of the evolutionary processes. . . . I'm bound to conclude, Hooli, that the Dark One's uncle, as you've so pithily described the occupant of the sphere, was also in that first alien ship to penetrate the gateway; that he, she or it escaped to its own universe, taking with it whatever was necessary to recreate Alphian life. In effect, Hooli, I've deduced the obvious: That our Alphians are the products of the alien's efforts to create a life-form subservient to its needs. As apart from those needs and as creature-humanoids, the Alphians are a mirrored caricature of a medley of tape banks filled with mostly *fictional* history and simple disc-lectures with more of the same. They are absolutely unaware of the peripheral areas of any supposed reality, what it is, how it got that way, what one can expect it to do. Example: An act of magick as practiced in front of an Alphian—and I spotted this at our first meeting—is accepted by him as equal to the results of, say, a servo-mechanism showing up at dinnertime with a platter of gog steaks. He hasn't the slightest idea of how either works, *and is not motivated to find out.* If he were, the contradiction would manifest itself eventually in independent thinking and a consequent inevitable rejection of the *sphere* as god and mentor.

"Our Alphians are dopes, and meant to be so, Hooli. The occupant of your sphere is indeed the Dark One's 'uncle' in that just as the D.O. before him, he too is incapable of organizing his power. He knows nothing of humankind; indeed, nothing of life. His very arrogance, the inability in this case to understand the peripheral but absolutely basic details of the *logical* development of *any* species, is his own death warrant!

"Do you understand me, Hooli? I tell you now that if that goddamned sphere and its occupant is not anti-matter, then by the *vulva* of the great mother, I'll end this war right where it started—on the military field of Glagmaron Castle, and on that hilltop where the alien rests his ship."

Hooli was so silent that I feared that he'd left his host and gone on to greener pastures. But then he said—and I'd never heard so soft a voice from him before, nor such a contemplative sadness—"Kyrie, in your own way, the humanoid way, you've come pretty close; indeed, you've grasped the particulars the alien overlooks when tackling you. Yes, Great Collin, and I call you that seriously, for you are now as much of Camelot-Fregis as you ever were of your *Foundation*. You've guessed it right. The sphere and its occupant are not anti-matter, and can, with luck in all areas, be destroyed by you. The other side of the coin, however, is still the catastrophic disaster if you fail."

"So? It's a chance I'll have to take."

"Not true."

"Hooli. You give me a pain in the ass like the original D.O. never did. I don't know what you know because you won't tell me; *can't* tell me. I do know what I sense, see, feel and hear each hour of the day—which is that a gang of test-tube freakos have been unleashed upon this altogether beautiful world and have introduced a wanton destruction and slavery upon the inhabitants of same. And all this under the protection of an apparently amoral, unconscionable life-form with almost infinite powers. I, too, am an Adjuster, Hooli. Remember? I've a job to do the same as you. Though I can't, for the moment, hit the source of evil, I can attend to its peripheral manifestations, preparatory for a final dénouement. The moment those preparations are completed, I will attack the sphere. Believe me, Hooli. You can count on it."

He said suddenly, solemnly, "*Would you believe that to do nothing is the best thing?*"

"Tell me *why* and I'll think about it."

"I can't, Kyrie."

"Then screw you, you miserable little raisinless brownie. All you're showing me is that when the chips are down, you offer a monkey wrench plus a refusal to help. I haven't forgotten the *Deneb* either, Hooli."

"What you say is not true and you are very unfair."

I laughed dramatically, bitterly. "Which *part* is not true? You never speak to the 'whole' of anything if you can possibly avoid it."

He glared at me, shook his head and said, "Well, I did snatch you out of old Charon's boat. That's a plus, or don't you think so? If I say that for you to do nothing is best, then deliberately allow you to live, knowing that you'll try to stampede these poor bastards into a bloody holocaust with damn little chance of winning *your* way, I most certainly have helped you. . . . To have allowed you to die would have been one helluva lot easier, buddy. For me, you would be one problem less."

I grunted. Who could counter that? "You did say that I could attack the sphere and, with luck, win. Right?"

"Sure. With a little luck you could also paddle across a lava lake in a paper boat."

"Would you prevent me from attacking it?"

"I will not answer that."

I sighed, drew the obvious conclusions; to me, that is. "Oh, ho, my little gog's bladder," I said accusingly, "we're beginning to see a dottle of a different color."

"Yup," he clichéd in turn—"a whole new kettle of fish."

"So you'd prevent me?"

"I didn't say that."

I quickly retreated to the original question. "But you did say the sphere had an energy tap through the gateway to a pre-nova?"

"Increments, buddy. No steady flow. He sucks up what he needs. Think of the converters aboard the *Deneb*. Took up space, right? Well there are no converters aboard the sphere. Just packs; batteries, if you will."

"Sounds archaic."

"Depends."

"On what?"

"On whose foxhole you're working out of."

"In other words, our D.O. in the sphere has no personal pipeline to the pre-nova, but can plug into *a* pipeline when he wishes. And this end of said pipeline—is on Alpha?"

"You got it, buddy."

I then asked smoothly, "Well then, Pooh Bear, other than saving my life, what else are you here for?"

He grinned his rodent grin, said silkily, "To suggest, in the words of your ancient carpenter philosopher, that you'd better 'pick up your bed and walk' and in a hurry. Get a move on. Time's a wastin' and all that. What I'm saying, buddy, is that if you don't get your ass movin' in the direction of Glagmaron your fairy-tale princess and her companion will be lost to you forever."

I laughed. "To that moron, Tarkiis? Hooli, whatever Murie would do or has done, she'd never be lost to *that*."

"Not lost, buddy. He'll eventually kill her and Caroween too. The signs are there. Which means you'll have to get both of them out of there, quick."

"But I saw them through Elioseen's mirror just a few hours ago. There was no indication of anything like that."

"You saw her two weeks ago, Kyrie. That's how long you've been ill."

"You knew I was dying, and you waited two weeks? Why, Hooli?"

He grinned. "Priorities."

"But why would he do that?"

"Well, he'd thought to keep them as bait for you, since the whole world knows now that the 'Collin' lives. But she's begun to mock him—among other things."

"Damn!"

"You've got forty-eight hours, at best. And remember what I told you before, too. If I have to call you in, it'll have to be quick; everything else to one side and no questions asked." He got up, stretched and straightened his mortarboard.

"Are you leaving?"

"I've done what I came to do; saved your life and thereby, hopefully, saved the lives of our two pretty princesses who deserve better than a laser in the belly, 'just for fun.' As for your posturings and all that, well, I've got better things to do, buddy."

"Why is it, Hooli, that I'm left with the feeling that you've actually told me nothing at all?"

He was beginning to fade.

"Where you going?"

"Actually, nowhere. Watch, Kyrie!"

And just like that the plain disappeared along with Hooli, and I was awake and scrabbling to sit up against the familiar pillows of my bed in the apartment in Gortfin Castle.

I looked wide-eyed around me. It was midmorning. The windows were full open. A warming sun flooded in to touch the furniture and to 'halo' the well coiffed heads of a half-dozen lords and knights, along with my usual stalwarts, plus the lovely Lady Elioseen. . . .

Seeing the absolutely pop-eyed looks on their startled faces since I'd returned from the dead, I said instantly aloud and strongly, "The one thing, comrades, that I could use above all else is a wash bowl full of gog stew, two loaves of bread and sufficient beer to wash it down. Now what say you all to that?"

Crying joyously, "By the gods, Collin, you're alive!" Rawl Fergis leaped instantly to his feet. Sir Dosh, on the other hand, went straight to his knees to begin a hoarse braying of prayers to Ormon, Wimbley and Harris, learned, no doubt, at his father's knee. The dark Lors Sernas—he'd had a jeweled flagon of wine to his lips—gripped it hard and stared over its rim in awe. Gen-Rondin but shook his head in a paroxysm of personal joy, then covered his eyes while my students who'd survived the flight before the temple, simply held up their hands and waved at me. Happy grins split their faces. The Lord Fel-Holdt stood stern, proud—and grateful.

Only Elioseen wept, softly and silently. Then she smiled through her tears so prettily in her joy that I lived, that I could not help but smile back and shed a tear or two myself.

And lastly, on a pillow at the foot of my bed, and with the pillow on a small stool, I spotted little round Hooli, the Marackian Court Pug-Boo. I now knew what he meant when he'd said that he wasn't going anywhere.

"Where," I demanded loudly, "did *that* come from?" I pointed to him deliberately, while he, unseen, crossed his eyes and dangled his tongue at me.

Gen-Rondin arose to say, "Why, we found him in the hall, my lord; just a few minutes ago. I'm reminded, sir, that in the great war of Dunguring, *all* court Pug-Boos left those countries with traitorous kings and came to Marack. 'Tis a good omen."

Oh, ho. I shook my head at Hooli. He'd done something else for our cause. He'd insinuated himself into the scene as a moral factor. . . .

The best tactic, I decided, was to ignore him. "What of my food?" I asked.

But they brought me broth instead, all crying and making over me in such a way that I knew that I'd indeed been dead for sure. . . . When I finished the bowl, quaffing it as I would a tankard of beer, I allowed them to lead me down to the great room of the chirurgeons; this, though being ten pounds lighter as a result of my illness, I was of the opinion that I could have flown the distance myself. As for strength. Well, with any encouragement, I'd have walked right through the apartment door without opening it. Moreover, I was as clear-headed as I'd ever been in my life before.

What had Hoolie said? That I must return to Glagmaron and seize Murie and Caroween from the jaws of their would-be murders? Well, why not? Other than Hooli's own reasons—the 'play within a play'—I would damned well do it because I loved her. I'd also do it as a part of our own plan to prevent the stabilization of Alphian power. After all, as I'd told Hooli, I, too, was an Adjuster!

On no single world of any I had ever visited had I ever found the equal of Camelot's 'room of the chirurgeons.' Galactic science can do many things, but the chiros, masseurs and gnostics of Fregis's curing rooms are in their own way, and for the purposes they serve, incomparable.

We made a party of it. Fel-Holdt joined as well as a goodly half of the off-duty officers and lords at Gortfin. All of us together in the great pool-bath, to be pleasured and relaxed by its warmth and cleansed in its curative waters. Wine, sviss and beer were served to make the camaraderie a true celebration of my return from ghast (the Fregisian hell) and, as a matter of fact, to be the only one on record to do this. They'd thought me dead. To a man, they wept in their cups for joy to find me living.

The chiropractic, the massage with heated oils and curative salves that followed, brought such additional euphoria that my Rawl was prompted to remark that my weight loss had given my profile a hawkish cast to strike fear into the hearts of my enemies. He vowed to follow suit, to make himself lean and mean, as did Sir Dosh. But not just yet, they agreed hastily. After the war, perhaps. As of the moment they had a serious need to build their strength for the struggle at hand. And, too, it was well known that both of them dearly loved their seats at table and the pleasures of the platter and bottle.

More broth, some fruit, and I slept again for four hours. This time when I awakened it was as if I'd never had an illness in my life. In the vernacular of an older time: I'd truly been born again.

In the solarium and in the company of most of those who'd joined me in the bath, I was briefed on what had happened during my two weeks' hiatus. Fel-Holdt was proud to report that a truly competent resistance had been organized throughout the north, along lines previously agreed upon. Moreover, the last of the thirty thousand Marackians who had fought against Hish in Om had finally made it from that far continent to the area of Corchoon in Kelb. Our sailors, alert to their coming, had contacted their fleet of coasters some hundreds of miles off shore and had then guided them to safety in the various inlets and lagoons of Kelb. From there they were being filtered in to Fel-Holdt's ever growing forces.

In this last respect the enemy too had had some success. He had created in each kingdom a subject army large enough to dominate the populace, at least in the major cities and towns.

The new temples, however, with their promise, was the prime enemy weapon. . . . The priests, interestingly enough, were drawn mainly from renegade sorcerers and warlocks; men whom we'd been unable to recruit. They'd been given a book, supposedly of holy writ. This book told of the one god, the only god, Diis, to be called by all, the *Unseen One*. Diis, it was explained, was everywhere and in all things (the pattern was all too familiar). He was the creator and the taker of life. To worship Diis was to accept the concept that Fregisians could again aspire to the heights from which their forefathers had fallen as the result of some great and unmentionable sin. The promise was that the day would come when their piety and service to Diis would grant them a return—if not collectively, then at least *individually*—to that pantheon of greatness. In the meantime the priest-sorcerers of

Diis would be the purveyers of *his* word; though the true *go-betweens* would be the immortal angels, the sky lords; *i.e.*, the *Alphians*!

The central temple, of course—and it was now under construction—would be in Glagmaron City in Marack. It was to be *the* site of the physical body of Diis—the abode of the blue sphere!

On the plus side, and despite this apparent consolidation of Alphian power, there had been many victories for the five kingdoms. A singular part of these, I was told, had been inspired by the "Collin's" return and his seizure of the temple of Ormon in the very heart of Glagmaron City. More! The villages and towns now rang with the name of Fel-Holdt, Marack's Lord Commander of the armies, and the enchantress, the Lady Elioseen, sister to King Caronne. And, to further plague the Alphians, it was now known everywhere that Fel-Holdt's H.Q., great Castle Gortfin, had simply vanished from Marack and the world, though the enemy sought it every day, and failed.

Fel-Holdt himself outlined the implementation of the strategy so far, and the tactics used.

With rare exception all villages were held by us. Traffic, in the form of merchants' caravans and the like, plus the entourages of those lords who'd taken the "white tab", even companies of the sky lord's troops, were generally denied the high roads. All were attacked. A goodly half had already been destroyed. Moreover, those who would camp at night to await the day for travel, would find themselves magicked and terrorized by the phantom images of wraith-like dead-alives—all ringing them in!

As for the Alphians themselves, well, wherever they rode, to inspect their domain, as it were, there clouds formed and rain, snow and hail fell in prodigious quantities. Wherever sky lords camped to picnic, a dank mist came. The water of a previously sparkling stream would turn brackish, its taste akin to raw sewage. No birds would sing for the sky lords; nor was there game for their weapons. Food, too, in any town or village, could only sicken them. What they had thought to enjoy had, in essence, become anathema.

I learned too that of the five ships, just three seemed active. This did not mean that the remaining two were incapable of lift-off, though the possibility of such was there. As Hooli's description of them had indicated, they obviously knew how to operate a ship. But, if a servo-mechanism failed for whatever reason, and was incapable of repairing itself, well, that was the end of the mechanism. The Alphians knew absolutely nothing as to the actual workings of anything. . . . Which led me to wonder about the possibility of disabling all of the ships without actually doing so—just *turning them off*, as it were. Matter-to-energy conversions, à la Elioseen, should work as easily in putting a man inside a skyship as it did in putting us in a square in Glagmaron City.

The key to it all was still the question of the sphere and its relationship to the Alphians. Since Hooli had essentially refused any solid data in this respect, I had no recourse but to continue to do everything in a way not to attract the sphere's attention. At the last moment, of course, we would do what we had to do; hopefully, we would knock out the Alphians *and* the sphere!

For the moment, then, we would continue to do only that which seemed feasible, while continuing to study the weak points that the struggle would surely disclose. As Fel-Holdt put it: We were halfway there. The sky lords controlled half the country by day. Marack and its magick controlled all of it at night!

While listening with pleasure to these facts, I'd noted a face in the group which, though familiar, still seemed a bit odd. His clothes were like those of most young lords, excepting that he wore a purple flat-cap to jauntily cover one eye. It was precisely that eye, merrily winking, that caught me as I turned to make some remark to Rawl. . . . *The eye was brown!*

I hesitated, peered sharply. Bloody *Jesu*! I arose and with hands on hips and a grin wide enough to span a tappimelon, said, "Well, now. I see, sirs, that with my death, you've at least recruited a good man to take my place. May I greet my good friend of the lost ship *Deneb*?" I promptly stepped down to grasp Kriloy in a firm embrace; for it was Kriloy! He'd dared to follow through, so I later learned; had actually picked up and delivered the Ferlachian and Gheesian sorcerers, as well as those of Kelb on his own and, in the face of my possible death, had volunteered the scoutship in certain other tasks.

I said simply, "Good to have you aboard, junior."

He shrugged, grinned. "Something to do on a rainy day."

Prior to dinner, and with most of my well-wishers drifting away so that, excepting Fel-Holdt, Kriloy and Elioseen, the only ones left were my companions of the attack on the temple, I quietly broached the subject of the danger to Murie and Caroween and the need to free them immediately. Not a one of them questioned me as to my sources, excepting Kriloy, who did so with his eyes.

Rawl grew pale at my words, and actually ground his teeth in rage.

"I propose," I told them bluntly, "to move on this at once and with a minimum of fanfare. To attack a temple within a city is one thing. To attack within a castle is another. Secrecy, under the tightest of circumstances, is seldom kept for long. As we have spies within the ranks of the enemy, be sure that he has spies in ours. There are always those who will sell themselves or their country for money or power.

Fel-Holdt, that grim old warrior, frowned darkly at this, telling me in swift rebuttal that security was tighter than it had ever been.

"Agreed," I told him. "Among those you control. But I speak of witches, warlocks and sorcerers, who are a breed apart. What of your magick workers, my lady?" I asked of Elioseen. "Can you honestly vouch for them all?"

She frowned. "Nay, Collin, I cannot. But if magick of any kind is at work upon these premises, I'll surely know it."

I took the opportunity to question her. "What of Glagmaron Castle? Does it function in an orderly way? Are there nightly feasts, a gathering where the new elite can mingle with the sky lords? And is there any kind of court held during the day?"

Her reply held the slightest trace of anger. "You are indeed recovered, my lord. You ask too much. To watch them that closely is not an easy task."

"But you do check from time to time?"

"I do."

"Then my question?"

"There's feasting every night as usual. As for holding court, there's no such formality."

"Not even council?"

"If 'tis done, it takes place within their ship. They have been seen to take Marackians and priests aboard."

"What of your mirror? Is the ship safe from its prying eye?"

"There's an aura beyond which we cannot penetrate. And we've yet to come up with the proper sounds." She laughed then, amused, sensing my unspoken thoughts. "Nor will we be able to spirit you aboard until we do. The problem's a hard one."

"But you can put us in the castle?" The question was rhetorical, or so I thought.

"Nay, Collin. We cannot. We risked too much the first time. You saw the condition of those of our coven before you, yourself, were struck down. Two died, sir, while you were ill. Also, and this is the more important since we've accepted the risks as soldiers of Marack: At the time of the temple attack, we almost failed the lot of you, *twice*! To fail now, when there's a chance to hold and then to win, would be terrible indeed. For you and your comrades to be lost *now*, to say nothing of the royal family who would perish with you, would be a disaster the like of which I doubt we'd survive."

"Well now," I exclaimed glumly, "there speaks an objective mind. I salute you my lady."

Her great eyes had filmed with tears so that I marveled at her intensity. But even as I'd spoken, a sudden strobe flash of the hidden tunnel down the three-hundred-foot cliff of Glagmaron's base prompted me to say, "But there's still a way, my lady, if you can do just two things: keep us within your mirror's sight from the first moment of sup and wassail to the last; and, at a given signal, materialize as many swords and shields in midair as we will need. If you fail in this, 'tis true that we'll most likely die. But if we win, why then, my lady, I'm bound to think that Marack will soon be rid of all its pestiferous 'angels'."

All of them seemed ecstatic.

"You think to use the passageway?" Fel-Holdt, his eyes alight with the adventure he immediately envisioned, seemed suddenly half his age. I knew he'd give his soul to go with us.

"I do."

"Both ways, coming and going," Gen-Rondin put in solidly. For he knew, as did we all, that that was the only way it could be. . . .

Except that it wasn't.

Rawl—his honest eyes had been screwed up painfully so that I knew he'd been thinking hard—spoke swiftly to Fel-Holdt. "My lord," he said, "our Kelbian ambassador reported three armed parties of merchants, new priests and the like to be on the road for Glagmaron. They no doubt ride with the permission of the sky lords, and will thus be received within the castle on arrival. As the ambassador put it, the first group should arrive at Glagmaron tonight. The second, with luck, will make it at the fifteenth hour tomorrow; the third and last, tomorrow night. "Now how would it be," and he turned to me with a hard gleam in his eyes—blood still flecked his lips where he'd silently bitten them at my news of Caroween's peril—"if our men in the area are ordered to attack the second group, and to slay them all? Then we, old comrade, will join the third and last group as the sole survivors of the second, the brave merchant remnants who dared defend themselves against the bandits and murderers led by the evil Collin and the mad Gen-Rondin."

His suggestion got a solid round of applause.

I joined in their enthusiasm. "It's good," I said, exuberantly, deliberately building on their fervor. "We'll do it! We'll need to disguise ourselves, in any event. And what better way than to adopt the faces and the purses of those already expected? We'll take their gear, dottles and goods—along with the guild blazonry of those we most resemble."

Elioseen had yet to reply to my request that she supply us with weapons. I chose the moment to again dwell upon the danger to Murie and Caroween. Again, none questioned me as to how I knew this, for I, too, in their minds, was a *wizard*; though my magick, inclusive of that of my new surrogate, the friendly sky lord, Kriloy, was simply but totally beyond their ken.

I'd sensed that Elioseen did know somewhat of the plight of our two ladies; for when I'd described the need and the form such a rescue should take, I could not help but feel that knowledge in her steady gaze.

She said finally to my previous question: "There'll be no problem with your swords and such, Lord Collin. But there could be problems elsewhere. You may gain entry to the castle, win your battle, and even flee safely with my niece and her friend. But, sirs! How will you return to Gortfin within an acceptable period? You must admit, Collin, that this is not the time to absent yourself from council. There's heavy fighting now in all the kingdoms. Draslich, Chitar, the lords of Kelb and Great Ortmund, depend upon you. You must know that we had not, indeed, dared not tell them of what we thought was your impending death. Obviously, had you died, we would have told them; tonight, as a matter of fact, if such had been the case. But surely you can see the problem."

Fel-Holdt said strongly, " 'Tis true, my lord. Our friendly enemies have done and will do things in the field that they would not do if they knew that you were somehow no longer at the helm with the rest of us. And, as our lady says, the next few days can be critical."

Elioseen picked it up. "Marack, Sir Collin, can scarce afford to have you wandering in the forest, or anywhere else at such a time."

Puzzled, I objected, "But my lady, you have the mirror. I can be contacted."

"Again, 'tis not that simple. One finds Glagmaron City with the mirror, and then moves from there. One traces the line of a road to find those who ride on it. To *find* someone just anywhere is at best extremely difficult. What we need, my lord, is a point of departure, a general plan—a map of the course you'll take. . . ."

I smiled wryly. "And if I know not that course?"

"Well, there's the problem."

But there was no problem, really; at least the kind they were concerned with. I turned to Kriloy, winked and said, " 'Tis that my comrade here will do the job. We'll use our own skyship to pick us up, the one we would have used to get us there and back had we not decided to travel with Kelb's merchants."

I stared solemnly at Kriloy, and waited.

Startled, caught off balance, he could only nod and mumble. "Hell, Kyrie. Of course. Why not?" But he'd swallowed hard. The shadow of fear again touched his eyes. Sir Dosh, and he'd been looking straight at Kriloy, saw it, and turned instantly to me. But I ignored his warning eyes, pretending that I'd seen nothing.

"What our Lord Fel-Holdt and our Lady Elioseen are suggesting," I said soberly, "and rightly so, is that the risk may be too big for the effort. Normally, I'd agree. In this case, however, I sense the presence of an outside force that has aided us in the past. I've a strong feeling that parallel developments beyond our knowledge require our being precisely there and engaged in exactly such an attempt so as to exploit our potential victory in other ways—should these developments mature. In all of this, comrades, you will have to trust me. For one thing, you must know by now that I am not a fool. I will, however, since my reasons may still seem more personal than objective, ask only those with a similar interest in the matter to accompany me. . . . These are: Sir Fergis, Caroween's betrothed, Sir Alten Dosh, her brother. And," I smiled grimly, "Sir Lors Sernas, to keep him from any serious trouble during our absence."

"My lord," Gen-Rondin instantly spoke up, his blue eyes twinkling in his heavy, florid face, "I'm not to be put aside, sir, like a used but ugly chambermaid. Moreover, other than your suggested 'force' and its supposed actions on our behalf—and, might I add that I'm pleased to learn of its existence—I say that there's still sufficient priority for such an attempt. You yourself, my lord Collin, together with our Princess Murie Nigaard Caronne, will eventually *be* the royal house. None can deny that. So I, too, will come with you—to guarantee that fact."

Our three students—they'd been allowed at my deathwatch, and had been with us all the afternoon—fell to their knees before Fel-Holdt. These were Rogas and Tadee, both excellent swordsmen, dottle handlers and trainers, and Kodder, a young would-be warrior-chief, for he dearly admired the many ways to prepare and serve gog steaks and chittygreens. At five-by-five feet of solid bone and muscle, his fighting style was the strangest ever; indeed, it had been Kodder's fal-dirk that had joined with Sernas's to slice the sky lord's throat in the square of the temple. Now they piteously beseeched Fel-Holdt that they be allowed to accompany us, pleading that they had fought hard at the temple and had damned well earned the honor.

Fel-Holdt, glowering at first like an unamused head waiter, shrugged finally, winked and agreed. He then turned to me.

"A last question in two parts, my lord: How can you possibly counter those weapons that the sky lords carry; especially since there will not be just two this time, but a roomful; and now can eight swords win against such odds as you will find there?"

I smiled. "Hopefully, it will be like this: First, I've a means to cancel the power of their weapons. Second, we have two of their weapons which can be used, though as a last resort only since I've no desire to taunt the real power, the *sphere* into action. That we are but eight, well, so be it. 'Tis not my purpose, sirs, to take on the whole garrison. We'll seat ourselves as closely as possible to the exit corridor for the royal chambers. It is within that corridor, so I understand, that the door to the secret passage can be found. It is there too that the sliding door, built to block all access to the king's chambers, can be used to block pursuit. Depending upon the time and the circumstances, we have but to take our ladies, and the king and queen, too, if they so desire, and make a running fight for that corridor. . . .'Tis not impossible."

"No it is not," Fel-Holdt said. He crossed the room to embrace me. "I would but ask, my lord, that you take good care."

Hooli, of course, had listened to it all and without so much as a blink of an eyelid, or the twitch of an ear. I'd mentioned the "outside force" deliberately; it was the first time I had done so, the first time ever that his presence had been hinted at beyond the hypnotic powers of his *flute*. Moreover, my little *rodentius drusis's* lidded eyes seemed dull as dull could be—except that this time, I knew better.

There is no stronghold of any kind on Camelot-Fregis without its secret passageways. Some have more than one. Indeed, depending upon the owner-lord's degree of resulting guilt-paranoia from mistreating his peasants and such, he may have as many as six, ten or even a dozen. Most, however, are satisfied with two.

I knew that Gortfin had one, at least. For I'd hardly retired after a hearty dinner and more table talk of new victories won in the south and west when that particular passage was put to use. In no way sleepy, I'd first opened the draped, stoneworked windows to the night breeze and wafted perfumes of flowers plus the smell of water from far below. In my bed again, I'd lain back against the propped-up pillows, the better to watch the ghostly moons of Capil and Ripple wending their liquid way across the star-filed skies. My mind was at ease with a sort of *Zen* contemplation when I sensed movement in the far corner next to a stairwell. The starlight, touching softly on the area, seemed suddenly then to withdraw; indeed, dissolved to a yawning blackness.

My spine tingled. A doorway of sorts had been opened by someone. Seizing my sword, I drew it slowly and silently to me while unsheathing it in a way so as to make no sound.

"Stay your hand, my lord." The softly imperious though hardly audible words were those of Elioseen.

"Well, now," I murmured just as softly, "here's a witchery I hadn't counted on."

My body thrilled throughout to the exciting sensation of a quasi déjà vu, a tingling feeling of repetition. For Murie, too, had come to me once in exactly this way, and with almost the same words.

Wasting not a second, Elioseen came swiftly across the few paces to my bed. Her form, slender, silver in the starlight, gleamed with a phantom shining. I threw back the furred sleeping robes, though I was quite naked. She in turn shrugged her single garment, a gossamer thigh-length shift, from her body. She bent to kiss me, lips and breath warm against my own. She then moved to lay beside me, but I took her completely in my arms so that her head was against my chest beneath my chin. One slim leg sought immediately to encircle my body.

I welcomed her as I would an expected, familiar lover. For some things are preordained, and this was one of them.

She knew it, too. She said huskily, her mouth searching my flesh, "Last night I truly believed you'd never see the sun again, Collin. Tonight—well to me it's as an extra few hours of life for which neither you nor myself need ever account to anyone." She spoke matter-of-factly, but with a certain sadness.

I laughed, squirmed into a more comfortable position above the heady warmth of her body. "You confuse me, my lady. If there's an ambivalence to your pleasure, why so?"

But she'd chosen the moment to run her lips over the muscles of my chest. The caress completed, she looked up. "Why, if you were dead," she said, "I'd not then be betraying my niece like this—" Her wet mouth roamed still further.

I told her hoarsely, "Elioseen, twixt you and me there's no betrayal of anyone."

"Oh? Why not?"

"Because as of this moment we are not of this world's reality. I am again truly from somewhere else; and you, too, for what you've become. This night and hour has nothing to do, therefore, with any part of the world of Fregis."

Her laughter came silver-sweet, mocking. "Hey, Collin? I'm bound to think from what you've said that things are not so advanced among the stars as you'd have me believe. Your rationale for illicit love is most interesting."

"It may sound so, on this world. Not out there. There, if I've chosen a mate, and she me, well, we may still enjoy the body of another if we so desire. There's neither guilt nor blame. 'Tis but a pleasant exchange, no more."

"But you are now in the kingdom of Marack."

"Nay. I am in this room with you."

"So what of my niece?"

"Why, that I love her. Nothing will change."

"Do you love me?"

"Certainly. But not in the same way; nor," I grinned, "do you love me, my lady."

"How do you know that?" She sat up to grasp my shoulders and to stare deep into my eyes. I winked immediately, phasing my contacts ever so slightly so as to avoid what I thought might be a quick attempt at hypnosis.

"If you did," I murmured, putting my hands upon the softness of her inner thighs to spread them, "I doubt you'd be here."

"By the gods!" she exclaimed at my movements, gasped as my hands touched further. "I'll most certainly take that option, to visit the stars—when this is over."

I rolled her gently to her back, raised myself to look down upon that soft female body of melded golds and silvers; her arms reaching, her legs wide-spread, her eyes so wide in the starlight as to seem like a Terran painting of a child I'd seen in the long ago.

"If Murie knew of us—" I said confidently. "If she knew that this was the way it truly was, this mutual but quite undemanding act of pleasure, I doubt that she'd be all that unhappy."

"Oh, ho. You but say now what you wish to hear. If my niece knew of this—" and she seized me in such an embrace of legs and arms as to make my eyes bulge—"why then, sir, I swear she'd have us both to the dungeons. And that's a fact. A last point, Collin, is that you talk too much. . . ."

"Perhaps," I said. "But still—"

And that is as far as I ever got.

The hours of a night such as that are long remembered; indeed, are set aside by some selective natural mechanism of the human mind for the later, dreaming years of age. The whole of it was a collage of flesh and limbs, tossed bedclothes, and a sweating, writhing, gasping; to be repeated and repeated with each dénouement, until the final exhaustion of two bodies holding hands and with limbs spread to the cooling night breeze. . . . Then after, the exploring and the sustained intimacies of the tastes of flesh that last interminably. . . .

There is usually, on such a night, and there was then, a last raging against one's ultimate end; a final melding of flesh in glorious battle. And that was it. And *that*, to those who achieve it—for those who can participate and still be free—well, let us say that it is truly they who have a right to the stars.

In the early hours, as a simple act of understood comradeship, she laid a hand upon my cheek. I touched each finger with my lips. And so she left me.

The attack went well the following morning, despite the fact that the Kelbian merchants and would-be priests were accompanied by two full companies of white-tabbed warriors and led by six knights. The order for battle was given with the use of the *mirror* and an accompanying audio effect. The voice was Fel-Holdt's own, to his men.

We watched the fighting. The enemy, ambushed and thus surprised, and with our numbers being twice theirs, was literally destroyed. The battle was short, bloody and brutal. In the midst of it all, when I saw that we were surely winning, I called to my volunteers, including one of our sorcerers, reputedly a master of disguises, shook the hands of all those who knew we were leaving and went quickly to thc mcadow in back of Gortfin, and the scoutship.

I'd kissed Elioseen's hand, a simple act. Gen-Rondin did

too. For luck, he said. A small glance of friendship and love then passed between the three of us. . . .

Another glance from me to that miserable Hooli, who'd appeared unannounced in the same magick-room, elicited a wink and a head bobble, from where he leaned on a monstrous, bubbling retort. Why was it, I'd time to wonder, that though I truly loved Hooli, usually, when I thought of him at all, my one desire was to boot his little ass over the nearest conifer?

Even as I pondered this transient riddle, a small voice said, "Screw you, too, Henry."

How, indeed, could I not love him?

Kriloy, taking the scoutship back to the protection of Gortfin's invisibility, left us at the scene of the battle. Later, two warrior students, familiar with the environs of Glagmaron Castle, would accompany him to our trysting spot on the river road below the cliff. That he'd be within three short miles of the dreaded *sphere* had brought no pink to the pallor of his cheeks.

"Don't sweat it," I told him. "No one ever takes the river road at night. We'll be there. I promise you. Moreover, those who'll be with you are fine swordsmen. A last thing: If we're not there, well, wait 'till the false dawn only—then get the hell out."

He said seriously, unhappily, "For Og's sake, Kyrie, don't be a fool. Use those goddamned blasters at the first sign of trouble, not the last. You know what I mean?"

I laughed. "I'll think about it."

"You've got a new admirer."

"Who?"

"Me. I confess that before, when I was aboard the *Deneb* and we'd get your reports, *see* you even, in this battle or that, well, it all seemed like a video—Captain Universe and all that crap. It's not that way anymore. Actually, for me it's too real. It scares the hell out of me."

"You'll get used to it." I slapped his shoulder.

"Kyrie. I don't want to get used to it. By the way, how come you no longer mention the drain on the CT tap, or that I've failed to contact the galactic grid? Change your mind?"

"I think I know where the stuff's going. I'll explain it later—on the river road."

"Hey, Kyrieeee."

"No time," I said gruffly. "Really."

I stepped away, watched the ship phase out and then trotted off through the trees and the sun-dappled undergrowth to the ambush site. Our waiting Marackian swordsmen were led by a half-dozen knights, among them the brothers, Sir Chat and Sir Vos-Agin, both good friends to Rawl. They'd expected us, no more. We had to tell them of our purpose.

"Well then," Chat-Agin said. "You're in luck. One Kelbian party was from the town of Hertz, just a few miles from the border. Take their robes and dottles with the heraldry blankets and saddles. You're nine, right? You match up perfectly. There was a priest, a knight, four merchants and three ostlers."

"We're eight. Our good sorcerer here will return with you. He'll aid us in looking like those we replace."

The swordsmen of the four knights and the Agin brothers then propped up the bodies of the Kelbian-Hertsian mendicants, with their accompanying knight and priest so that our sorcerer, Ter-abs, could match us up properly, and then sat down all around us to lunch.

Amidst encouraging remarks, catcalls and much head-shaking from those around him, Ter-Abs sat each of us next to his appointed likeness and went to work with paste, colors, hair and sticky putty-glue. When it was over and we were bidding each other good-bye, we were no longer recognizable. Gen-Rondin, the oldest and most portly, had become the merchant leader. Sir Rawl was the Kelbian knight, Rettish. *I* was the red-eyed, ascetic warlock priest and our students were the three ostlers, or dottle handlers. Other than riding dottles we also had a dozen loaded with bags of sea salt and dried fish. These were for the trade-mart in Glagmaron City which we would supposedly visit the next day—to buy and sell.

It went so smoothly, we could hardly believe our luck.

We'd arrived at the site of the ambush at noon. The battle itself had taken place at eleven a.m. At the sixteenth hour the *third* Kelbian caravan came wending its way toward Glagmaron—to be met by myself, a distraught priest who moaned and cried of ambush, slaughter and the fact that so few had survived. I then whistled the others out of the trees. With the exception of the unbending Dosh—he was now a merchant, as was Lors Sernas—they did a right good job of crying and bemoaning their fate.

I begged the leaders of the new caravan to allow us to ride with them as protection against more forays by the "Collin bandits." They agreed, but sneeringly, noting the interesting fact that whereas all other trading dottles with heavy packs, bales and the like of merchandise had seemingly disappeared into the forests, *ours* were still with us. The cost of their protection, they told me, would be one half the value of our goods.

Young Sernas—he was a born trader, or so we found out—became furious at this and actually dared to challenge the knight-captain of their troop of one hundred warriors so as to defend our goods, until I managed to calm both him and the captain down.

Gen-Rondin, in an aside to me later, was for demanding that the irresponsibile, money-grubbing Sernas lose himself in the forest immediately. But Sernas, hearing, apologized profusely for his outburst and was given a second chance.

"Collin," Rawl said to me while we trotted along through the lazy afternoon—I'd known he felt queasily uncomfortable at the idea of parting with his weapons before entering the great hall—"to enter thusly, into the very heart of our enemy's camp, does my heart no good. I'm bound to think, old comrade, that should we be discovered, we'll be stuck like so many gog babies."

"There's always your fal-dirk," I told him grimly. "I'd concentrate on our purpose, sir. Caroween, I swear, will be most happy to see you."

"Not so," he remonstrated sadly. "For I'm thinking, too, that the head she'll see when it's been parted from this pinto body, will be that of a stranger. Mind you, Collin, I've nothing against big noses and pendulum ears. But in no way can my dearest associate these attributes with the well-loved profile of her true love. I'd not thought to die a buffoon playactor, and that's a fact."

He carried on this way until we were slowed by the ford of a river crossing. I said, as our dottles bounced their big fat paws and waited their turns impatiently, "I've a mind to agree with you, my old companion. But I do assure you that if we are found out, there'll still be time for the weapons to appear; time, too, for you to rid yourself of that nose and those pancake ears to disclose your true self to your lady. I must confess, however, that I'm bound to think—and perhaps you should ponder this—that your new nose and ears are not all that unsightly. Given free choice, our Caroween might well choose the man she sees rather than the one that was."

"By the gods, Collin," he hissed in reply, glancing about him the while, "you do most certainly choose the wrong place and time for such a joke, though in *your* case it could be true. Those quivering jowls and puffy cheeks, sir, do resemble a flimpl's ass after mating. Yet I'm bound to believe that for our Murie the change could indeed be welcome, if the truth be known."

Sir Dosh, an inadvertent party to our conversation, felt a need to enter the lists at this point. He said, as an act of serious mediation—and at that point we were waist-deep in the waters of the river—"My lords, as my lord of Fergis says, this is no time for differences. Still, if I must judge the two of you as you now are and have been, I'd have to say that both have gained some points and lost others; this, with your new guises. I, on the other hand, have been most foully tampered with. I've been made to appear a clown, sirs; given a round, red nose akin to a deformed plum-wit, in place of the great and generous one passed on to me by my glorious father. His was a stately nose, sirs, before which all of Ortmund was wont to tremble. I do pray the gods that I'll not be made to suffer long."

As we rode up the cleft of the far bank, drenched and mud-spattered, Sernas, our Hishian lover, could not help but seize the chance to enter the arena. . . . "For such obvious clowns to boast of points on either side," he muttered loudly so that all could hear, "is an insult to the name of beauty. A *man's* beauty lies in the workings of his brain, a well-kept lean and supple body, and a lance and ballocks in proportion to make a gerdess kick her heels with joy. Why I've allowed myself to be cozened into such an adventure for lovesick schoolboys I'll never know. If ever you doubt your manhood, sirs, I challenge you: Run not to your mirrors, but rather, reach down, grasp your parts firmly and pray that our good and gracious Hoom-Tet will get the juices churning. *That's* what the ladies want—a constant and deep, gut-level reassurance that they are forever desired, wanted; now. RIGHT NOW! They'd care not a fig if your heads were fern pots; for all the primping and tweezing in the world will never substitute for the visibly aroused male who's coming at them, doodle in hand, to have his way with them. Enough! You tire me. The world of Hoom-Tet is admittedly small. Its rewards, however, for the use of simple common sense exceed those of all other gods."

I report this as a typical Marackian conversation while on the way to battle. . . .

As the twentieth hour, with great Fomalhaut setting fast behind the range of forested hills to the southwest, we entered Glagmaron City from the east road. We were one hundred Kelbian warriors, at least half again that many merchants, ostlers, pack-men—and ourselves. Glagmaron had changed. Two things especially were more than disturbing. The center of the city, the great square and temple for which we had fought, had been completely destroyed, along with at least ten square blocks of buildings, warehouses, inns and dwelling places. In the enlarged "square of destruction"—and it covered a good twelve acres now—there was nothing but blackened, stone-like lava, from the heat no doubt of the cruising ship's great laser guns.

People, watching our passing from semi-ruined buildings, seemed hungry, disorganized, but still fiercely independent. Children played or searched through the ruins for whatever they could find. Some shops were open; guildsmen still practiced their various trades. Inns and hostelries did a thriving business. For Glagmaron City was still the capital of Marack.

One thing I'd noted, too. Construction was beginning in the destroyed square; a new temple to house the *sphere*; the house of Diis, the Unseen.

Sending our goods-laden dottles with the pack animals of the other merchants, and under the care of their ostlers, we proceeded on up the familiar castle road to the great mound of stones that all of us knew so well. Rawl, at my shoulder, could barely contain himself. Tears wet his cheeks.

The great plateau of the jousting field was barren to the very entry of the first stones of the mighty bridge. In all the time I'd known or frequented Glagmaron Castle there'd not been a day, winter or summer, without some half-dozen pavilions, tents or the like, present for the testing of the skills of this lord or that. On a summer day there would easily be as many as a hundred tents, and the field would be green. There was no color now. It was all bare earth, stone, dirt. Alive to wassail and constant tourney to lighten the hearts of the most martial in splendor and deeds, and the most gallant in minstralry and poetry—and most true warriors were proficient in both—our field was a desert now; a graveyard. . . .

The Alphian ship sat silently, somberly, two or three hundred yards to the south. We eyed it askance, as did the others of our Kelbian troop. For though they now swore allegiance to the sky lords, we'd gathered, in the bit of conversation we'd had with them, that they feared them more than they'd ever feared the Dark One.

Normally at any facsimile spaceport—which this military field was assuredly not—there were a few servo-mechanisms for loading, off-loading and the like, as well as a spate of ground cars to take passengers and crew wherever they wished to go. Not so with the Alphians and their ship. The Dark One's "uncle," as shortsighted as his predecessor, had not provided for such. The Alphians, with no previous experience at anything, were unaware of their loss.

The incongruity then—to one who had known the complexities of a starship and a thousand ports—was the sight of a dottle pen within a few tens of feet of the skyship.

We then saw that which fully endorsed the concept of the field as a "graveyard." At a few feet to the right of the entry to the bridge was the beginning of a double line of sharpened stakes upon which as many as forty bodies had been *impaled!* I had heard nothing of such an act, nor had Gen-Rondin, Rawl, or any of ours. Still, they had obviously been there for some time, since most were shrunken, dried by the sun and wind. Scavenger birds sat on collarbones or stake tips. Whitened ribs were exposed where the flesh had been torn away. Skulls were picked clean. Over it all was the sick, sweet, cloying stench of rotting death. We raised our sleeves before our noses as we passed.

Among the bodies, according to the tattered signs of heraldry remaining, were those of the lords Rekisto of Gleglyn, Gen-Giaos of Feglyn and Per-Kals of Longven; all with their ladies, knights and squires. I also noted the cabalistic rags of the aged sorcerer Per-Looris. Rawl, Gen-Rondin, Dosh and our three students raged silently, fighting the tears that brimmed their eyes. After a single look, I rode straight onto the bridge and then to the wall gates to turn left along the inner wall.

Only a few white-tabbed guards had been at the bridge; a handful more were on the walls. Less than a dozen were at the gates of the inner wall, hardly enough to man the great locks and the portcullis. No trumpets sounded at our entry; no kettledrums. All was quiet, silent. The very atmosphere seemed dead.

Inside, with our dottles stomping the flagstones of the familiar courtyard, we were hit by the first faint smells of a different decay . . . Having killed a goodly half of the castle help, and frightened off the greater part of the remainder, the new rulers were just now getting things back to some degree of normalcy. Dour ostlers took our dottles. They didn't want to leave. Indeed, sensing something awry, they *wheeed* and *whoooed* dolorously as they were led away to the stables.

With twilight already setting in, we were taken at once to one of the many, now empty, apartments. Since it was large enough to house the five of us comfortably, I asked that our ostlers stay with us to act as our personal pages at sup. The castle page guides shrugged. They couldn't have cared less. Indeed, their attitude and general slovenliness made me wonder just who they were responsible to these days. For I'd also noted the colors of poor Dors-Riis, the castle steward under Caronne, as having been one of those on the stakes. . . .

Our apartment being half way up the southwest tower, we were also in a direct line with the hill of the sphere. I went to the balcony to view it, shifting my contacts to ten mags and to infrared, too, to have a close look in the fast-growing darkness.

Gen-Rondin, to my rear, declaimed upon the manner of execution of those without the gates. His past as a jurist and interpreter of the king's law lay heavy on his shoulders.

"Never," he said with some heat, "in the written history of this land, has a prisoner of war or a plain criminal been treated thusly. Marackians," he cried. "Nay! Fregisians of all stripes, though admittedly ferocious in battle, simply have no history of such cruel punishment. . . ."

My eyes on the sphere, I whistled the others out to join me on the balcony. " 'Tis that I wish to check my eyes against yours," I exclaimed. "To me that damned blue-bubble seems alive, even breathing. What do you see?" Actually, the sphere's activity was more a pulsation, a giving off of heat with a resultant distortion effect, or so I told myself.

Sir Dosh, the first to speak up, cried, "My lord, you've named it exactly. That's what it's doing, breathing."

Like the others, he had fantastic eyesight.

The others agreed, staring hard, as curious as I but for different reasons. In truth, they were not far off the mark, for in previous conversations they'd spoken or referred to the sphere as the "creature," not viewing it as they did the Alphian ship, as some kind of vehicle, but as a *thing* in itself. . . . I glanced across to the skyship. Its sensor pods, fore and aft, were also aglow. I wondered: Were they communicating? Obviously the pods had such a capability, but that was not their purpose. A communications system was much more direct; except that the sphere might be different—mental, perhaps. I studied it some more. No, by the gods! It wasn't breathing, not even pulsing. The damn thing was actually sort of bouncing up and down, but within just a foot or two of ground-zero.

The hell with it. It was tomorrow's problem. In the apartment again, we broke into our various packs to see what raiment our Kelbians had brought to impress the sky lords. My erstwhile priest, I found, had been the recipient of one of the Alphian garments that went with the office. Apparently the robes had been made beforehand. The stuff was silken and of an unknown weave, of a shining azure blue trimmed in white. The dress itself consisted of a jumpsuit, a surplice-like surcoat with flowing sleeves and a brimless kepi for one's head. The kepi had a precious stone fitted to its center. The legs of the jumpsuit were designed to be shoved into metallic half-boots. . . . I found the "book," too; indeed, I took it with me as a measure of my devotion.

Since it was already late, I was not surprised when we were almost immediately called to sup.

Not knowing quite what we'd find, we'd steeled ourselves in more ways than one for our entry. The steel referred to was of the finest mesh. It had also been hardened in the best of Marackian smithies. We wore it beneath the borrowed finery. It would stand us in good stead. As a last point before leaving, I snatched up the ponderous new bible and sliced its guts out with my fal-dirk so's to make a nesting place for the two weapons captured at the temple. I then placed the "book" in the center of a large pillow and carried it as I would a votive offering.

It is one thing to come home again in the accepted sense, to family and fireside. It is another to return to a home that is occupied, desecrated and despoiled by strangers, *aliens*!

Glagmaron Castle was now my home, *our* home. My family was Murie, our fireside, the huge, indented stone crypts sunk into the walls on each side of the great hall. Built to hold whole tree trunks, they were banked now because of the heat of summer.

Though we were the last to arrive, our small section of the Kelbian caravan—a knight, a priest, three merchants and three squires (I'd elevated our students in rank)—earned us a seat but two tables from the still-existing "high tables" of Caronne's court. These high tables consisted of a line of three placed on a raised section of stone slabs at the hall's north end. At right and left angles from the high tables, two additional lines of from four to five tables each extended the length of the hall.

At the height of the summer—holidays, marriages, feast days, tournaments and the like—the lines on either side were doubled so that the great hall could actually seat some six hundred all told, a quarter of whom would be below the proverbial *salt*.

On this night, though it was the height of summer, there were fewer than two hundred. And, too, the gathering seemed more a Walpurgis Eve than happy wassail.

The three high tables were occupied by twenty Alphians, an equal number of lords and knights from the five kingdoms, with their ladies and two priest-sorcerers, one for each of the tables flanking that of the sky lords. The center Alphian table was a sight to see. . . . Tarkiis, Marquest and the others had evidently taken to the pleasures of the flesh quite rapidly (I'd long forced the pictures of their first sampling of this delicacy from my mind), for there were at least forty of the most beauteous daughters of the erstwhile Court of Marack with them, all in various stages of quasi-nudity, and seeming to be quite happy about it. The overflow from the Alphian table, in terms of girl flesh, wound up at the adjoining tables of lords and ladies. The result was a study in the maintenance of poise in the face of the obliteration of all accepted Fregisian mores.

The rows of tables at right and left angles to those on the dais were more or less filled with others like ourselves. New visitors from the kingdoms around, or lords from Marack's countryside, all come to make their peace with the sky lords and to give obeisance to Diis, their new god.

A small thing but important: Whereas, in the court of King Caronne, those who had come to dine and take their pleasure had occupied both sides of the long tables, now they occupied but one. This, apparently was a better way to see and be seen. It was also a good security measure. As of the moment, and this within the open-ended rectangle between the tables, a trio of sad-eyed young harpists was playing. Their instruments were deliberately muted so as not to interfere with the pleasure of the company. The result lent an oddball balance to the sometimes wild laughter and shrill screams from the high table.

The decay, I think, was manifest in the care—or lack of it—of the hall itself. A few shields and pikes had fallen here and there and had not been replaced. The discolored blank spots cried for attention. The varied flags and banners now seemed unkempt, faded, though it was difficult to believe that such could happen in so short a time. But the most glaring sign of the absolute contempt of the new rulers for the old, was the great laser burns on walls, ceiling and floors.

These, I was told, were the result of the playful Alphians shooting wantonly at frightened bats whenever these poor beasts would wander in out of the night. The sky lords thought it great sport. No matter that a number of humanoid casualties were also the result; no matter the searing of aged polished wood or the burning of this thousand-year-old tapestry or that. . . .

Normally, as an Adjuster, I would be acutely alert to the reactions of the newly invited merchants, etc., as well as to those who'd by now become acclimated to the modus vivendi of their guardian angels. Now, except for an on-the-spot evaluation and an automatically pigeonholed analysis, I lent most of my efforts to checking the hall for our own purposes; the prime one being the rescue of Murie and Caroween.

Neither had made an appearance, and if they failed to show altogether it would be, as Hooli had quaintly put it, "a whole new kettle of fish."

The heavier and older of the two priests then made a lengthy speech on the potential wonders of Diis, which few listened to, and the meal began. We ate, talked and socialized. Those at the high table, the Alphian table that is, talked only to each other and socialized only with the girls; their socializing being the kind that one would find in any cathouse from Terra to Assine II.

As the meal tapered off and the effects of the wines, sviss and beer grew, the fat priest would arise from time to time to introduce the name of this visiting lord, priest or merchant, and that worthy, in turn, would arise, go to stand before the Alphians, bow obsequiously, say a neat little piece and retire to his table. Seldom if ever did the Alphians say anything in reply.

Studying this quite gauche phenomenon in how *not* to win friends and influence people, or creatures, I devised a quick and simple paragraph of greeting and obeisance for when it came my turn, which we could all agree to use, and upon which we could elaborate if necessary.

The occasional shriek from the girls, the constant chatter and murmuring from all other areas became a sort of *in* thing with each group. I wondered at it, but took advantage too. In this way our closeness to each other was not considered suspect. From time to time new guests came, others left. The new arrivals from the city below disclosed drenched furs and cloaks. The audible deep rumblings from without had brought a natural rain again.

Sir Rawl, being our Kelbian knight, Sir Rettish, was called first. He went dutifully and soberly to stand before the Alphians while his status and background were described. I'd clicked my contacts to six mags, the better to observe Tarkiis while this went on. The Alphian overlord hardly listened, at least not to the priest's description of Rawl. His ear was rather cocked to a series of ooohs, aaahs, and titters from one of three silken couches placed to the rear of the high tables. On this particular couch an Alphian had stripped a girl of her quite diaphanous shift and was engaged in an act of frenzied copulation in full view of all. Tarkiis seemed only amused by the sounds he heard. . . . Rawl, watching bug-eyed, failed completely to respond when it came his turn to speak and had to be reminded.

Gen-Rondin was next, as our chief merchant, Dos-Dreglan. By the time his brochure had been read, there were three naked pairs, all coupling on the couches. When prompted, Gen-Rondin woodenly spoke his piece and retired. . . . I could not help but note that those who had left the hall so far seemed to have been from the two flanking high tables on the dais. Both were mostly empty now so that only the Alphians and their girls remained.

When it was my turn the cries from the girls on the couches, plus accompanying shouts from the quite uninhibited Alphians—and they had no reason to be otherwise, considering—fairly drowned my introduction. The fat priest ended it simultaneously with the climatic fulfillment of the copulators. They were, for the moment, exhausted and their moans tapered off. Since their performance had been the central attraction, a vacuum-like silence ensued.

I took advantage of this to bow to the priest and to the overlord, Tarkiis. I then said my words of greeting.

Finished, I waited the few seconds of protocol lest there were questions from any source. Tarkiis, also aware of the vacuum, was finally prompted to say something.

"Why, priest," he asked disinterestedly, "do you have red eyes when all the rest have blue?"

A good question. I hadn't the slightest idea.

So I improvised. "My lord," I said, "before I became a priest of our new and gracious god, Diis, I was first a warlock. Warlocks, the better to work their magick, make use of the tistle-weed. 'Tis smoked, inhaled into the lungs. This results in dreams and freedom from all worry. With this weed, my lord, we feel no restraints, no ties—no nothing! The price we pay for this pleasure is that the weed makes our eyes red."

He thought about that, then said, "We of the *Kentii* have no restraints; and this without your weed. Still our eyes remain blue. But we, of course, are superior to you. What magick did you work, Warlock?"

I hesitated. He apparently now knew the word but not its meaning. "Small things," I told him. "Our work in no way compares to yours."

He accepted my compliment contemptuously, as I'd known he would. He said sneering, "Show us one of your tricks."

I bowed, pressed my belt stud for the ionizing effect, careful to widen the beam but still keep it directional for focusing. I then pointed at the nearest table where sat a large metal tureen—and the tureen *glowed*. I doused the beam, turned, pointed to another tureen. And of course nothing happened. I shrugged in deprecation of my own abilities.

This act of failure in so small a thing elicited exactly what I wanted. A ripple of laughter came from the Alphians, to be joined by the snickers of everyone else. Good. One seldom fears that which he despises. I was waved away by the languid hand of Tarkiis. I bowed low, backed away and returned to our table.

Sir Dosh, amazingly thick at times, was the first to comment, but in commiseration. He said stoutly, "Pay them no heed, my lord. A bit more practice and we'll come at them again, turn the tables, as it were."

I smiled. I couldn't help it.

Then, from the king's corridor that led to the room of the privy council and the erstwhile royal quarters, there came a tramping of feet. The doors opened, the drapes were pulled aside and the king and queen were ushered in by armed guards, along with Muric and Caroween, and four daughters of certain slain Marackian lords, all quite young and fair. The four, as opposed to our two princesses, were white-faced, regal—and *terrified.*

Murie and Caroween in pantsuits, sleeveless blouses and leathern half-boots, were as beautiful as ever, except for one thing. Their faces were flaming red and a splash of black dots ranging in size from a pea to a penny covered their foreheads, cheeks, arms and throats. These blemishes continued, obviously, to belly, breasts and loins. By the looks of them, I could only assume that they had some sort of pox. . . .

The king and queen were still arrayed in what was once royal garb. Unfortunately the clothes were the same as those worn on the night of the coming of the Alphians. They'd been allowed no access to their wardrobe; still, the cloth of shirt, pants, gown and stockings was neat, though frayed; clean, though faded.

The Alphians were applauding the sweating, red-faced threesome who had returned to the tables from the couches. A smattering of additional applause circled the tables. Some of this last may have been for the king, himself, we couldn't tell. That he was alive at all was a surprise to our Kelbian contingent. A place had been kept for them at the upper part of that table which was at right angles to the high tables, the angle nearest the corridor to the royal chambers, which they apparently still occupied. . . .

Good. I relaxed somewhat. It was the ideal setup.

The four daughters of the former lords of Marack were marched to the center of the open rectangle and forced to stand before the sky lords. Hearing the hissing of indrawn breaths from some tables and seeing the glittering eyes and florid faces of certain lords and merchants, I had the presentiment that what we were about to see was nothing new in this Alphian court.

The priest-spokesman—and I'd already marked him as one to whom I'd devote some serious attention if the opportunity arose—cried out, "Well, now! The *mounts* have arrived. Where are the riders? Who among you, sirs, has a wish to play tonight? Our sky lords, who dearly love the game, have called for three races to be run, the winner to receive—" and he held up a great diamond on a golden chain for all to see—"this princely bauble. *This* to the man who's still aboard when all others have failed! What say you all? Who'll be the first to volunteer his prowess?"

Four mattresses with sundry silken, down-stuffed pillows had been brought by as many lackeys and placed directly before the center high table. Tarkiis, Marques and another whose name I'd heard shouted as Coriad all leaned forward in unbridled anticipation of what could only be a coupling of the four girls with whomever would volunteer themselves.

I was not amused. The initiation of the likes of Tarkiis to sex was like introducing candy to a spoiled brat, honey to a Terran grizzly, or red meat to piranhas. There was no controlling it. I was reminded of a Terran historical work having to do with the inmates of an asylum taking over the asylum. The Alphians were not rational; ergo, there would be nothing rational in anything they did. The D.O.'s "uncle" had neither known nor cared that a smattering of knowledge derived of infantile tapes and discs "does not a human make"; especially when the clay itself has long been spoiled.

Some things are like character and ethics: a social morality is not just talked about. It must be lived, nurtured across a millennium of time. The truism of the relationship of theory to practice crossed my mind.

Watching the developing tableau, I also wondered about the two hundred guests from the five kingdoms. There were some, I'm sure, who would accept a Tarkiis as they would a long lost brother; for just as there are changelings, bad seeds and those who can destroy a man, a city, or a world without a qualm, so are there weaklings who but wait for someone to follow. Still, whatever they thought, they were here now and had little choice but to play along with Tarkiis's game.

The four young ladies in their white virginal shifts were thrust forward to await their would-be lovers. Tears wet their cheeks; this, despite their aplomb, poise and their downright contempt for the murderers of their fathers.

A young Ferlachian had arisen, stocky, heavily muscled, brutal. "I'll have a try, my lords," he cried, while eyeing the four lewdly. "Just let me pick mine first."

Tarkiis's face grew instantly red. "You will take the one nearest you, scum," he shouted, "and ready yourself."

Two more then leaped the tables to join the first; a heavy shouldered, black-furred rascal from Ortmund, and a small red-fur from Gleglyn who licked his lips and found it hard to keep his eyes from the well-rounded bottom of his appointed victim. A fourth man then came running from around the last table on the left. He yelled, "Well now, by Diis, since I've made up my mind, let no one deny me a right to the joust."

The burly priest, satisfied with these first four, cried out: "You will strip and present yourselves, sirs. All bets," he announced to those at the tables, "must be down and covered ere the race begins." The twenty Alphians were already examining the four as they would pit-bulldogs or pure-bred stallions in an elder time.

Then Murie called out. And oddly enough, I'd half expected her to do something. "It would seem to me, Sir Tarkiis," she said clearly and *loudly*, "that sky men too should compete in this game which is yours alone. Not that the bastards would win," she laughed. "Oh, no! But we of Fregis, who are true men and women, would at least see some comedy—in a charade that is lacking in anything else."

She stood alone in arrant defiance, eyes glaring. And at all the tables the "guests" had arisen to their feet. Whatever their reason, the action honored her.

"Woman!" Tarkiis raged back. "Do you really seek your death so soon? Take your foulness from this hall, and now! Lest you contaminate us all."

She laughed again. "This foulness, I got from you, sir. So you, at least, are safe."

Tarkiis went white. He reached for his blaster, yelling, "By our great Diis, you bitch, you do tempt me."

"Oh? But not *enough*, apparently, for I still live. Cease your lies, sir. I and my companion are alive for but one reason—and all the castle knows it. You hold us as bait for my lord the Collin and his sword companion, my cousin, Sir Rawl Fergis. Your god orders it. So much for your personal anger." And she dared to snap her fingers.

There was quite a muttering at this forthrightness. And there were some, I'm sure, who, sensing the direction things were taking, would have liked to have gotten the hell out of there. Their fear, however, of what would happen if they tried was greater. I sensed too a resentment against Murie. Her very defiance was a threat to their own possibilities for power and riches as offered by the new god, Diis, and the sky lords.

I'd felt the first tingling when Rawl was introduced and had gone to speak. It had been with me all this while, the sign that Elioseen was watching. . . . We had no set plan as to when I was to begin our move. Actually, I have always believed—indeed, been taught—that events will unfold of themselves and in certain ways, dependent of course, upon the objective and subjective conditions of the moment—plus one's ability to insert the proper fulcrum and/or monkey wrench at the right time. An Adjuster's teaching *begins* with the hoary Machiavelli—but moves on to greater things.

And then the unexpected; though not necessarily for me. Gen-Rondin, our paragon of legal and moral virtue, arose to walk around the tables and to say directly to Tarkiis, "Oh, great lord, if you would indeed rule in this land and world, think then on what you do. It is not right to prey on the children of the unjustly slain, who have no sword to speak for them. Nor is it meet, sir—"

Tarkiis, in one liquid movement, drew his laser, leveled and fired. Nothing! He fired again. Nothing! Angered, he threw the weapon from him, drew his blaster and fired that—still nothing.

My belt had long drawn the power from every energy pack of every weapon in the hall, save two: those captured weapons inside my bible from which the packs had been withdrawn and were no longer in positive negative contact.

Others of the twenty white-robed angels had also drawn

and fired; with the same results. They stared in puzzled wonder at the useless metal in their hands.

Then it was truly the proper moment so that I too stepped out and took my place at Gen-Rondin's side, while signaling my companions to stay where they were. To orchestrate it properly was the thing.

The Alphian called Coriad looked haughtily down at me and fingered his useless weapon. Ignoring him, I called bluntly to Tarkiis: "Tell your men," I said, "to sheathe their weapons, for your day, sir, is over. And what you have done to this world of Fregis you can no longer do."

I spoke more for the ears of those at the tables than for the Alphians. To hear a challenge such as mine go unanswered, or at the very least to hear it and see me alive and preparing to fight, could only point up the potentially "clay feet" of their new gods. . . . I would immobilize them *if* I could.

The Alphians' answer was to look at each other and laugh; Tarkiis, especially. His brow a storm cloud, he shouted, "Well, now, you red-eyed beast, you've played a trick on us for sure." He threw his blaster at me. I dodged it. He raised a hand and snapped his fingers.

And from all sides to the rear of the tables, from vestibules and corridors, there stepped more and more fully armed Marackians with the white-tab of the new god Diis upon their harness. There were at least two hundred, all led by burly sergeants and priests. I'd not thought there would be so many. Whatever. My prime concern was still limited to those swords that would place themselves between my group, with Murie, Caroween, and the king and queen; for it was obvious now that all must escape simultaneously, and to the corridor to the royal chambers. In that direction, I counted but fifty.

"Hold!" My roar to the gathering warriors was sufficient to shake the wall tapestries. At the same time I signaled the others to me. They came, in a line to either side. "Hear me, all of you. You were *men* of Marack before ever you raised your blades to defend this mewling scum in white. I tell you now that they are not angels, and that their god's an abomination. Look on us! We are but eight. Still will we dare to defy these murderers of the helpless; these despoilers of temples. We will do this. And we will take the king and queen and our two princesses from this place. But we, sirs, will return. For I spoke the truth. The days of the sky men

are truly numbered. I therefore ask you to either stand aside or die with them, as you so please—or to return, now, to Marack and your rightful king."

On my signal, we then retreated some ten paces from the high tables; upon which I called, "Now!" and we held our hands wide in front of us. . . . Almost instantly there came a tingling and a roaring all around us as of a great wind from without. It was quite real: a gusty screaming across the courtyard to torture the very eardrums; a blasting and shrieking as of Terra's fabled Erl-King, tearing at the mighty towers and crenellated battlements. Inside, a blackness grew to damp the glow of the torches, to weaken one's vision. Like a monstrous distortion, great shadows marched down the walls, evil, grotesque, deformed. They appeared to reach out to touch the amazed Alphians with phantom fingers of ebon-blackness. Then there was a great keening so that the wind suddenly died and the shadows, too. The torches blazed up, sun-bright!

And there, suspended before each of us, was a gleaming sword and shield. . . . A whistling sound of indrawn breaths circled the tables like the rustling of autumn leaves in a graveyard.

Being basically practical, we snatched at them quickly lest Elioseen's magick weaken and they fall to the floor. From the corner of an eye I'd spotted two smaller swords and shields appearing in the area of the king's table. These were grabbed just as quickly by two pairs of slender hands. A couple of graceful leaps and the owners had joined us, Caroween and Murie, to take their rightful place in our small shield front.

Tarkiis, his eyes bulging more with amazement than fear, yelled out, "Who are you, you red-eyed bastard?"

"I'm who you're looking for," I yelled back. "And among these with me are the Lord Gen-Rondin, King's Justice for Marack, and Sir Rawl Fergis, our King's Champion. We'll test those weapons you still wear, my Lord Tarkiis, if you've the courage for a real game. But I warn you, though we are ten and you are twenty"—I'd deliberately omitted the two hundred Marackians in the hope that phychologically they would then omit themselves—"we deem it that you've been rightly judged by our good Gen-Rondin and have been found wanting in every way. His sentence is death. We intend, sirs, to carry it out right here and now. I therefore ask you to come down."

Ah, the bravado of it. And all of Camelot-Fregis loved bravado. No matter that he who had taken the mask for his very own, *me*, was beginning to sweat the wrong kind of sweat, i.e., the sweat of fear, they loved it. How now, indeed, could our Marackians take the Alphian side? Unfortunately, I knew the answer to that, too. We'd win some and lose some. The question was—how many would we lose?

But Tarkiis had fallen strangely silent, staring; his brows knit at something he apparently saw beyond my shoulders. The remaining Alphians, some with swords half drawn, stared, too. Indeed, all the court, including the many white-tabbed men-at-arms, were gazing hypnotically to our rear.

I turned to risk a look. I had to.

The great iron-bound doors had been flung open, wide. Little whirlwinds, zephyrs and a rain-washed breeze tore past us, bringing leaves from somewhere and a spate of perfumed raindrops. Touched by these seemingly disparate wind gusts, the candles and torches on every side now truly guttered, and the black shadows, as created by the downright witchery of Elioseen's magick, returned, albeit this time quite ominous. Now they were possessed of life. In the entrance all was dark except for a number of guards straining to close the doors. They could not. The ponderous double weight of timber seemed wedged, and this by no human hand.

And then I saw him as I'd so often seen him in my dreams. He came strolling toward us with a quite natural aplomb; two feet, three inches of warm brown fur. His shades were gone. He wore no booties; no clothing of any kind. He held a single item in one paw—his flute. I thought, my god, would he dare to play it now? He did and he didn't. He but placed it to his lips once as he walked and blew one small, melodious, ululating note—and the flute disappeared.

I'd long known that one of its purposes was to trigger previously implanted suggestions, similar to the post-hypnotic kind. But what that single note had keyed in the Marackian's subconscious this time, I didn't know. Damn Hooli!

Making his way around our sternly martial group, he paused for the briefest of seconds, to stare owlishly at me. He then continued on to climb the table leg where the royal family sat and to deposit himself into the lap of King Olith Caronne. He then deliberately extended a small paw to touch the hand of poor Queen Tindil; this, with a soft and loving pat.

Already I could feel the "goodness" spreading.

The question, however, was why? Why was he here? Why now?

He had never in the past gone anywhere near the action. He'd even created the mind slogan which all northerners learned to repeat as if it were gospel: "Gentle Pug-Boos do not go to war."

Whatever the signal, most of the two hundred men-at-arms had got it; hard and clear. Some two dozen or so, for reasons of black deeds already committed with and for the Alphians, moved woodenly to align themselves with the sky men. The handful of merchants and such still at the tables flanking Tarkiis's made haste to withdraw to the tables below. They dared not flee the hall entirely.

Another twenty of the white-tabbed swordsmen filtered through to us. If Hooli's signal *and* presence, like my bravado, had been to neutralize the majority and to intimidate the minority that chose to stay with Tarkiis, well he, or *we*, had partially succeeded. . . .

The ensuing battle inside the great hall of Glagmaron Castle was as none in which I'd ever fought before. We actually maneuvered, exchanged insults and glared at each other for some minutes before the first sword was ever raised. The Alphians, though unafraid for reasons of pure stupidity, were still reluctant to come down from behind their table. I think that they actually had such contempt for us that even to contemplate a mano-a-mano engagement turned their stomachs. . . .

Seizing the time to take Murie into my arms, I said lightly of the steel long-shirt which I felt beneath her blouse and pants, "I see you came prepared, my love."

Hearing, she kissed me again and shoved me back to stare into my eyes. She said, "Gods, Collin. Did you think I didn't know?"

"Know what?" I used the moment to rip the fatty paste of my disguise from off my face, while she wiped at me with a swatch of pocket cloth.

"That you would be here, great fool. Elioseen is my father's sister. She's of my blood. Gods, Collin, I am the heiress to Marack's throne. Do you think she'd do what she's done, and *I'd* not *know*?"

I frowned, suddenly angered at I knew not quite what. "She never told me."

"I will *be* Marack's queen, Collin."

My anger had grown. "Whatever you'll be, my dear, is dependent upon what happens now and after. Which means we have first a war to win, in which I've been named your leader. Would you change that too, without informing me? If so, why then, when this immediate bickering's over, you may have my sword."

There was some shouting then to our left, but nothing happened. Muric was saying, "Hey, love. I'm truly sorry, and my pride is oft like your own, a burden I'd dispense with. There was no time. She told me but short hours ago. You were already here."

What with the winds and the guttering candles, the hall had darkened further. A few bats had flown in, too, and an Alphian, seeing them, got off two more empty "clicks," then hurled the useless weapon at my student-warrior, Tadee—who picked it up and hurled it back.

"My lord," Muric continued, "you *are* Marack's commander, and there's not a one of us who'd have it another way." She squeezed me tight, kissed me one last time, snatched Caroween from Rawl's arms and both of them ran to the four proud daughters who stood shivering beneath the high tables to pull them away to safety.

It was at that point that first blood was drawn. An Alphian, seeing the prey being taken, made some laughing remark to the grimly glaring Marques, vaulted the table and seized the last girl's arm. She screamed and struck back; upon which, with one quick, raging move, he cut the poor girl's throat.

Whether he would have grabbed for a second girl, I do not know. He wasn't given that chance. Rawl Fergis covered the intervening space in one mighty leap and before ever the sky lord could make his move to escape, whirled his great blade and split him straight through the skull and collarbone.

In the ensuing awful silence, while he cleansed his blade deliberately on the "angel's" robe, Rawl shouted to the still-raging Marques, "As he is, so will you be, you bastard. For I tell you now, sir, that whatever happens here tonight, 'tis *you* who will not leave this hall alive!"

Marques stayed where he was and Rawl returned to our ranks where there'd been an instant drawing together. Murie and Rawl's redhead—they'd given the girls over to the king and queen—had returned too. Tarkiis, watching it all, his eyes smouldering, still held back for whatever reasons—and I would not be baited to attack them.

Of the twenty white-tabs who'd placed their swords with us, I directed ten to the service of the king and queen. "You will escort them immediately," I ordered, "to yon exit to the corridor which leads to the royal quarters, and await us exactly there. If we are slain, they will then tell you what to do."

If we had tried to make such a move ourselves, which I would have preferred, Tarkiis would have attacked, instantly. This way, he dared not strike, lest we take him in the rear. The question then was: What would the uncommitted white-tabs do who still barred the way?

A sergeant of the ten saluted me briskly . . . At the king's side, he made known my instructions. Caronne arose, *Hooli riding his shoulders*, to wave a hand in acknowledgment. Then, with his small band of the queen and the three daughters, and protected at front and rear by our white-tabs, he moved toward the exit.

The uncommitted white-tabs, and there were at least fifty of these to the rear of Caronne's table, still barred the way. I roared instantly and in my most menacing tones—and my voice was amplified by Hooli, you can bet—for a path to be cleared, and for swords to remain in their sheaths. . . .

And they stepped aside, muttering.

Indeed, to a man, when the king and his guard had passed, they began slowly to make their way toward the south end of the hall to stand around in small groups, watching. As is so often true of people when given any kind of leadership, many chose instantly to duplicate the act. The two hundred or so merchants, priests and the like fled almost precipitously toward the great opened doors through which the night wind still blew, and with an occasional mist of rain. And after them, though at a slower pace, went the remaining hundred white-tabs.

Odd paradox. Though fleeing the proximity of bloody battle, the lot of them—and they were now a great half-circle of frightened faces—were still afraid to leave the castle; to trust that somehow they could make it past that ship out there. They stayed, hypnotized by what they watched, and terrified by what they knew would happen—either way.

I asked suddenly of Murie, "My love, have you been aboard the sky ship?"

"Indeed, I have."

"How many men, then, would you say are there?"

"Perhaps forty, no more."

"Surely they have some means to communicate. It makes no sense that these here must fight alone, without the others knowing."

"Well I know, Collin, that they can speak from ship to ship, but not from man to man except by voice."

I shook my head in disbelief. It truly made no sense. I was again sweating profusely. My mental picture was of the Alphian ship ending this entire charade of posturings and threats by simply blowing ourselves and the castle to hell in a single second—it was by no means pleasant.

"What?" I asked curiously, "is this god-awful pox upon yours and Caroween's faces?"

"Nothing, my lord," she smiled, "that won't come off with a few crisp latherings."

I shook my head again. It was unbelievable, their stupidity. But then, they had nothing at all to relate to. Even a native intelligence must have some experience.

We'd been stomping our feet, shaking our shoulders and dressing our shields for what we knew was coming. Steel mesh settles that way, and will not, thereafter, bunch and prevent the free movement of one's limbs; especially the sword arm. To our front the thirty or so Marackians who'd chosen to remain with the Alphians had been ordered to the fore. They'd dressed a line directly opposite us. But then the Alphians decided to move down too, forcing the thirty to split so that they could take the center position.

Tarkiis called out something which became unintelligible for the sound of a great wind which suddenly raced through the hall. Half the torches were immediately blown out. We were left, *all* of us, with illumination scarcely better than bright moonlight.

But again Tarkiis called out. This time his words were a shouted command. *"On them!"* he shrieked . . . *"Kill me this scum who dares oppose our almighty Diis!"*

Only twenty feet separated us. They came across it like a surfer's dream of the "perfect wave"—and broke to a boiling foam against our shield-front. The Alphians, without a doubt, were fine swordsmen. It was probably *the* single thing they'd honestly worked at; been truly trained to do. As with everything else connected with the original Dark One and this new facsimile, however, their knowledge, like their weapons, was flawed. They fought as individuals. A duel between Alphians would, I'm sure, be a sight to see. But that was the extent of it. They hadn't the slightest understanding of the coordinated attack, mutual protection and the like. Their greatswords, though devilishly sharp, were of so light an alloy that there was simply no weight behind their blows. They carried no shields. But a shield is not just for defense. It is also a weapon to supplement the prime weapon, the *sword!*

So when I say that they "boiled against our shield-front," I mean just that. They landed twenty blows to our one—and accomplished absolutely nothing. We killed two sky men and seven white-tabs in the first assault. I killed an Alphian with a simple thrust from between Murie's shield and mine.

The left wing of their front, made up mostly of white-tabs under a damned good sergeant, then drove around us to turn and smash back against Gen-Rondin, Sernas, Kodder and five of our new Marackians. They were met with an unbelievable fury, as is usually true of defenders who have already consigned themselves to death. The opposite is true of an attacker under the same circumstances. He, as a rule, knowing he has the edge in numbers, holds back, confident of victory, but wanting to be around to enjoy it. . . . After a minute or so of this, and we were almost a complete circle now, we simply locked our shields tighter and marched this way and that, driving the enemy before us and stepping over the bodies of the slain.

Tarkiis finally had sense enough to call them off. And, since we were in the exact spot where the fighting had begun, I whistled our men to stop, too, not to pursue. There were now *twenty-nine* bodies on the bloodied tile of the great hall. Just two of them were ours, brave Tadee and one of our white-tabs. Of the other twenty-seven, *ten* were sky lords.

Sweat, blood, and soot from the torches made all of us as ghastly gargoyles where we stood panting and leaning upon our weapons. A quick glance around me revealed that what with the wind whistling through the eaves, an occasional mist of driven rain, and torches reduced to but a quarter of those we'd started with, Glagmaron Castle's great hall looked now like some hellish inferno. More bats had joined us, their shadows a grotesquerie of flapping corpse-shrouds.

"Tarkiis!" I yelled. "I repeat what I said before: Lay down your arms, sir, for your day is truly over. You may even survive a Fregisian Court, though I'll not guarantee it. Surrender your men—or we will kill you all!"

"To *you*, you damned animal?" Tarkiis screamed his hatred; actually ground his snow-white teeth in rage. He was like a boy of ten or twelve, spoiled rotten; accustomed to having his every word obeyed. "We've forty comrades on our ship, with weapons that *do* work. We have four more ships with full crews, and *you* ask *me* to surrender?"

"My Lord Marques," Rawl intruded suddenly to Tarkiis's companion, and I could not help but note that his features were all twisted in the flickering torchlight, "whereas our Collin offers you life, I, sir, have nothing but death to give you. Hey, now?" He raised on his toes to squint. "There's no use hiding, for I see you there behind your betters. Come out, sir, now, and face me, for 'tis said that you've given my lady some hurt, you craven bastard, and I will *not* let you live."

Marques stepped forward, pale, resolute; his fear in part conquered by his hatred of the taunting and the taunter. He whirled his sword but once around his head, to hear the whistle of it, and said proudly, "You have it wrong, Sir Animal. No man of the great race of *Kentii* duels with that which is born of filth and slime. Will I deign to slay you? Certainly—as I would a gog in the pens. . . ."

Rawl loosed his shield from his left arm. The Alphian smiled. I called with some alarm, "Hey, comrade. You're giving him the advantage."

But my sword companion, brash, unheeding, angry, stepped from our ranks to whistle his own great blade in an arc made shimmering by the torches. He stamped his feet on the tiles and said bluntly, "Come."

And Marques *came*. And he, like Rawl's sword, was also a glittering whirlwind of light, a living blade to touch my stalwart five times for each glancing blow returned. Watching, I thanked the gods that my men had not been forced to fight them individually. For when given room, Marques, like the Alphian I'd slain in the temple square, was a veritable death machine.

Rawl was no fool. He knew what I knew in the first few seconds. He therefore wasted no more efforts in parrying or swinging wildly in the hope of a lucky hit. He simply stood solidly, turning always to face his enemy, accepting cuts on shoulders, arms, and thighs—and waiting stolidly for the error. He told me later that unless he bled to death first, which would have taken some time, since Marques's cuts were shallow, the only way he could be killed was by a straight thrust right through the mest of his hauberk. And that, he said, could not be done. One: The Alphian hadn't the strength to deliver. Two: It was the one blow he *could* parry, and with ease.

And he was right. Indeed, the first time the Alphian tried was his last time. The thrust came. Rawl, his shield-hand used but lightly in a two-hand grip on his greatsword, left the grip to deliver instantly a smashing blow to the Alphian's sword-flat, catching it on his forearm. The sword went flying. The Alphian, off balance, could only turn to his right; upon which Rawl plunged forward to seize him in, as Hooli would put it, "a Terran, double hammer-lock" (he'd dropped his own blade). In but seconds, as we all watched with something akin to awe, we heard the snap of Marques's neck, and that was the end of that. . . . But not quite.

A second Alphian, enraged, came boiling out to avenge him (a case in point of a developing loyalty—or simple frustration). My quite heavy-handed Sir Dosh—he'd personally slain four of the white tabs—stepped pompously out to greet him, and like a fool also threw down his shield.

Within what seemed like seconds the Alphian had accomplished what Marques had failed to do. He'd run Dosh through the midriff by throwing his full weight behind the thrust. Dosh, a puzzled look in his bulbous eyes, fell, skewered to the hilt like some stricken giant kaati.

Gen-Rondin then moved to go to his aid. But our lewd and lecherous Lors Sernas, putting his heavy shield to one side and snatching Murie's from her arm, himself leapt out to straddle Dosh's body.

"Hey, now!" he yelled to the Alphian victor. "I know you, you bastard who've slain my friend. And I've noted, sir, that you are one who profanes our Hoom-Tet laws of *love* by abusing such pleasures for sport and money. Now, I, sir, intend to take your parts, once and for all; for you truly don't deserve them . . ." He went on in this vein. And the Alphian, having not the slightest idea as to what he was talking about, was still sufficiently confident because of the success of what he thought was his first killing, to seize Marques's sword and come at Sernas. . . .

Our Hishian who now had a protective device but half the weight of his own, danced his opponent measure for measure. He brought it all to a stunning halt, finally, by the use of the Omnian dirty-trick expedient of kicking his opponent square in the groin and then taking his head when he'd dropped his weapon to double over in screaming pain.

Two of ours, Kodder and a White Tab, then rushed out to seize Dosh's body and pull him to our circle. He was still breathing. Indeed, he looked up to bat his eyes at me and say huffily, "By the gods, Collin, I've a stomachache to end them all. Would you have a potion on you, sir, or perhaps a faldirk to the jugular?" I knew he was in great pain. I said, "Let be, old comrade. We'll tend you shortly. Believe me." But he was again unconscious, which eased my own feelings of inadequacy.

All the while, in this mad and sulfurous atmosphere of hell-fire, *duellos*, whistling winds, graveyard shadows and a cold reality of bloodied tiles and sword-slashed bodies, I too, was shuffling my feet and shrugging my harness, preparing for my personal challenge of Tarkiis which, since I was Marack's champion, was as fated as the orbits of Capil and Ripple.

It was more than a question of personal revenge for Murie. If I could strike Tarkiis down, slay him, well, what with all that had happened, that could be the end of it. With the Over-lord dead, no white-tab would oppose us. I doubted that the remaining Alphians would either. But even as I procrastinated, for that's what my hesitation amounted to, a couple of things intruded. The first was Hooli. The second was Tarkiis, himself. . . .

There'd been such a roar of wind tearing at the battlements that I'd thought a sudden buzzing in my head was a part of it. Not so. Nor was it a product of the communications node buried at the base of my skull. Only the *Deneb* and Kriloy had access to that. The *Deneb* was long gone, and Kriloy used a dit-da-da warning. I turned toward the king and Hooli—and Hooli's voice exploded inside my head with full amplification—"*Damn,* Collin! Stay open. You've a natural blanking ability you know."

And at that exact moment, Tarkiis led his remaining swordsmen in a sort of kamikaze charge!

I yelled mentally: "Hooli! Not now!"

"Yes, *now*. It can't wait, Collin."

"Get—out—of—my—bloody—head!" All around me, I could sense and vaguely hear, but not see, that a fight was raging, a howling, screaming melee of flesh and steel.

"Just cool it, Kyrie. There's something I've got to say."

"Say it."

"Use the belt laser. Take 'em out now. If there's a reaction from the sphere, *I'll* handle it. We've got to get you back to Gortfin, have Elioseen put you aboard the skyship where you can then seize the controls. After which, you're to blast anything of metallic alloy that comes within scanning distance."

"Just like that?"

"Yup. I told you, Kyrie. I warned you that this would be a possibility."

"*You* warned me." In my instant anger, I, too, had begun to ignore the no-quarter fighting around me. "I'm suddenly thinking, Hooli, that it never was just a "possibility," but rather that it's been a fact all along, just waiting to happen. The only question, brown-bag, was when? How's about the sphere? Will I be blasting that, too?"

My mind, caught in the crazy maelstrom of Hooli's making, was at a white-hot heat. The little bastard had used me again, every step of the way. Sure we were winning; we'd also been dying all over the five kingdoms of the northern continent for the last three weeks. Even now, though others were risking their lives to protect me, Hooli's robot, standing like some overstuffed scarecrow in their midst, was unable even to lift a sword arm.

He was saying strongly, "You go after the sphere and we're dead, Kyrie. *I'll* handle the sphere. If *I* fail, then we've all had it, and you'll still be dead. *For there's simply no goddamn way in the world that you or any combination of forces on Fregis can take the sphere!*"

"But you said—"

"I lied—"

I said coldly, "Well, now. It's a whole new ballgame. You also said that as a Universal Adjuster you were incapable of lying. . . ."

"Attend to your lady, sir. I think she needs you."

"*Damn* you!"

"Time's a'wastin', buddy. I still love you."

"I've a man over here who's dying."

"Not to worry. . . ."

And he cut me off, and I staggered and fell, disoriented at the release. I'd fallen on poor Dosh. Struggling to my feet with the help of Caroween, I saw that we were the center of a protective circle. Around us the fighting had died again except for a clash of weapons beyond our group. Caroween, shoving my rescued sword back into my hand, and with her shield's edge to my back to steady me, said concernedly, "Are you all right now, my lord? For a few seconds there, we thought you were gone."

Seeing five newly slain bodies to our front, I mumbled, "*This*, in just a few seconds?" Our lovely redhead shrugged. Except for her fur and hair she could have been a clone to Murie, in every way. Blood dripped from her cheek and chin now; her own or someone else's.

Immediately beyond our circle Gen-Rondin and Murie each fought separate battles, Gen-Rondin with the largest of the Alphians, Murie with *Tarkiis*.

Even as I was introduced to what was happening, Rondin, that veritable *gerd* of a warrior, literally drove his shield ahead against a myriad of blows from his defending opponent—and stopped, deliberately to throw his man off balance. Indeed, the fellow had to stand stock-still for the briefest of seconds just to keep from falling. When he did, Rondin brought his own great weapon around in a one-handed blow of such strength and power that he actually cut the Alphian in half. Before ever the torso toppled, the man's eyes had seen the severing of his one part from the other. Then, mercifully, he was dead. The cry of horror arising from the throats of friend and foe alike at such a stroke, was something I've no desire to hear again.

Murie and Tarkiis, caught up in the fury of Rondin's attack, had paused to watch, leaning on their swords. With the sky lord's death cry, however, another "angel" leaped from his group to the aid of Tarkiis.

I'd been facing them directly. There was no time to reach the book with the hidden weapons. But I did have the belt. I positioned myself to fire, my finger poised over the laser stud. I *froze*! I couldn't do it. And it was no longer a question of what the creature within the sphere would do—if he actually could know of the act, and I was beginning to doubt that seriously. The deed would be un-Fregisian. In essence, northern chivalry would accept it—but never understand it. For I was their Collin, *sans peur et sans reproche!*

I'd used the laser beam but twice before in all my time on Camelot-Fregis. Once, to blast the sorcerer Fairwyn from off his high tower. But that had been understood, for Fairwyn had been directing lightning bolts at us. The second time was when I'd imploded the Dark One in the eyrie of his dread pyramid temple in Hish.

With twice the strength of any Fregisian, and with a certain practiced agility, too, I cleared the intervening space in one giant leap. I'd have aimed myself at Tarkiis, but Murie was in the way. So I came down square on the challenger, knocking him flat to the tile. He never had a chance. I bent, seized his half-conscious body by the feet, whirled it—and flung it straight at the sword-swinging, cursing Overlord.

The time consumed was five seconds at best. Infighting is like that. There was then a tableau which I will remember all the days of my life. The Alphian I'd tossed at Tarkiis was out of it—unconscious or dead; a pool of blood was rapidly forming beneath his head.

Tarkiis, though down, was in a sitting position, supporting himself with his two hands. His expression conveyed total terror, and with good reason. For Murie, eyes blazing hell-fire, stood over him. In an altogether beautiful five-feet-two of splendidly coordinated bone and muscle, her pose was that of a dancer, her legs apart for balance and purchase. Her left hand was raised. Her sword arm, from shoulder to sword-haft to point, where it touched on Tarkiis's throat, was one single, rigid line. . . .

The entire hall, as if in response, seemed enveloped in a sudden cold shroud of silence. Even the wind had ceased. The torches no longer wavered. The encroaching shadows were now immobile, lifeless.

Tarkiis, eyes bulging, managed a whisper, a hiss, really, that caromed, ricocheted, rebounded from all the walls, like some voice from a witch's cabal in an ancient Terran play. "Tell me what it is that you want, my lady," he forced the words, "and I'll give it, that I may live." Spittle damped his chin. There was a trembling in all his limbs. He looked less than a god now; indeed, less even than a man.

Murie's gaze had turned flat-eyed; her face expressionless,

except for the faintest of curls at her lip. She murmured, almost sweetly, "But you've nought else to give that I want—*but your life.*"

He screamed. "But I *must* live."

"That, you shall not."

His face went ashen. He pleaded. " 'Tis that I know so little of death. . . ."

"For one who's given it to so many, I'd have thought you knew a great deal."

His voice became sickeningly servile then, obsequious. "Let me live," he begged; tears even coursed down his cheeks, "and I promise that I shall surely study it."

His throat was so constricted now that he could scarcely speak, and I marveled at him as a thing not truly human. I'd seen robots, servos, and "droids" more sensitive, more understanding.

"Murie," I called suddenly, for a thought had insidiously touched my mind. "I intend seizing his ship. I may need him."

She turned to observe me calmly and to say, "Well now, my lord, if that's the case, I'm sure you do. But why not those?" She pointed with her free hand to the remnant sky men who still held bloodied swords. "Now hear me, Collin," she continued, "and I say this before my mother and my father, who still rule in Marack; and I say it before all of you who have fought so bravely, and before all those in our northern kingdoms who have done likewise: Though you remain my love, Collin—and we will surely be wed, and soon—you, too, are a sky lord. I know this now. And though you've risked much and fought well for all of us, still, you've fought your battles in part for other reasons.

"And so I'm obliged to tell you now that it is not you who has been harmed here in the castle of our fathers, nor in this land and world of Fregis. It is our people, sir, and *me*. For I, too, have been harmed by this thing who dared to call itself a god. I have been harmed both as a woman and as Marack's future queen. And so I say for all that he shall not live. And that's a fact."

And she dispatched him with one deft slash of the blade.

She came to me then, her cheeks all wet with tears. I held her, and all I could think of was the *Deneb*, and the hundred of our crew, and Ragan, my comrade, and the starship's commander, Drelas Niall—none of whom had ever thought to die so soon, and in so strange a circumstance.

Which snapped me back to the still existent *sphere.*

"What you did was right," I consoled her. "And Gen-Rondin, too, will agree. Your father offered peace. Tarkiis gave him not even war, but *murder.* There are some things, Murie, which are beyond the pale; for though they seem as human, or as life-respecting, as *we* would say, they are not . . . Not allow me," I told her softly. "I must end this." I gently broke away, retrieved the blaster and laser from the bible, fired a single blue beam at a larger than usual bat and missed, then ordered the remaining Alphians to lay down their swords. They did. The ten white-tabs had already done so. They stood now, heads bowed, awaiting their death.

I put them to work instead; first to collect the useless blaster and laser guns; second, to strip the dead Alphians of their clothing and to see to it that the bodies were taken to the courtyard and the hall immediately cleansed of its battle scars. Assembling the power packs for a recharge, and my belt was capable of this potential, I showed Kodder and Rogas how to use the Alphian guns and sent them to the turret towers above the bridge gates to stop any Alphian effort to enter the castle, should they attempt to do so.

Gen-Rondin, in the meantime, went to those merchants, priests, white-tabs and the like still gathered at the hall's south end. Their fear of the skyship had held them there. He told them that from now on they would be judged by what they did and how they conducted themselves. All who had castle apartments were told to go to them and await his orders. The white-tabs, other than those not on clean-up duty, were sent to the barracks. The worst that could happen, he told these last, was that at their future trial those who had *killed* for the sky lords and the false god, Diis, would be imprisoned, while most others would simply be banished to the countryside and dropped forever from service in the royal army. The last was a greater blow than one might imagine.

Rondin then joined the king and his party, who'd returned to his table and was now surrounded by my original handful, including a somewhat shaky Sir Alten Dosh. Dosh refused to accept the fact that he was alive, insisting rather, that we, too, had obviously been slain, and that somehow this castle and the scenes around us were but a view of Ormon's heaven whereon we'd actually won instead of lost our battle. The idea of a Hooli dispensing a special kind of cure-all *goodness* would have made less sense to Dosh than his own bizarre conclusions. I therefore allowed him to cling to his nonsense.

Time continued to run out, Hooli's time. I quickly buzzed Kriloy before joining the king, hoping to catch him before he'd moved to the secret passage exit on the river-road below. I got him—if for no other reason than that he'd delayed leaving the safety of the ship until the last moment. Considering our victory, I forgave him without ever accusing him.

"New orders," I told him bluntly. "Return to Gortfin immediately. Inform Fel-Holdt that we have seized the castle, slain Tarkiis and that our next move is to capture the Alphian skyship, the details to be worked out when he gets here. For this last, you will pick up Elioseen, Fel-Holdt, and a half-dozen of our best swordsmen. Tell Elioseen, too, to prepare six of her wizards for transit. You'll bring these last to Glagmaron on your second trip, along with an additional ten swordsmen. . . ."

"Christo!" Kriloy audibly sucked in his breath. He asked hesitantly, and I could sense the guilt of his own procrastination, "Was it—difficult, Kyrie?"

"Yes and no. You'll be briefed with the others. Now move."

At the king's table, I told them that Elioseen and Fel-Holdt would arrive shortly and that I had informed the two of them that I intended to move against the Alphian warship without delay.

Rondin asked sharply but straightforwardly, "And just how, exactly, do you propose to do this, my lord?"

I poured myself a cup of wine, drank it, sighed my pleasure and poured another. Hooli was again in Murie's delectable lap, but by no means asleep. I sensed an alertness, a sharp awareness of me and what I was up to. Good! I had a couple of surprises for him.

"Well, for one thing," I said, "we're in luck. A sky lord has told me, though I've yet to question him at length, that his comrades have developed such a penchant for *love* these days that they now have a stable of lovelies aboard their craft with them. So. 'Tis simple. We have twenty sky-lord uniforms from which the blood is being cleansed. With Fel-Holdt's swordsmen, plus ourselves and two guides, we'll simply enter the ship and take them prisoner. The assault, whatever the resistance, will, I assure you, be a great deal easier than the melee we've fought here tonight. The true test will come after. . . ."

"Which is?"

My eyes fixed hard on Hooli. That I intended entering the Alphian ship with laser and blaster weapons and in sky-lord uniforms hadn't phased him a bit. He even dared to do his pendulum tongue trick as a sign of his acquiescence.

"What else? We will attack the remaining ships."

And now came the real challenge, for I intended telling them everything that would happen while withholding the source of my information. Hooli would either interfere, or he wouldn't. "It goes," I told them, "like this: Tomorrow, and at any time after sunrise, we can expect at least two if not all of the remaining skyships to come to Glagmaron field, at which point it is my intention to destroy them with the aid of the skyship which we will capture. We must achieve their destruction as rapidly as possible, for tomorrow, too, the *sphere* will move. What it will do is beyond my knowledge. I would remind you, however, and all who were there will verify this, that the *sphere* was capable of destroying the great ship of my comrades. That is all I can tell you."

Gen-Rondin scratched his nose, sniffed and poured us both another drink. Sighing loudly, he said slyly, "It would seem to me that you've said enough. Still, if we cannot win against this last and obviously most dangerous of our enemies, then I suggest that we fall back to our original strategy: disperse, stay alive, and patiently continue to study the enemy for his weak points; this, though it might easily take the rest of our lives. In essence, Collin, other than yourself and those you choose to fight with you, there's no reason for the rest of ours to remain in Glagmaron. The city, too, should be emptied lest the *sphere* take vengeance for his ships and men."

"Except for the one thing I've yet to tell you."

"Oh, ho? Tell it then."

"I speak now of the *force* that I've only hinted at so far. If, as a result of our destruction of the *Kentiin* fleet (I'd deliberately used the Alphian name for themselves), the *sphere* decides to attack us, this *force* will then enter the arena. Hopefully," and I stared hard into Hooli's little bright eyes, "it will win. If not, well we, myself, all those in the ship;

indeed, all in this world could conceivably die. Still, I've no way of knowing this for sure. As for an evacuation, well I seriously doubt that it'll make any difference now."

I bowed then to the king and queen. The latter had indeed been touched by Hooli's healing paws. She looked alert. And though she wasn't all that "chipper," she was at least "with us," whereas before this was simply not the case. The problem was that though he could cure her physically, it would take time for the brain to avail itself of the cleansing.

The royal family retired to the royal chambers and to the royal wardrobe that had been denied them for so long. Murie and Caroween went with them, "to cleanse themselves of the pox," as they so merrily put it. The rest of us retired to the great room of the chirurgeons below, hoping to get ourselves in shape for the coming of Fel-Holdt and Elioseen. They arrived, unfortunately, while we were still in the baths, so we were not present at the meeting of the king with his sister. I'm told it was more of a familial love scene than one of strain and accusation. I was scarcely concerned with that anyway, being more intent on observing myself critically in the mirror—in my new attire as a sky lord.

Our ablutions completed, we were ready; and I now wanted it over as soon as possible. Arriving in the hall of the privy council, I found that the second shuttle of swordsmen and sorcerers had been safely delivered. And, too, Elioseen, wasting no time, had made a mental contact with the main resistance forces in Glagmaron City, so that a couple of hundred of our best would shortly arrive through the secret passageway to aid in holding the castle for the king—or so they thought. One thing was certain: If all went well tonight *and* tomorrow, why then, except for the many slain by the Alphians, things would be back to normal in short order.

In the council room, I greeted Fel-Holdt warmly with the Marackian abrazo and handclasp. I also embraced our beauteous Lady of Gortfin and received a kiss on the cheek and a glance of love from wet eyes as my reward—all this under the stony glare of my dearly beloved. Fortunately, Gen-Rondin's quite passionate embrace of our lady took the edge off somewhat, as did her response which was equally unrestrained and effusive.

But, as stated, there was no time and those who had begun our little saga were destined to end this part of it now. These were: Myself, Rawl, Gen-Rondin, Sernas, Dosh, Rogas and Kodder, called in from the wall; our two valkyries, who'd have it no other way, nine of the newly shuttled swordsmen, and two of the captured sky lords as guides. We were twenty, dressed in sky-lord uniforms and carrying sky-lord weapons.

With everyone around a long-table in the great hall, I explained the simple mechanisms of the Alphian weapons. Each had a safety, an intensity gauge and an automatically synched scope. While still inside I had them do a little dry firing to accustom them to the trigger. I also promised eternal hell-fire if they didn't keep their fingers out of the guard unless they were actually drawing down on someone.

Outside, in the great courtyard, I set their laser beams to *burn* and let them fire off a few practice rounds at the walls. They were pleased as punch with the new toy and would have seared every brick in the battlements had I not called a halt to it. Their enthusiasm being what it was, I feared for what they would do inside the Alphian ship if there was the slightest resistance. All blasters, I concluded, would be left behind. Anything that might harm or even immobilize the ship was out!

While they practiced, under the care of Kriloy, I had time to question our two chosen Alphian guides further.

"What," I asked, "can we expect in terms of a night watch?"

The Alphian who had previously volunteered information wrinkled his brow at that. "What," he asked, "is a night watch?"

"A commander and a handful of men, in the command room."

Our particularly limited sky lord with a video star's features, then said in puzzlement, "But the ship is at rest. There is nothing for anyone to do . . . So we do what we please."

Probing further and somewhat stunned by his answers, I asked, "How many officers have you, other than Tarkiis?"

"None."

"I see. And *he* was your commander?"

"Yes."

"And if he had been killed?"

"Someone else would be. Perhaps Diis would say."

I jumped on that. "And how is Diis contacted?"

"*He* contacts *us,* through the *god* communicator."

"But how would *you* contact *him?*"

"The same way. But it is never done."

"Why not, if he is your god?"

The speaker looked at me blankly. "Why he is a god. There is no reason. It is not done."

"When were you last contacted?" I was onto something, though I didn't quite know what it was.

"This morning."

"What did Diis say?"

"That the others of the fleet would join us here, for a few days."

Oh, ho. Hooli'd tapped the *god* communicator. "Why?" I asked.

"He didn't say."

"Well didn't he tell you anything else?" My exasperation was a tingling anger. What little respect I'd had for them as sperm-bank types with an extremely limited education was fast slipping down the drain.

"He said that he would talk to us then."

"When?" I grated the word.

"When the ships come."

"But can he not speak to the ships wherever they are, at any time?"

"Yes."

I tried another approach. "Did he speak of trouble? Did he warn you of—other ships?"

"We are fully warned of that. All ships other than our own will be fought when *he* is near—and gives the word."

"And if he is not?"

"If he's on the *other side* we are not to bother unless we are attacked."

"That is why you attacked our ship?"

"Others of ours attacked your ship and were lost; that was before we came through the mists to here."

The "mists" I took to mean the warp. I shook my head. Gods! What did it look like through his eyes, really? "And on this side?" I continued. "When you attacked us on this side, too; what of that?"

"But we didn't attack you on this side."

"But Diis, the sphere did. Were you not ordered then to attack us too?"

"No."

"Because Diis attacked for you, right?"

"No. Diis didn't attack, and we were not ordered to attack."

A hot chill shot down the length of my spinal cord. "You mean that our ship was not destroyed?"

He looked at me curiously. "Not by us. We fled from it. Diis let it live."

"Where did you go?"

"To the south of here. To that other land beyond the water."

I was sweating all over, but I got back to the original problem. "So he now thinks that *other* ships will come tomorrow, right? And that is why the others have been summoned?"

"No. He didn't say that."

"But he wants them here, just in case—of danger?"

"I don't know. He will talk to us tomorrow."

I chanced it. I asked, "If he talks to you tomorrow, what do you think he'll say as to what has happened here tonight?"

By now the man was exceedingly uncomfortable. I warrant he'd never been asked to think, to *reason* on anything before. I'm sure his head was hurting.

"I do not know."

"But even if I allow you to tell him, what then?"

"But no one talks to Diis."

"Do you think he already knows?"

"Yes. He is a god."

"But do you *know* he already knows?"

He shook his head and repeated again: "He is a god."

The practice firing over, Kriloy, the only true alien among us, had sat silently, stolidly by my side and heard nothing. His single desire, it seemed, was to make himself invisible. I sympathized with him. I really did. I'd long categorized him as the basic intellectual clerk, the kind who'd choose to live in a small Anglicized cottage not far from his job, have a rose garden to dawdle in, a library with all the right books, the best of sound equipment and season's tickets for everything worthwhile. He hadn't changed across ten centuries. He was what he was—and I liked him for it. He'd been given a room not too far from my own, though I'm sure he'd have preferred the scout ship.

I dismissed him and we moved to go about our business.

Bright moonlight and the tail end of Ripple just making it over the horizon. The sky boots we wore were like those worn by the *Deneb's* crew, light, silent, and feather-soft. We passed like so many wraiths over the great bridge; phantoms, racing the coming sun, drained by the excesses of some grand Walpurgis Eve. From the bridge it was but a few hundred yards to the ship.

Its design, as stated, was almost standard; which says a great deal for the effects of the parallel technological evolution among all sentients. The main body was a duel-level ovoid, with control room, sensor pods, sleeping and recreational quarters and the like. To the rear on corridored shaft appendages were the great CT converters. The nuclear engine was suspended below, something on the order of the leaded keel of a sailing ship.

We seized it without a shot being fired, and it was as simple as that. I used Tarkiis's pack to open the prime exit, a simple device, also on the sound-vibratory principle. A door swung out, the ladder-platform mechanism came out and down. We climbed it and entered....

It took myself and Rawl just thirty seconds to find the control room and to witness that it was just as our Alphian said it would be—empty!

Then we split, Gen-Rondin with nine of us going down the right half-circle corridor, and myself with the remaining nine going down the left half-circle corridor. We found our first Alphian and his lady, *en flagrante sexualis extremis;* which, in this case, meant in the act, as it were. We disarmed him, then marched them down the corridor to the next sleeping pod, collected our second man, etc. I hardly need add that my comrades, together with the half-dozen or so Marackian swordsmen given us by Fel-Holdt could scarce contain their hilarity after the first two. It was like a surprise raid in a brothel; what would we find behind the next door? And we *were* surprised. For in this area, at least, the sperm samples of the great race of Kentii had been quick to learn.

The two corridors met in the rec-room to the rear. We arrived almost simultaneously with our forty naked Alphians and their forty naked ladies; upon which Murie demanded furiously that all of them be sent immediately back to get their clothes, though she hadn't been all that modest during their capture.

Not a one of them had put up a fight or asked a question. They were unhappy, however; though irritated is more the word, for what was happening to them. Their ladies exhibited a similar irritation. I was prompted to remark to Murie upon this most interesting phenomenon, saying that even though our Marackian lovelies were here because they'd been brought here and had no choice in the matter; still, that very lack of choice had also relieved them of a proper responsibility. In effect, I told her, grinning the while, the old adage, relax and enjoy, seems to have been on the order of the day. I even reminded her that, as she herself had put it, the standard sky lord as opposed to the standard Marackian, well there was just no comparing. One was perfection; the other, a ploughboy. Why *not* then enjoy them, while they had them?

Rawl, listening solemnly to what I had to say, could not help but agree, profusely—and got a slap in the face from Caroween to equal the one I got from Murie at the undeniable correctness of my analysis. . . .

And that was that. And if one dared to think about it, he could only conclude that Murie, who'd introduced this Achilles heel of simple sex to the Alphians, had been quite knowledgeable of its potency as a weapon to be used against them. . . .

Kriloy, as my surrogate, slept aboard the ship. He was fresh. I was dead on my feet. He was instructed to familiarize himself with its armament, since on the morrow it would be him and me at the weapons controls. As a last point before tearing myself away from his unhappy visage, I suggested softly that he cheer up—that from now on we had nothing to fear from the sphere.

He grew very solemn; screwed up his eyes and studied my face. He simply couldn't accept my statement as a fact as any Marackian would. He had to ask, "Why, Kyrie? Just why the hell do we suddenly have nothing to fear from the sphere?"

"Because I say so, buddy. The missing pieces are coming together. And that's all you're going to hear, except that with a bit of luck, by this time tomorrow there'll be a lot of singing in Marack and perhaps some dancing in the streets."

I bedded with Murie in her apartment high in the east

tower. We didn't make love. We were too drawn out, too drained. That would come later. Bathed and relaxed, she just sort of put herself within my arms, both of us propped against the pillows and mother-naked against the soft and oh, so sweetly perfumed night breeze.

She said just once against my chest, "Well, my lord, would you like to hear now of all the things that have happened?" I grimaced. "Another time. I'm still male enough to pass on that for now. Still, there is a parallel from my far world, of a lady called Godiva who rode the streets of her capital, naked, to free her people from unjust taxes. Her fame, my love, lived on in saga long after those with little minds and priest-ridden souls had gone their way . . ."

"Why, now." Murie sat up, pleased with the tale. "That one seems a queen as she should truly be. But still, my lord, there are things I must tell you."

"Nay," I begged. "Later—mayhap when this pelt of yours is more gray than gold."

"But there's a thing, great fool, that I must say."

"Must?"

"'Tis that I'm pregnant, Collin."

"The hell you are."

"By god!" She reached to grab my ears and to stare into my eyes. "What, my lord, do you mean by that?"

"Just that I hadn't thought it would be so soon."

"You are disturbed, you bastard?"

"Nay, my lady." I grinned wickedly. "But you might be."

"Explain yourself."

"Well. I'm reminded that you showed distaste for those of my comrades aboard the *Deneb* for their lack of fur."

"But you have fur."

"Indeed I do. But 'tis a thing of science-witchcraft. A *child* of ours could very well be furless. Moreover, their eyes were generally brown, or dark. Remember?"

"But yours are purple-blue, like my own."

"Nay, my love." I passed a hand before my eyes and dropped the contacts. "*Voilá!*" I said. "Brown!"

"By Ormon's grace!" she exclaimed, peering closely. And then, "They *are* sort of pretty, my lord. Indeed, one senses a softness, a kindness not too much visible before. There's even a hint of understanding, too, which I swear has been hidden all these months. Well! So you have blue-purple *and* brown. You must make me a pair of brown, too, my lord. It is not well for a queen to lack that which her consort has." She smiled happily. "We'll be a pair. And if all goes well tomorrow; well, 'tis still summer. The height of the 'season' lies before us; what with our brown eyes—*and* our marriage, we'll be the rage."

I sighed, said, "Come. Sleep. There are still a few things left to do. . . ."

We breakfasted aboard the Alphian ship, now christened *Ormon's Bliss,* since it had had no name of its own. The naming came from our stout student-warrior, Kodder, and was a bit of a double entendre, referring to a famed brothel, now destroyed, which had held forth for many years right next to the king's collegium.

Great Fomalhaut I arose and nothing happened. It climbed the eastern sky until the tenth hour, and still nothing happened. To the southwest the sphere's surface continued bluely iridescent. Nothing had changed there except that it also seemed, for whatever reason, to be growing ever smaller.

To say that nothing was happening, however, is not exactly correct. Something totally unexpected was happening. For purely Marackian reasons—though Rondin and Elioseen, joining us on the Alphian ship, said not to worry since it would in no way interfere in what we had to do—the king and queen, plus a few of the remaining lords of Marack who had not been slain and were filtering back, were making a festive occasion out of the engagement to be; of ourselves with the alien ships. This *savoir-faire* of the royal house, considering, was remarkable; their trust in me, unconscionable, since if I lost, and survived, I'd then have no other recourse but the Terran anachronism of *hara-kiri.*

The Alphian weapons were: CT pencil-shells, which became clouds and could only be used in deep space. Two batteries of laser beams with a range of a hundred thousand miles or better. Two batteries of ion-projectors with a tremendous implosion potential, and a double bank of heavy weapons with plain old nuclear warheads.

The laser and ion beams were at speed of light. They were, therefore, in terms of in-atmosphere fighting, unobservable by any scanner until after the fact. In essence, at speed of light in an atmosphere, release *and* impact are simultaneous.

I knew this. Hooli knew it. Even my unhappy, and therefore quite dopey Kriloy knew it. If the Alphians knew it, well that was the extent of it. They presupposed nothing and were therefore prepared for nothing. . . . Their two ships—and the rumor of a malfunctioning on the part of the remaining two was apparently correct—came sailing in on anti-gravs around high noon, at about two thousand feet.

I'd had all bridge communications switched direct to weapons control—so that if either or both of the ships made contact it would be with me. They did, but only to appear on the viewer to say that they were coming in. That I didn't reply bothered them not a bit. It was as if they hadn't expected me to.

Kriloy was at one weapons computer bank, I was at the other. Each bank fed two heavy lasers. On target, we hit the data-fire bars almost simultaneously. Four great laser beams, two to each ship, instantly destroyed the enemy anti-gravs and all of his sensor pods.

They hadn't a chance. Their automatics cut in with an attempt to switch to mag-line power, or CT-nuclear. But at two thousand feet, no way. Before ever they got a positive wobble, they'd smashed into the ground through the thick foilage of the forest southeast of Glagmaron City.

And that was it.

Crowds from the city had gathered on the far edge of the field to watch. They cheered hysterically. King Olith Caronne and his sister, the Lady Elioseen, with Queen Tyndil and sundry lords led by Commander Fel-Holdt, then came down from the bridge towers to advance toward our ship. Their intent? To salute us personally and with the proper accolades.

Hooli—and this was another first—rode with the king. He had a reason. It was made known immediately; to me, that is. At the skirt of the bridge where it was anchored on the plateau side of the chasm or ravine splitting the field from the castle, the king's dottle halted—*seemingly of its own accord*. Those of Caronne's entourage immediately followed suit; though with puzzled, frowning expressions.

Caronne, seeing that the dottle would respond to neither his verbal nor his physical commands, baton, spurs, and the like, simply shrugged and relaxed against his saddle's high cantle. He then awaited the outcome of whatever the dottle had in mind, with a purely Fregisian form of patience.

The dottle bowed its head as if in an act of genuflection. Its silver mane covered its great blue eyes. *Hooli* then tightroped out from where he'd been clinging to the saddle horn to position himself at the point of the animal's descending neck. Again he held the silver flute. . . . I switched my contacts to ten mags so that I was but a few feet short of eyeball contact. I received no friendly wink, nor even the slightest attempt at fun and games. The little black eyes were wide, solemn. Again he blew but a single note. To me it lasted scarcely a second. To the others? Well, apparently he'd gone far beyond my frequency, for they still listened. Odd that I would learn precisely then that Fregisian hearing could approximate that of a Terran dog. . . .

Nothing happened. I mean that, literally. Everything simply stopped, dead. Even the usual midday breeze from the west was just suddenly, gone.

All those around me seemed in some form of stasis. Everything and every one, singly or in groups, were as a series of silent tableaus in a monstrous wax museum that stretched to infinity. Were our dottles and Marackians even breathing, I wondered? They were; slowly, imperceptibly. Were their hearts beating? Yep. At five beats per minute. Those nearest me on the small platform remained as they had been, standing, relaxed, and staring straight ahead. . . . All except Kriloy who hadn't slept for a full twenty-six hours. Coming up from weapons control he'd fortunately collapsed on a couch in the rec-room. One of the ladies still aboard—and why this was I do not know—was then sent by Gen-Rondin to attend him. She did so, holding his hands, massaging his neck, shoulders and body, and bringing cool cloths for his brow. Murie, an inadvertent witness to the more intimate aspects of the body massage, frowned her disapproval and complained to me of a growing "looseness." "Sooner or later, my lord," she said, "we'll have to attend to it."

I was frankly glad he was asleep. For like myself, Kriloy was not subject to the balm of Hooli's flute. I'd fully earned my front row center, and I'd no desire to share this very personal thing I had with Hooli, and he with his sphere-opponent, with anyone.

As for what would happen now, well, whatever it was, Hooli would handle it. He'd already left the genuflecting dottle to make his way across the field to me. He did this, I might add, at a much greater speed than his little legs would ordinarily propel him.

He climbed the stairs to the platform, looked me square in the eyes and said, "Well, it's about that time, old buddy; the end of the line. Tell me, have you guessed any of it?"

I grinned. "Surely you must know. You do have mind control."

"I do. But with you, Great Collin Adjuster, what with our being friends and all that, I use it as little as possible. Again—what have you learned?"

I sighed. "That you are alike, just as you and the Dark One were alike." Even saying it mentally caused a chill of sheer terror to slice at my spinal nerve ganglia. Still, I could not have said it if I didn't believe in his essential *goodness*.

He nodded. "Yep. All true, buddy. And it's time, too, to grab the old tiger by the tail. You won't like what you're going to see," he cautioned seriously. "And I adjure you, *tovarich*, that it could easily make a zombie out of you for a week or so. I can change that if you wish, enter your mind and make it like a couple of boxers going at it; or maybe a couple of lady wrestlers?"

"Cut the crap. Am I the only one who'll see this, Hooli? The only one in the whole damn universe?"

"You are."

"Then let 'er rip, brown bag. Lay on," I quoted, "And damned to him that first cries, *hold, enough*!"

His beady eyes glittered, his real way of smiling. He said, "Well, then, I'll be leaving this for a bit," (he meant the host Pug-Boo). "But it shouldn't take too long."

"A last thing," I asked deliberately.

"What?"

I grinned. "Where's the *Deneb*?"

"*In orbit, where it's always been.* You'll see it—after."

And he was gone. And the little *rodentius drusis* sat, kerplunk, upon the platform and went instantly to sleep.

I swept the horizon, searching. The blue sphere remained where it was, as if it neither knew nor cared what had happened to the two Alphian ships. . . . Nothing, nothing, nothing. Except, unh-huh, just there and above the great forest to the southeast was a *second* hovering blue sphere. Why that little bastard. It had arisen from almost the exact spot where I'd first damped the *Deneb* scoutship.

Without the slightest hesitation it came directly toward our tournament field, a fitting place, perhaps, for whatever it had in mind. It landed between the bridge with its mass of unseeing viewers, and myself on the platform of the Kentii warship. . . .

I looked toward the south hill. The first blue sphere was already airborne, as if surprised; caught off base, but heading quickly toward its brightly shimmering companion. Its bulk, for whatever reason, had decreased still further. Both were now but half the size of the Alphian ship.

For the record, the first ship, from the hill, was, as Hooli had put it, the Dark One's uncle. The second was Hooli, himself; the real *Hooli*. They were entities, living organisms; I knew that now. They needed no ships, just a shimmering shield, a part, actually, of their own substance to ward off meteorites, or sunburn, perhaps—the kind you get when you're but a few thousand miles from sun-surface. No doubt the shield could also keep mosquitoes away, or even Fregis's ubiquitous thousand-legged bugger-bugs. . . .

It came to ground just thirty feet from Hooli.

There was nothing then for quite some time. Indeed, thirsty, I even took a chance on missing something by running to fetch myself a drink from the command room.

And then—and then there occurred a tingling in the air and a sudden darkening of all the heavens around us. It was as if some great electrical disturbance were building; but without clouds. The very horizon itself seemed suddenly to shift, to blur. Checking Fomalhaut I, and it was now approaching high-noon, I was in no way surprised to see that it, too, seemed but half its usual size. There was an obvious and most powerful distortion factor present. Looking toward the castle, I saw that its battlements were now rounded in all the wrong places; its four towers, twisting, melting, as would a butter frieze beneath a brace of candelabra.

The tingling became audible, tactile, even. The skies grew darker still so that the stars and constellations were faintly visible. With the enveloping darkness there came a flashing everywhere, a whirling kaleidoscope of pyrotechnics resembling warp. . . . And suddenly, it was as if we'd fallen straight through from *somewhere*, to another set of values in another place, in another time. The sky now was a purple black, and there were no longer any blue spheres. In their place; and this on a red sand plain that sparkled with a million varied crystal jewels, there were two entities. I saw them through a myriad of bursting, dying, color points. . . .

There is no way to truly describe what then ensued. Extra-dimensional factors were obviously present. They had to be. For where the entities, or *beings* were, one could still see the spheres as being vaguely superimposed upon them, and vice versa. The very sight of this changing, of all things becoming something else and back again, forced a vertigo that made me physically ill. The entity-beings grew and diminished and grew again while I watched, and retched—and vomited the contents of my stomach. I could not, *would* not take my eyes from them. And I would have sold my soul to every humanoid-worshipped devil in all the systems for a potential to get the stuff on videotape. But such was not to be. . . .

There was still no sound beyond the sound, and I'm not even sure now that it was such, of the tactile tingling. I looked just once at my arms—and saw a transparency of cloth, meat, bones and veinal structure. I dared not look at the rest of me. Instead I forced my gaze to hold on the two beings; to watch what now was a mingling of tentacular appendages, *whole groupings of them,* like unto a monstrous snake pit! Moreover. To see them fully was also to see them from the inside out! For that is precisely one of the ways I saw them; this, while I was outside looking in! Unknown internal organs, a series of great hearts beating and pumping everywhere, juices, effluvia, intestinal tubings, a myriad of eyes looking both in and out at me. . . . To view it all at any length was to guarantee madness. To hasten the process was the insidious knowledge that *one* of the two was diseased, its parts a rotting corruption which but clung to life by the sheer will of its owner. One's olfactory senses could attest to this last, as well as one's eyes could attest to the four-dimensional qualities of the beings. It was this ultimate knowledge, I think, that finally pushed me over the edge. I simply gagged one last time, and fainted.

How long I was out, I don't know. Hooli said later that it was only for seconds. And that may be so. But when I revived it was to see that once again there were *two spheres.* The one, a gray-blue-silver now, was lifting, lifting, to shoot suddenly like a dying star toward that section of sky—and it was all blue and beautiful again—which led directly to Fomalhaut II and the Alphian gateway. . . .

The second, smaller sphere, gleaming with hard diamond points of white within the shimmering luster of its iridescent blue, appeared to be watching; to be saying a last good-bye.

After awhile his voice asked softly inside my head, "Are you all right, Kyrie Fern?"

"I'll live," I answered weakly. "Where did your uncle go?"

"Home to die. He was dying anyway, you know."

"I see. And about the *Deneb*? What—"

"No problem. It's up there. Just give 'em a buzz."

"It's really been there all this time?"

"Yep. It thought it was somewhere else, and so did you. But no mind, buddy. It's all right now."

"Is it really—all right?"

"Well, yesss—except that—"

"Hooli! For fucking Buddah's sake—"

"*Calma, hijo.* It's just that I thought you'd like a certain memory erased. I could make it so that every time you thought on the little scene you've just witnessed, well maybe your mind would switch to Christmas trees and candles."

"I'm an adult, Hooli. I'm an Adjuster! Moreover, I'm a survivor type. It's a print for my old age. I might even learn something. Old age. That's a laugh. I'm thirty, Hooli. With luck I'll make it to a hundred and fifty—and you're already five thousand."

"Ten thousand."

"Oh, bloody Magus."

"I must leave you now, Collin. There are some things I must do."

"So soon? Will I see you again?"

"Of course. I owe you."

And the shimmering sphere with the crisp diamond-point lights rose neatly and disappeared over the southern horizon.

At the exact nano-second of Hooli's disappearance, things sprang to life all around me. The parallel image of a dead video screen and a tape suddenly clearing, slid across my mind's eye.

I wasn't ready for it, really. But still I held them all for the brief seconds necessary to ask that they look toward the south hill. "The last great enemy of the world of Fregis, and of the land of Marack," I told them, "is gone forever. Our world is now at peace. 'Twill be our duty to maintain it. Hail Marack!" I roared. "Hail Ferlach! Hail Gheese! Hail Kelb! Hail Great Ortmund! And hail all those of our brothers on the great continent of Om!"

And they did so, raising their voices enthusiastically for the northern kingdoms, and woodenly for Om. For after all, they were and would continue to be, men and women of a fighting race who had still to get their feet truly planted on the first rung of the ladder.

To me, other than the peace of Murie and the close companionship of Rawl, Caroween, Sir Dosh, Sir Sernas, Gen-Rondin and now, Elioseen, it was anticlimax. I felt drained, tired, old. I knew something, or rather I knew just a small bit of something that few in all our galaxy would ever know. It was still difficult to accept; especially, since it remained unclear. He'd said he would explain it when he returned. I could only hope—and wait.

And so there was a great and sustained singing and dancing in the streets of all the northern cities; this, of course, after I'd also done a fly-over of the remaining two Alphian ships and blew the both of them to hell. We took as many as fifty additional prisoners who'd not been aboard and tossed them into Glagmaron's dungeons along with their buddies. The celebrations went on for days.

Kriloy and I also visited the *Deneb-3*, our comrade Adjuster, Ragan Orr, Admiral Drelas Niall and the hundred-member crew. As they told it, they had been living in a gray mist for all this time. They said that no single instrument aboard the *Deneb* had worked except servos and those needed for the maintenance of food, heat, and (Hooli's humor), a working video mechanism for the running of old movie tapes. This last, Commander Niall told me, was a most interesting phenomenon, while still being a part of the insoluble problem.

I, in turn, told them what had happened, which was little enough when you get right down to it. I promised a more complete report, hopefully, when Hooli returned.

Kriloy was his old self. All was most definitely right again in his world. Indeed, as he saw it, to coin a cliché from the past, he'd been *reborn*. He even volunteered to shuttle the kings, Draslich and Chitar, from Ferlach and Gheese, respectively, plus the appointed regents of Kelb and Great Ortmund to Glagmaron for the major victory celebrations. Each of them had a train of at least fifty lords and knights, together with their ladies. No small task at all. Kriloy was roundly praised.

The victory feasting lasted a full week, and culminated in the marriage of myself, Kyrie Fern of the Galactic Foundation, known for all time in Marack as the Collin, to the Princess Murie Nigaard Caronne, soon to be queen in Marack. We were wed simultaneously with the young Baron Rawl Fergis, cousin to the queen, and his betrothed, the Princess Caroween Cey Hoggle-Fitz, soon to be queen in Great Ortmund . . . And all this with the one-hundred man crew of the *Deneb-3*, and her Commander, Drelas Niall, in attendance.

There had never been anything like it. I doubt that there'd ever be anything like it again; not with *that* feudal splendor.

I hadn't given up on Hooli returning. In a way, I think, he was simply allowing both of us a breather. I appreciated that. I'd fought through two great wars, a hundred battles, the recent and quite bloody little conflict; and with a deep-space war tossed into the pot; and then witnessed the dénouement of Hooli and the sphere. I'd indeed *had* it for awhile. My thoughts were on a leave of absence—two years, perhaps, of absolute relaxation, and in a Camelot-Fregis at peace. I'd introduce the game of chess; perhaps, fly-casting, too. Maybe the Terran game of baseball. It was still being played, so I understood; a proof of its staying power. I also wanted to visit and spend some time with Great Ap and the Vuuns again. And finally, I wanted a few hundred hours of sack-time with Murie. What else? Oh, yes. Despite being a vegetarian, I'd become addicted to gog-meat stew. . . .

And there was one final and very important thing. But only Hooli had the answer to that.

It wasn't until autumn that he came again. He'd waited a full three months. The leaves had already changed, were falling, covering the surface of the Cyr and being blown in swaths by soft zephyrs over the great flagstones of the castle courtyard. . . . It was indeed that time again. Even the greater part of the dottle herds were being released into the forests to seek their winter forage. It was quite a ceremony, and one in which the dottles themselves participated. To watch it would make a Druid out of anyone, if he was half a man.

I'd been hawking with Murie at the time, a sport both of us dearly loved. Indeed, we were fortunate in that we dearly loved doing many things together, especially now, since Rawl, Dosh and Caroween had gone off to inspect their kingdom, get things set up for a visit by us on Wimbely's Night before the coming of the solstice. . . . Even Lors Sernas had finally departed. He'd pledged me his undying friendship, but explained, too, that Hish needed him; that he'd received a message that the worshipers of Dark Tuums, an evil god of sacrifice, was attacking his Hoom-Tet, with the help of certain greedy lords and willing priests. He hinted, too, that he'd been too long from his well-rounded and oh, so willing, Buusti. The tale was all too familiar. I bid him a most affectionate good-bye. . . .

Our hawks, grown much too fat and lazy for the fantastic amount of poor pitty-docks they'd knocked down and eaten, had lost their enthusiasm for the hunt. And so we lunched, and Fat Henery, my court dottle, broused alongside Murie's little Tarditi, named for a court seductress of olden times. After lunch we dozed. Murie with her golden head on a downy pillow, myself with my head on her thighs; my second favorite spot, the tummy having been taken over by a small stranger. . . .

The warmth of the sun and Murie's thighs, the sound of insects, all of it was conducive to a total relaxation. Except that suddenly I heard a boat whistle. Nothing shrill, mind you. It was more of an inoffensive "toot," the kind one might hear on the upper Thames at the height of the boating season. I squinted without squinting. with my eyes closed. Sure enough, there was the river and there were the boats. And there, coming around a bend of rushes and the branches of overhanging English elms, was *himself,* a very familiar figure. He was working a one-man scull, wore a brimmed beany and had on a shirt in the colors of a very famous English boy's school. He deftly maneuvered the little craft to the river bank which was directly in front of me, rested the oars, pulled it up a bit so the current wouldn't carry it off, looked up, waved, and called, "Hellooo, buddy!"

I waved back, said straight-faced as he approached me, "More of the post-Victorian, right, nougat-head? You do have your predilections. But you're entitled."

"You're forgetting the source, buddy; to wit, *you*. Still the milieu, gaslights, bowlers and Doctor Jekylls, has its attractions. . . ."

"Touché."

"Well, buddy." He took a seat on the grass and fired up his Holmes pipe. "What can I do to put your mind at ease?"

"Just tell me the story, round-ball, about who did what to whom, and why."

"You figure it's about that time, huh?"

"Yep. It's about that time."

"No matter how dull?"

"Hooli—Get on with it."

He grinned his cheshire grin, made the pipe disappear, adjusted his purple shades and placed his paws in back of his head so's to rest both head and paws against the bole of an English oak. . . . He said, "Well. It goes like this, Kyrie:

"Once upon a time, two beings from a universe beyond the comprehension of intelligent life in your galaxy were sent as watchers to another, dying universe; specifically, the one beyond the gateway. Their purpose? To observe and record the process of its death. The objective? To eventually control that process, to be able to reverse it, to keep it in stasis, or to speed it up, depending upon the requirements of its varied life forms. I generalize in this case, buddy, since there were no life forms in the universe beyond the gateway."

"*Magus Og!*" I couldn't help exclaiming aloud.

"Bear with me, buddy. There are many such universes. Too many, perhaps. But all must have their watchers. In the case of the two beings, however, the single small galaxy of that quite simple universe was possessed in its final stages of an inordinate amount of pulsars and collapsars—these last, if you remember correctly, Kyrie, are the *black holes* of all your warp-punching nightmares.

"The years passed, eons of your time. The simple phenomenon of beta-decay, indigenous to the intensely powerful magnetic fields of pulsars and collapsars, had an insidious effect upon our two beings; the more so because of an unawareness on their part of its overall potential as applied to themselves. Their lives, bordering on immortality, were shortened; their minds, ruined beyond all hope of repair. Indeed, the creeping totality of the effect was such that they could no longer remember from where they came, or who and what they were. One of them, however, and for whatever reasons, experienced a remission sufficiently strong so as to allow him to grasp for a short span the vague outlines of his glorious past. With this sole bit of knowledge, and knowing, too, that the process of their decay was irreversible, he prevailed upon the other to join in two things: To produce a third entity of their kind and then to flee with it to a safe universe, along with the data so long collected.

"Ill as they were, and we are androgynous, by the way, though this is not as simple as it sounds, they produced *me*, and then began to create the gateway. Allow me at this point to state that normally, for such entities, no gateway is needed. In this case, however, he who was *wholly mad* could no longer project himself; thus the need. The first, who was but partly mad, was bound by unimaginable ties to save him.

"We succeeded—and by this time it *was* we, for I had already achieved my first five thousand years, in your time sense. Indeed, we succeeded, but only to find ourselves in the very heart of that greatest of humanoid tragedies, war; and this time in its ultimate and most destructive form, a boiling holocaust of nuclear obliteration. To paraphrase your Bard with but one slight change: We were the victims of a 'tragedy of errors'. . . .

"He who was but partly mad escaped back through the gateway. He who was completely mad escaped to Fregis in an Alphian host; physically, I mean; and I'll not go into the details. He did this, of course, in one of the very ships that *I* had renovated for the rescue of the Alphian remnants.

"Unbelievable as it may sound, I did not know for tens of decades that he who was wholly mad still lived. And then, a new phenomenon. . . . Though his madness was irreversible, free of beta-decay, he was regaining health—and power. I could only watch the process fearfully. A monster was being born on Fregis, the like of which this galaxy, even this universe, if not protected, would long remember. And I, by the very nature of my being, could not destroy him; whereas he could, and most assuredly *would*, destroy me—if he knew I lived.

"Then you came, Kyrie. And both of us, working together

for disparate reasons, but mostly for the same goal, destroyed him. Unbeknownst to you, however, the first being had again come through the gateway. His purpose? To *live* and to search for me; this, though in his mind he was convinced that both I and the other were surely dead. Sick, and more so than ever now, he created his humanoid-servos from Alphian sperm and ovum banks; rebuilt and renovated the Alphian ships that have lain so long in the buried ruins of underground cities. They would work for him, protect him, provide that which he could no longer provide. . . . Might I suggest that he and they were truly 'the blind leading the blind'? I knew he had returned. For as you have seen me, Kyrie, *I* need no spaceship to cross the void, *any* void. I had hoped to prevent him from leaving Alpha; to accost him just there with the fact that I was alive. *And then to demand my right of maturity!* But he, too, was not sane. Remember? He'd searched the planets of Fomalhaut II. I was not there. He would therefore go to Formalhaut I. His first choice, without a doubt, was Fregis. And he found the still living Alphian-Fregisians there. Remember the two-day hiatus? It allowed for a briefing of his 'robots' as to who they were and why they were here. . . .

"But though he sought me, Kyrie, I still feared him. I repeat, he was not sane; indeed, could easily be more dangerous than our Dark One. My intent, therefore, was the same: to present myself to him only at the time of my *maturity*, which is a period in the life of such as we that lasts for hours only, but which must be used for a melding with another of our species who is already *mature*. A part of the mature one is then passed to the immature one so that he becomes a complete being—*able to fully reproduce himself*!

"And so, whether on Alpha or Fregis, I had but to wait for my maturity; indeed, it is what I've been waiting for all this time. The act of melding, a step higher than merging, *cannot be refused*. It is an inherited, conditioned, *must*. It is the priority; the only priority of all our race. In this case, by presenting myself then and only then, I would achieve the following: He could not refuse me; nor could he harm me. I would become a complete being. He, because of what he had become across the eons of beta-decay, would not survive the meeting. . . ."

He paused to observe me through a pair of merry, self-confident, Pug-Boo eyes. He then snatched his Holmes pipe from nowhere, knocked out the ash, filled it and fired up again.

I said, "Hooli. You're sure the one for detail."

"Oh, well, look, I just wanted to hit the high points."

"I mean that pipe, brown-bag. So that's the way it was. You were fooling around on Alpha, decided to check me out, and found yourself in the Pug-Boo aboard the *Deneb-3*?"

He grinned and blew a perfect ring.

"Scared the shit out of you didn't it?"

"Sure did. I had to do that business with the *Deneb* to keep your admiral from blowing my boy into dust-bunnies. But first, I had to get you to get the *Deneb* back to Fregis; get you out of the ship and down to Marack. Without your being there, Kyrie, things could have been a helluva lot rougher—for the Fregisians, I mean—when my boy and his surrogates landed."

"Well, thank you."

"On the other hand, if you had just let up when I told you to. . . ."

"Gog shit! You saved my ass, true; and I'm sure you would have done that anyway. But *then* you touted me back to Glagmaron to rescue Murie, *so you said*. In reality, I was your ace in the hole, to keep the Alphians from zapping you in case your boy had gone sufficiently nuts to ignore your *maturity syndrome*. Even with them out of the way, you still couldn't come down on him if he came at you. But you damn well knew I'd have to, and *would*! You had it all worked out, brown-bag."

This time his grin of pleasure literally split his hairy little face. "You hit it, Collin. I confess. He had a presentiment of peril. He *knew* I'd be coming. He just couldn't believe it. A contradiction. He distrusted his own, limited sanity. You see, like me, he knew the very hour and minute of my birthing; therefore, he also knew the hours and minutes of my *maturity*. . . ."

"Wow!" I said, in contemplation.

"I owe you, Kyrie."

I switched. "So you put a power drain on my poor Kriloy's bypass to back up that weird story of a pre-nova CT sun being tapped through the gateway. . . . You are the one, Hooli."

"I had to, otherwise, you'd have been screwing things up all over the place. Besides, no one got hurt beyond the usual."

I asked, curious, "What is your energy source?"

"For just everyday living? Solar power. Any sun within a billion or so miles. All I have to do is breathe. Anything beyond that, well, I'd have to go to work. I don't store all that energy."

"Like the Dark One did?"

"Yes and no."

"We're back to 'no comment'?"

"Not really. It's just too damn complicated to explain."

"And the *Deneb* could have destroyed our boy?"

"Yep."

"And you, too?"

"Only during the hours of my *maturity* period; when the Alphians could have got me—when *you* could have got me—otherwise, it would have had to pin me down and that's next to impossible. I've got mind control, Kyrie, and not just over minds. And when you get right down to it, that's about ninety-nine percent of the ball game."

"Hooli. What would have happened if I'd not been there to take out the Alphians, etc., and you had been killed? Give me a straight answer."

He said solemnly, "Barring the quick death of the remaining being, I cannot imagine a survival of this system, or of that of the binary. And he would have gone on, too. For when I say he was dying, I'm thinking within our time sense, Kyrie, not yours. He could have been around for another thousand or so of your years."

"Question, and I'm just hitting around now: If you are your own space vehicle—and even our most recent visitor made it to Fregis from Alpha on his own—even considering a space-warp jump—why then couldn't the first D.O. return to Alpha and the gateway on his own?"

"I honestly don't know. My conclusion is that since he was the craziest of our trio and had automatically assumed our deaths, that he'd simply extended this conceptual flaw to the gateway, too."

"Weird."

"Elementary. He was as mad as a hatter."

"We've dumped the Alphians, you know. Dropped them

off in a valley in upper Om. We left food, clothing and shelter for a year or so, plus the tools to survive. But there are no women. None would volunteer."

Hooli shrugged.

I decided to hit him with the big one. "What," I asked slyly, "of the powers of the Lady Elioseen, of Goolbie, Fairwyn, Gaati? It seems to me that their witchcraft, their sorcery went somewhat beyond the ordinary."

"The ordinary?"

"You know what I mean."

I'd caught him again. And if I hadn't asked, he'd never have told me. I wasn't so sure he'd tell me now.

He made noises, frowned, blew a lot of smoke rings and finally said, "Well magick, Kyrie, that is in the accepted sense of the word, is unacceptable to all you straights, right?"

"Yup."

"Well. Look at it this way: What would be true magick to you is not true magick to me—or to the D.O. and his uncle. And there is simply no way to explain that."

"Try, Hooli. Real hard."

"Well I can cast a *real* spell. I can turn you into a flimpl or a dust mop. I can put you into a sound sleep, and with my personal guarantee that only a princess with one blue eye and one red and weighing one-hundred-seven-and-one-half pounds can wake you up, etc., etc. . . To you, that's magic. *To me it is not.* It's all a part of the same big picture. You see, even with yourself as an undeveloped humanoid, the potential for an understanding of what I'm saying is there. This being true, the potential for doing it is there too. All one has to do with that inactivized frontal brain mass is to—"

I was staring at him in absolute awe, it had hit me that hard. I whispered hoarsely, "Hooli? You didn't do that, did you? You didn't mess around with Elioseen, Goolbie, and those others?"

He looked as sheepish, then, as a *rodentius drusis* could possibly look. He said, "I'm afraid I did, but only a little bit."

"To how many, across the years?"

"Maybe a thousand or so. I had to give the north a weapon, Kyrie; something that my insaner third couldn't trace to me. Then, given time, and if he got to me first, and if they developed it properly, well, then they could beat him on their own. They were just beginning to really learn. . . ."

"That wasn't very adult of you, Hooli."

"Who the hell ever said I was an adult? And I'm not sorry, either."

"You can reverse it, right?"

"Nope. It's irreversible. Not only that, it inevitably becomes an hereditary factor."

I sighed. "Bloody Jesus! And *this* is your gift to us before you go off to play among the stars?"

"Kyrie," he then said flatly, and I could see he was dead serious. "Look at it positively. With magick you can't implode a sun or vaporize a world; nor can you poison a planetary ocean, or make a desert out of teeming forest lands. There are serious, natural limitations to magick. I wouldn't worry all that much. Indeed, from what I've seen inside your head and those of some of your constituents, if I were you, I'd prefer the magick any day to what you have. . . ."

I sighed again. "But the greater part of it is still dependent upon sound and the mag-field and its use, right?"

"Right," and he winked. "*Fregis*'s mag-field."

"Good enough. I'll stick to that as your story. Hopefully, our Elioseen who, with the Lord Gen-Rondin, is going to Foundation Center and from there to other places, will play it cool."

He grinned again. "Not to worry. Most of it will be linked forever to Fregis anyway."

I brightened. "Hey! I like that. A World of Magick, unlike any other. And it will always be that way . . . What will you do now, Hooli?"

"Relax. Observe. Go galaxy hopping for the next few thousand years. After that, well, I've got to find my roots. That means universe hopping. They're out there you know, those from whom I came. I must find them."

I sighed again.

He got up and stretched, and I saw that one of his legs was missing. He'd already begun to fade.

He said, "I love you, Kyrie."

"I love you, too, Hooli. Will I ever see you again?"

"Sure." His eyes glittered. He bobbled his head and his tongue came out to do its pendulum swing. He dearly loved to make me laugh.

Then he straightened his jacket and his brimmed beanie and said softly, "Tell ya what, buddy. If you ever want me, I mean *really* want me for something, well all you have to do is to say these numbers. . . ."

And he came to where I sat, also leaning against a tree bole, stood on his one visible tippy-toe, put his small paws on my shoulder—and whispered them in my ear.